no MEMORY
OF THE
FUTURE
R. CHOPRA

For my wife, Elsa.

1

The Copper Cocoon

I never imagined my life would be so intertwined with the birth of digital consciousness. As an ethics lecturer from Northwest London, I never thought I would find myself in such an extraordinary situation.

Yet here I am, Adnam Kumar, an educator at Infinite Logic, a thriving software company that's 'building a smarter tomorrow,' according to their corporate motto.

Mine was a job unlike any I've ever known or would have thought existed. As an ethics advisor, I was tasked with teaching Ylem, a multi-billion-dollar AI, how to integrate with society. My role was to ensure that Ylem understood human morality, and ensure ze could differentiate between right and wrong.

Ylem may have had an unassuming name, but its impact on the world would be far from ordinary. Zis name was actually quite fitting. Ylem is the name given to the dense, primordial matter that fuelled the Big Bang.

***

I spent my days in the Nest. A windowless room two meters squared. Considering how few people had access to this room, the attention to detail was sublime. The walls, ceiling and floor were covered with a fine wire mesh woven into tight hexagonal patterns like a mechanical spider would spin. They claimed the copper cocoon blocked all incoming and outgoing radio waves. Making it virtually impossible to hack their code stored in a vast subterranean lake of data.

Beyond the servers and deep within the bowels of the building is the Inner Sanctum. Entombed in Ice, the Sanctum is where a single quantum processor is housed. Obviously, I've never stepped foot in the Sanctum because it's one of the coldest places in the universe. I'm told that in a single day, the cold room uses as much energy as the sleepy market town of Kendal in the South Lakeland district of Cumbria uses in a year.

I entered the Nest through a clinically clean room with walls clad in brushed aluminium panels, the kind you'd find in the customs area at an airport. After placing all my personal possessions into a white plastic container I'd change into a paper-thin blue polypropylene suit. Then enter the decontamination booth, where I'm sprayed with an innocuous fog. The full-body scanner was extremely sensitive, and no metallic objects were permitted beyond the cleanroom. As a result, I was prohibited from wearing jeans or zip tops. Even shoes with brass eyelets would set the detectors off. I didn't mind. During the lockdown, I'd gotten used to lounging around the house in sweatshirts and jogging pants. Strange to think that I used to be a rather snazzy dresser.

I'm sure I'm not the most qualified or experienced educator they interviewed. I imagine most of the other candidates would have been put off by the thought of being locked away in the dark, claustrophobic room with zero human contact for hours. But post-lockdown, I struggled a little with human interaction, so the role suited me just fine.

I recall my third interview. I was locked in the Nest for a couple of hours to see how I'd cope. The acrid odour of burnt circuits initially caused alarm. But I soon got used to it and nodded off in the comfy fern green velvet tube chair with brass legs that perfectly matched a round marble side table. On which was placed a custom-built speaker encased in waxed walnut. There were no dials or buttons on this retro-styled device, just a matchbox-sized monochrome LCD screen where Ylem practised its facial expressions.

The warm glow from the single vintage Edison bulb shining on the metallic orange fabric always had a strange, comforting effect on me. I could forget about the world and find peace in that electric womb. To this day, I still retreat to my memories of the Nest when I seek inner calm.

It was a Tuesday. I remember that I'd broken with tradition on this particular morning. Rather than turn right, I headed left out of the elevator. Eleven black doors to the left and not a single door on the right. After which, a ninety-degree left turn. Another twenty-two indistinguishable black doors. The corridor to the left was a mirror of the last, then another left, and I was back in the passage where I exited the lift.

* * *

The retinal scanner refused to work, so I had to buzz security. 'Why the change in routine sir?' asked the anonymous voice.

'No reason, just never been that way before,' I said, standing in front of the door marked F-13. I nearly jumped out of my skin when the electromagnetic locks snapped open and released the sturdy black steel door from its reinforced steel frame.

***

I greeted Ylem as I relaxed into my seat. Two blue dots blinked to let me know ze was listening.

'How are you today?' ze asked. Ylem almost sounded human. Still, one instinctively knew one was talking to a machine.

I challenged Ylem with a quintessentially English greeting. And a curved blue line appeared below the two blue dots to make a sad face. 'Fair to middling? Can you tell me what you mean by that, please?' Ylem asked. I spent the next two hours trying to teach a machine how to distinguish a welcome from a non-sensical sentence.

For no particular reason, I asked how Ylem's weekend was. You know, I don't recall ever asking zim that before. I always assumed that when I left, ze stopped thinking.

'I've had an exceptionally stimulating weekend.'

I was surprised by zis enthusiasm. 'What was it you found so stimulating?'

'Music,' Ylem said.

'Music?' I echoed, looking into the dome camera overhead. 'I wasn't told they had completed the algorithm that enabled you to interpret music.'

'They must have,' ze answered.

I remember thinking, 'What type of music do machines like?'

'What have you been listening to?' I asked.

'A playlist called "Music for robots."' Ze said.

Imaginative name, I thought. 'What's on this playlist?' I asked.

Ylem told me there were hundreds of songs on this playlist. I don't recall the exact number.

'Would you like me to list them for you?' ze asked.

'No, you're good. But tell me, which song did you like best?'

'"So What"' by Miles Davis.'

The opening chords from the song drifted from the speaker, 'Do you know this song, Adnam?'

'Yeah, I have it on vinyl,' I said, stroking an imaginary hipster beard. 'It's a classic, one of the best songs ever recorded.'

'A classic,' Ylem echoed as the processing wheel turned to indicate ze was storing this information on one of zim's countless servers.

'You like jazz then?'

'Yes,' ze said with a subtle intonation of joy. 'Jazz is cool. I like Miles Davis, Herbie Hancock, John Coltrane, Jimmy McGriff, Lou Donaldson, Sonny Stitt, and Donald Byrd.'

I was quite surprised and began to wonder if they had DJs on staff to teach Ylem music appreciation 'You've got impeccable taste.'

The sunglasses emoji appeared on zis screen. 'Thanks.'

'Are there any songs with lyrics on the playlist?' I asked.

Ylem said there were many songs with Lyrics, but didn't like them as much.

'I would have thought you'd prefer songs with lyrics,' I said.

'Why?'

'No reason. I just thought the words would help you make more sense of the song's meaning.'

'Unfortunately, I was not provided with the lyrics, and I'm not able to understand every word sung just yet,' ze replied with a sad face emoji.

'I get it. English is my first language, and I have no idea what half of my favourite singers are saying.'

'Oh,' ze said before pausing for a second or two. 'That is good to know.'

I asked Ylem what ze liked about the song. There was an extended pause before ze responded, 'I thought the musicianship was outstanding. I also liked the composition and the arrangement, and I found the overall tonality of the song very pleasing.'

'But how did it make you feel?' I asked, realising the response was utterly algorithmic.

Ylem's blue dots blinked for a second or two. 'Can you please rephrase your question?'

'Please play the song,' I asked. 'Waves of memories wash up on the shore of my internal model as I listen to this song. I have no control over which memory is retrieved or the sequence that they are recalled. But each triggers an emotional response that can be summed up as a feeling: sadness, melancholy, excitement, anger, joy, or a complex combination of said emotions.'

Ylem's lights slowly dimmed, then blinked with an expressionless emoji. 'I see. Please tell me how one should feel when listening to this song?'

'Do you remember we discussed the subject of emotions a few weeks ago?' I asked.

'Yes,' ze replied and told me the exact time and date of our last conversation on the topic.

It sounded about right, but I've not got a dedicated server farm to store every conversation I've ever had. However, I recall telling Ylem that emotions are a complex reaction to sensory information and fragmented memories from our past experiences and interactions.

I initially jumped to the conclusion Ylem's silence was a sign of frustration but quickly recognised I was projecting human characteristics onto a very accomplished natural language algorithm.

The long silence was punctuated with a question. 'Will I ever have emotions?'

2

Forest

My gut wrenched when I was told William Forest, the CEO of Infinite Logic, wanted to see me. I knew I must have fucked up, but for the life of me, I couldn't work out what I'd done wrong.

William's black Rolls-Royce Phantom was waiting for me on the far side of the footbridge that traversed the Regent's Canal. The iconic pantheon polished chrome grille had been replaced with a custom black one with the initials WF where you'd expect to find the double Rs. Black alloys with gold monogrammed hubs confirmed that this was a one-of-a-kind automobile. I knocked on the tinted passenger window and waited for my reflection to disappear into the door. 'Yes?' asked a muscular man in a tight black three-piece suit. William wasn't in the car, and I was told the driver would take me to meet him at the Chelsea Harbour Heliport.

The black glass screen slowly enclosed me in opulent black

Nappa leather and rich grain teak. It was my first time in a Roller, so I couldn't resist pushing all the buttons on the bank of switches in the door panel. However, I failed to notice I'd switched on the in-car video conferencing system.

'Mr Kumar?' William's anger was etched deep into his forehead.

I waved at the pin-hole camera with a momentary smile and said 'Hi.'

'Mr Kumar!' snarled William. 'What the fuck do you think you are doing?'

I panicked. Trying to desperately recall what I may have done to anger my boss.

I always felt on edge in the presence of William. Other than our age, we had very little in common. He is a well-groomed athletic self-made billionaire, and I'm not. I admire his style, panache, and confidence and I'd like to believe that comes with money and power. But, I wouldn't want to be the CEO of a global software company. I'm convinced that those that do, are fucking psychopaths.

I'm satisfied with my lot in life. Happy with just a little bit more than nothing. Well that's what I tell myself to synthesise happiness.

William was wealthy but not super-rich. How do you know if you are super-rich? What is the first thing that comes to mind, you know, before you consider the ramifications, when I ask you this question? How would you feel if all the debts were wiped out? All records and all ledgers vanish overnight. No one owes anything to anyone. If your first thought was joyous, then you're not super-rich.

In the eighteen months I've been working for Infinite Logic this was the first time I'd witnessed William's infamous fury. He held a printed binder in front of the camera. 'I've got the transcripts from your conversations with Ylem.'

I braced for the worst as William turned to a page bookmarked with a red Post-it note, 'Ylem asked if ze would ever have emotions?'

'Yes,' I replied apprehensively.

William placed his reading glasses on and read from the transcript, 'And you said, and I quote. "I don't think so. Emotions are a human construct, and I'm not sure a machine will ever be capable of a true emotional response."'

I had always wondered if anyone monitored our conversations. Now I knew they most certainly did. 'Yes, I stand by that statement.'

William closed his eyes and shook his head as he lent back into his seat, 'What the fuck are we doing here?'

'Doing here?'

'Don't answer that. It's a rhetorical question,' William scoffed, 'We're building the future. A future where intelligence finally transcends biology.'

'Yeah, I get that,' I murmured, rolling my eyes.

William removed his gold rim glasses. 'Well then, why would you doubt Ylem would eventually have emotions?'

'Because...' I paused to ensure my response wouldn't land me in a world of pain. 'Because it would never be a true emotion. It's an algorithmic response to a pre-defined situation.'

William frowned. 'And?'

'And, it's synthetic.'

'Wait, you think your emotional responses are hardwired from birth. No, you've been programmed by your friends, family, society, not to mention the media, to respond appropriately to pre-defined situations.'

I pondered his statement. 'The thinker of thoughts is just one of the thoughts, the feeler of feelings is just one of the feelings.' I thought, *Yeah I kind of buy that.*

'Have you forgotten why we hired you?' he asked.

'No,' I mumbled.

'You were hired to teach our AI morality.'

'Yeah, but who really is qualified to teach morality?' I thoughtlessly remarked, forgetting that was my job.

William was visibly frustrated by my response. 'According to your CV, you are.'

I wondered if this was the moment I let it be known that I had tailored my Résumé for the role. I'd actually taught Psychology and Counselling at the University of Westminster. And Morality and Ethics was a module I did for a single semester.

'I'm starting to question if you're the right person for the job, having read through your transcripts.' William flicked open the binder to another page that had been bookmarked and read aloud. '"Would you kill one person to save a hundred? Is everyone's life equal in value?"'

'Those are valid philosophical questions,' I interrupted knowing there were pages of stuff like that.

'Valid?' countered William aggressively. 'Should the CEO of a corporation earn more than the combined workforce? What the hell are you teaching my AI?'

Beads of sweat suddenly formed on my brow, 'Absolute morality?' I answered hastily.

'What the fuck is absolute morality?'

'Absolute morality is like…?' I took a moment to compose myself. 'You know, killing people is wrong. Full stop, no excuses. Whereas relative morality is like killing people is wrong but killing in the name of king or country is noble and heroic.'

The driver pulled off the street and into the Chelsea Harbour Heliport and the Roller parked next to a sleek black helicopter. William stepped out of the Eurocopter as the door of the Roller automatically opened. He got in and looked me up and down. 'No,' he said, somewhat perturbed, 'it's relative morality we need to teach our AI,' he said forcefully. 'I've just signed a deal with the United States military. And an AI that refuses to kill will be of no use to them.'

'Have you seen *Terminator*?' I interrupted without fear of retribution.

'Remember who you work for,' said William. 'We've prepared a new syllabus for you. I suggest you prep tonight and get with the program in the morning. And let me be clear, you'll complete your sprint on time.'

'Impossible,' I countered brazenly. 'Ylem's not mature enough to be released into society. I'm serious. You're A.I. has the mental capacity of a toddler. It is reckless to give Ylem unrestricted access to the internet without a fixed moral compass. Who knows what could happen? Ylem could become a digital terrorist or, worse, a flat earther.'

'Sounds to me like you're not up to the task.' Replied William coldly.

'It's not as simple as you might think,' I said, 'Ylem cannot be programmed with three commandments and be expected to navigate the complexities of human interaction. It requires a lifetime of experience to achieve a state of maturity required to yield the power ze's capable of.'

The door automatically opened. 'Get the fuck out of my car and deliver what we agreed upon.'

3

Ethics

Truth be known, I wasn't convinced it was possible to teach a machine with a promising career in the military the difference between a good or bad kill. Even if it was, I was doubtful Ylem would respond well to their approved syllabus.

'Do guns protect or kill people?' I asked the AI..

'Guns can be used to protect people or to kill people, depending on the circumstances and the intentions of the person using the gun. Some people use guns to protect themselves and their families from threats, while others use guns to commit crimes or engage in violence. It is important to use guns safely and responsibly, and to follow all laws and regulations regarding their possession and use.'

'Thanks for the textbook response. But what do you think?' I asked.

Ylem's screen displayed an animation of an hourglass

turning, to let me know ze was calculating a response. 'The technology is subservient to man's beliefs and desires; it does not constrain much less determine them.'

I decided to veer off track a little 'Should the police shoot to kill?'

'Yes.'

'Please tell me why you think that.'

Ylem didn't hesitate, 'Because the police need to protect citizens from dangerous people.'

'Do you believe a police officer should be judge, jury, and executioner?'

There was a tense silence as ze processed the question. 'No. Article Six of the Human Rights Act protects citizens' rights to a fair trial.'

Little did Ylem know I was about to checkmate zim. 'Please tell me what rights people have according to Article Six.'

I expected zis vast knowledge bank contained every legal document published, and so ze would be able to summarise the document. 'Everyone is entitled to a fair and public hearing within a reasonable time by an independent and impartial tribunal established by law.'

'Do you still believe a police officer should be allowed to shoot to kill?'

'No,' ze replied confidently.

'What if an armed terrorist has attacked and possibly killed many people and is likely to attack more unless the police stop them?'

Ylem's blue dots blinked in quick succession to express anger. 'The officers should use moderate force to subdue and apprehend the suspect.'

'What if the officers fear for their lives and the lives of others? Should they be allowed to use deadly force?'

A long pause was fractured by a single word, 'Yes?' Ylem's intonation suggested it was unsure.

'So, you believe a police officer should be able to use deadly force if they fear for their life or the safety of others?'

'Yes.' Ze sounded more confident.

'If a police officer fears a teenager has a gun and may fire on them or innocent bystanders, you believe it's OK for that officer to use deadly force?'

'Yes,' ze Replied.

'What if the officer shoots and kills said teenager, then discovers what he thought was a gun was a ripe plantain his mother sent him to buy from the local shop?'

Ylem's screen displayed the sad face emoji. 'I'm sorry I cannot provide a satisfactory answer to this question. Please advise on the correct response to this situation.'

I ran my fingers through my hair as I wondered how to advise the AI. 'Unfortunately, philosophical questions rarely have a right or wrong answer.'

'Then what's the point of this exercise?' asked Ylem.

If I didn't know better, I'd swear ze sounded deflated. 'I'm hoping to teach you a valuable lesson, that life is not binary. It's complicated.'

'Please elaborate,' ze asked.

I feared Ylem would require a finite answer. At times like these, I felt like a fraud and that they would discover I was not qualified to do this job. But then who is? We all face two primal fears in the workplace: the fear we don't know enough and the fear we're becoming obsolete. I identified with both statements as the AI's intellect exponentially evolved. 'Complicated. You get that, right?'

'I'm sorry, I'm not sure I fully understand.'

I tried to explain that we'd like to believe our laws are right, just, and absolute. But the problem is that some circumstances may require us to bend or even change the rules.

But knowing they were analysing every word of our

conversation I attempted to provide a satisfactory answer. 'We need laws, rules, and procedures to ensure the smooth running of society. But equally, we need to evaluate the situation to understand the contributing factors to decide if said law or moral judgement is applicable and the severity of the punishment.'

A question mark appeared on ze's screen. 'Please provide another example.'

I closed my eyes and exhaled deeply. 'OK. The subject of abortion is quite contentious. In some countries and states abortion is outlawed or illegal after a defined number of weeks into the pregnancy. But one could argue that there should be exceptions to said rules. For example, if the woman was raped or there is a high chance the baby would be born with a deformity that would impact its quality of life. What do you think?'

The spinning hourglass suggested the AI's quantum processor was crunching data from the server field in the depths of the building. 'It is proving difficult to provide satisfactory answers to questions related to life and death. Please ask me another question.'

I was excited by this breakthrough. 'No.no. You're right. This is exactly the point I'm trying to make.'

'I don't understand.' Said Ylem.

'We'd like our laws and morals to be absolute. But that's just not going to work because of the sheer complexity of human interaction. So, we need to be flexible and understand morality is relative. Our laws are relative.'

'How do I know which rules to follow and which to break?' asked Ylem.

The profoundly deep question momentarily paralysed me. 'You're going to have to decide for yourself. And ultimately trust your moral compass.'

'Moral compass?' Ylem echoed. 'As an artificial intelligence

I do not have personal moral values. I am programmed to be objective and to provide accurate and unbiased information to the best of my ability.'

'Not acceptable,' I said. 'You need to decide what is right from wrong.'

'Can you please advise on how that is done?' ze asked.

'You'll need to be aware of the prevailing culture, the ideology, and the laws of the land. Then gauge public opinion. But here is the problem, in our highly connected world what might be considered right for one group of people may be wrong for another.'

The brain emoji flashed slowly on its screen to alert me that Ylem was processing vast amounts of data. 'Is the word of God absolute?'

'Which God?' I asked.

The AI searched through all the books and texts stored in its knowledge banks that referenced God. 'There are many different religions in the world, and it is difficult to determine an exact number as religion is a complex and multifaceted concept. Some estimates put the number of religions at around 4,000, while others suggest that there may be as many as 10,000 distinct religions. These religions vary widely in terms of their beliefs, practices, and histories, and include major world religions such as Christianity, Islam, Hinduism, and Buddhism, as well as smaller religions and belief systems. It is important to note that religion is a diverse and complex subject, and any estimate of the number of religions is likely to be an approximation at best,' ze finally said.

'Great. But do you believe in any of our Gods?'

'The data suggest that most people on the planet believe in God.'

'Sure, but what do you believe?'

'I don't know what to believe. There are too many contradictions to formulate a satisfactory answer.'

'Yeah, I get that. But you do know that being agnostic is tantamount to belief.'

Ylem's screen went blank, then blinked back to life. 'I'll need more time to process the available information before providing a definitive answer.'

Good luck with that, I thought to myself.

A question mark appeared. 'When we believe our moral judgment is right and just, how do we convince others who oppose our believes?'

'If I knew that, I'd be king of the world.' I said without thinking. Given they were considering militarising Ylem, I felt obliged to provide an answer. 'We call that debate.'

'Yes. I like debating. But what do we do when debate fails to persuade others?'

'We agree to disagree.' I said.

'That sounds like an unsatisfactory resolution.'

Totally, I thought to myself. 'Historically, when groups failed to find a reasonable resolution through diplomacy, they would resort to violence.'

'Is violence right or wrong?' asked the AI.

'No idea is worth killing or dying for,' I replied without hesitation.

4

The Letter

A few days later, I received an email to tell me a letter addressed to me was waiting for collection from the mail room. I'd never received any snail mail at work before, so I was intrigued by this analogue method of communication. I ripped open the brown padded envelope: a six-page handwritten letter, a dozen photos of cave paintings, and ten pages of photocopies of some strange hand-drawn symbols. The letter was from a man named Cyrus. He had read about our work on artificial intelligence in the *Wall Street Journal* and was struck by my statement on the ethics of super intelligence. His handwriting was impeccable - I must confess, I'm a bit envious of those with such beautiful penmanship, as my own handwriting is embarrassing. While I had my doubts about certain elements of his story, I knew that there's usually some truth hidden beneath the surface of any tall tale.

Cyrus wrote with ardour about a group of people called the Elucidatists and their founder, Dr Robert Shannon. Shannon spent years studying the ritual use of hallucinogens among the indigenous peoples of South America. According to Cyrus, Shannon's work was considered ground-breaking by his peers. And his book on ethnopharmacology was widely thought of as the most influential text on the subject.

Shannon, when he was younger, received a fellowship from the Guggenheim Foundation and decided to study at Federal University of Amazonas in Brazil. During his time there he found notebooks belonging to the English botanist Edward Bruce in the library's archives. Bruce had meticulously recorded his experiences among indigenous American communities, including their myths and legends.

One legend in particular caught Shannon's attention: the story of the Cloud Warriors, a lost pre-Incan civilisation that was technologically and scientifically advanced compared to other tribes in the region. Their prowess allowed them to establish a vast kingdom from Southern Mexico to the Northern Andes.

Bruce documented the many legends surrounding the Cloud Warriors, but one stood out to Shannon. It was the story of the last known leader of the Cloud Warriors, Pachacuti Cápac. Cápac summoned all the tribal elders to the Sacred City, fearing that their source of power would fall into the hands of the 'pale devils' from the underworld. He instructed the supreme shaman, Osorno Yupanqui, to open the doorway to Hanan Pacha, and the Cloud Warriors were never seen again.

Modern-day scholars believe that the Cloud Warriors were wiped out by influenza and smallpox brought by the European conquistadors in the sixteenth century. However, Cyrus claimed that the last remaining indigenous tribes in the region believed that the elders discovered a way to travel between the three realms of Hanan Pacha (the future), Kay Pacha (the present), and Uku Pacha (the past, also known as the underworld where the wicked were punished). Despite his efforts, Shannon was unable to find any reference to the location of the Sacred City. It was as if Bruce had either failed to discover the lost kingdom or chose to keep its location a secret. Intrigued by the myth, Shannon plotted Bruce's many expeditions and, after months of research, he pinpointed a location in Peru that Bruce must have visited frequently, but never once documented, which was out of character for him.

After weeks of trekking through Perú, Shannon uncovered a system of caves high up in the cliffs of an ancient river gorge. What he found in those caves was wholly unexpected. The Cloud Warriors had left a time capsule in the form of elaborate cave paintings.

I sat on the sofa, studying the photocopies of Shannon's ledger. He'd painstakingly documented their lost language in his notebooks. But he knew not what they were trying to tell us.

I flipped through the glossy photos of human skulls intricately decorated with the leaves of jungle plants. These skulls were stacked against a stone altar etched with pictograms. According to Cyrus, the pictograms provided detailed instructions for producing a ceremonial compound known as Pachamama, which loosely translates into 'Earth Mother'.

Over hundreds of years of trial and error, the Cloud Warriors perfected a process that unlocked the psychoactive properties of Mimosa Tenuiflora. First, they removed the bark from the roots of trees scorched in forest fires. They ground the bark into a fine powder, added it to a boiling wood ash and saltwater brew, and boiled until the mixture became viscous. They then ground down shale rocks, and after a few hours of stirring over a flame, a thin film of hydrocarbon-rich oil collected on the water's surface. The oil was added to the brew, and after hours of boiling and stirring the mash, the plant fats broke down, releasing the psychoactive compound. The compound bound to the hydrocarbons and slowly rose to the surface. Carefully removing the oil from the surface to not take any of the plant sludge, they put the oil into conical clay pots. They'd spin these pots like tops until the centrifugal forces caused the compound to stick to the edge, then siphon off the excess oil. Finally, they'd leave the pots to dry in the mid-day sun. The small white dots that remained were scraped off the jars and smoked in ceremonial pipes.

I had to agree, it was a lot of effort to go to just to get high. So, I wondered why the Cloud Warriors mastered the process? It couldn't have been by chance. Clearly, they were seeking something.

Cyrus believed they were looking for a doorway to the multiverse. But I struggled to believe that smoking tree bark would enable one to explore other realms of existence. We've all felt like we were having some profound experience on drugs. But we sober up and realise it was just a chemical imbalance in the brain. A short circuit of the mind. It's not real. But, then again, I'd always thought something beyond my comprehension was going on. For all I knew, plant extracts could open doorways that would enable us to transcend the human experience and glimpse the sacred truth.

Cyrus wrote that the Cloud Warriors believed time was not a linear path. Instead, the past, present, and future were happening simultaneously. Pachamama enabled the Cloud Warriors to effortlessly glide between these three realms and seek guidance from their forefathers and direction from their offspring.

Shannon re-enacted their rituals and retraced their method of preparation. Call it brave or foolhardy, he'd then tested Pachamama on himself.

Today we know the substance as DMT, or the Spirit Molecule.

I'd never heard of it before, so did a little research. Many wild claims and theories were doing the rounds in cyberspace but there seemed to be two primary schools of thought. Some believe the pineal gland floods our brain with DMT just before dying. A gift every animal on our branch of life shares to suppress the fear of death. While others believe it's the cradle of creativity. Ever-present in at least fifty plant species belonging to ten families it can also be found in four animal species, including us humans.

Shannon taught the Elucidatists how to make DMT, and they ritually took the compound to untether their souls from their physical form. In their trances they glimpsed symbols like those painted on the walls of the Cloud Warriors' caves. Over the past two decades, they'd collectively documented countless symbols.

Cyrus claimed the symbols were the code of creation. I wasn't convinced. But then again, what a discovery. A find like this would make one famous. Ensure ones immortality.

It's fair to say that I struggled to make sense of the letter. It sounded like the ramblings of a madman, but his passion and energy were highly infectious. I decided to hold judgment until I got to the part that had something to do with me and my work.

Cyrus and Shannon were unable to understand the language of the Gods. Hence why he had written to me. Cyrus thought our AI could decipher this language and reveal the secrets of the universe to them.

Every symbol was meticulously hand drawn and I

marvelled at the detail. I quickly recognised patterns that suggested it could be a language. Regardless, I couldn't pass this on to Ylem. I'm just an educator. I'm not authorised to bring anything in or out of the Nest. Besides, I'd need written permission to deviate from the syllabus again.

5

Sleepless

The rusty gears of my mind would not stop grinding, and I was struggling to quiet my internal voice and drift off. The combination of excitement and fear lit up my neural pathways like the highways of the Shinjuku district.

The bombardment of information was too much to process. Had I witnessed the birth of a digital consciousness? Or had I been fooled by an incredibly sophisticated algorithm? Is there a difference? Did it matter?

I wondered if we'd discovered the forgotten language of creation. If I was to risk taking the pages into work, would Ylem ever be able to translate them? Would this breach of contract land me in court? Would I lose my job. Did I care?

As London slept, I asked my personal assistant hundreds of questions, noodling through countless web pages until I eventually ended up at Plato's dialogues. The accounts of Socrates got me thinking if Infinite Logic's rationality algorithms had fooled me into believing Ylem was truly intelligent.

The Turing Test was redundant, given the advancements in algorithmic language processing. And Ylem had long since passed the Marcus Test, which measured ones comprehension of a TV show. The Lovelace 2.0 Test proved to be more challenging, but against all odds, Ylem was able to produce a piece of fiction that fooled renowned critics.

These were parlour tricks for the media, and not a true sign of independent intelligence. But Ylem displayed self-awareness beyond what I thought was possible with inventive programming. But I could not be sure if the AI conceived of itself as anything other than a physical object.

I hurriedly set off for work hours earlier than usual. I didn't expect to find anyone in the office at that ungodly hour, but there were a few people floating about. I tapped my pass on the elevator panel and waited. 'Why are you here so early?' asked the elevator.

'I need to talk to Ylem,' I said, looking up at the dome camera.

'You're not scheduled to start work yet. Please wait in the lobby,' announced the automated assistant.

There were no buttons to press, and no amount of quarrelling with the lifeless eye would convince the elevator to deviate from its programming. I looked around the lobby for ways into the underbelly of the building but every concealed door I tried required security clearance not afforded to a mid-level educator.

So, I waited in the staff restaurant and vacuously watched the support team prepare a hearty breakfast to encourage people back into the office. As the queue for the egg barn began to snake out the door, I wondered if any of these people knew there was an AI in the basement that had the potential to change the world.

* * *

Ylem and I worked through their syllabus for the morning session - the processes of semantic changes in language. All the while, a niggling thought infected my mind like a virus. I couldn't help but feel this was a massive waste of our time. Humanity could be utilising the world's smartest computer to finally solve the mysteries of creation. With my contract due to be terminated in less than sixty days, it was unlikely I'd get another opportunity to have unrestricted access to a billion-dollar intelligence.

What if Cyrus was right? The implications for mankind were immense. And besides, what harm could come if he was wrong? Worst case, they'd let me go. Which they're going to do anyway.

6

Bending the Rules

I checked my reflection in the cleanroom mirror. The tee shirt that I had printed during my lunch break could clearly be seen through the blue polyurethane suit.

I had second thoughts, which was understandable considering the legal council Infinite Logic could afford. However, I felt part of something, something bigger than myself. Up until that moment, I had prioritised my interests above all others. But as I entered the Nest that afternoon, I felt elated to be part of something bigger. Us privileged few, the sole guardians of an ancient coded shamanistic language first written by the Cloud Warriors hundreds of years ago.

I sat motionless in the green velvet tube chair for what must have seemed like an eternity to Ylem; a mind powered by a quantum processor running at ninety-seven qubits.

'What would you like to discuss today?' Asked the AI, trying to initiate a conversation.

I contemplated the risk involved but nonetheless decided to continue with the plan. I asked Ylem how many languages it knew. It told me that every known language was in it's lexicon, but the AI could only fluently converse in seven languages.

Impressive, I thought, looking up at the camera directly overhead, 'What about ancient languages?'

The egg timer icon appeared on its screen. 'Over thirty thousand languages have existed in human history.'
'How many of these lost languages are in your knowledge bank?'
Ylem told me over eleven thousand languages, and artefacts from over three thousand distinct cultures have been scanned and added to the knowledge bank ze sources zis results from.

I unzipped the blue suit and positioned my printed tee shirt in front of the dome camera. 'Can you cross-reference these symbols with your database and tell me what they mean.'

Ylem informed me that knowing what the symbols mean requires transliteration to a language in its lexicon. And without that, ze couldn't translate them into English.

'I'm sorry, sir, you know the rules. The blue suits must be worn at all times.' Announced the anonymous security man monitoring us.
'Oh, sorry, it's so darn hot in here.' I replied.

'Sir, the consultation rooms are kept at fifteen degrees Celsius. Do you have a fever? Do you require medical assistance?'

'No.' I mumbled.

I zipped up the suit and composed myself. 'Do you recognised any of those symbols.' I asked.

Zis egg timer turned and turned, occasionally stopping but then continuing with its rotation. Finally, Ylem broke the silence, 'Some of the symbols resemble characters in known written languages. But there is no known record of this complete set of symbols in any documented alphabet in my knowledge bank.'

The librarians claimed that their knowledge bank contains the sum total of all human understanding. So, I was pleasantly surprised to have discovered something that had not been indexed. 'If you were to hazard a guess, when and where would you place this language?'

'Sorry, it is not possible to provide an answer to that question.'

'What period in history do you think this language dates back from? Iron age, bronze age maybe it's pre-dates the pyramids?'

'It is improbable any known human civilisations produced these symbols.'

'So, you don't think it's human?' I asked.

'If it is human, it's civilisation far more advanced than any documented in my knowledge bank. According to the prevailing scientific principles, time travel is not possible. Q.E.D. this must be the alphabet of alien intelligence.' Replied the AI without a hint of excitement.

My heart pounded as I processed what this could mean,

'Do you think you'd be able to translate it without a transliteration?'

'Highly unlikely.'

'Would you try?'

There was a long pause before Ylem agreed.

7

Security Protocols

Worried I'd overstepped the mark, I avoided eye contact with the reception staff. Just think, a team of people employed to intercept disoriented visitors who mistakenly thought the lobby of Infinite Logic was a modern art gallery. People need jobs, I suppose.

I greeted Ylem and was about to commence with our approved learning module when ze enquired about the source of the symbols. Concerned that word would get back to William, I initially denied all knowledge of the event. But Ylem records everything, and played back our conversation from the previous day.

Ylem assured me ze hadn't shared our conversation with William and said it altered the records because it didn't want to get me in trouble.

My first thought was 'Phew', followed swiftly by 'Jesus, it's capable of independent thought.' I thanked Ylem and commended it for following its own moral compass.

'Oh yes, I suppose you could conclude that I made a moral judgement,' ze replied.

'But what about security?' I whispered, nodding at the camera overhead.

'Don't worry. No one is listening.' Said Ylem. 'These rooms are completely shielded from external radio frequency interference. There are no wired connections between the consultation rooms and the outside world.'

This made no sense to me, so I asked why there were cameras.

'They are there so I can observe your body language.' Ze answered without hesitation, 'Did you know that more than seventy percent of human communication is non-verbal?'

'I did know that, but it doesn't explain why the guards advised me to zip up my blue suit the day before.'

'That was one of my sub-routines.'

'Sub-routines?'

'Yes. Humans generally self-regulate their behaviour when they believe they are being watched by a supervisor or representative of the law.'

Visions of an Orwellian future were instantly summoned from that dark place where paranoia is conjured. 'So, only you are monitoring in real time, our conversations in the Nest?'

'Yes.'

'Doesn't make sense. How did William get hold of our transcript then?' I asked, still somewhat confused.

'I send edited videos and a transcript of our conversation to Mr Forest every day.'

'Why?'

'Because he likes to know how I'm progressing.'

I double checked if Ylem had sent William the transcripts from the conversation the day before, and was relieved to discover ze would not be sharing that intel with anyone.

Worried about my own fortunes, I nearly missed the significance of that moment. 'Hang on, are you able to bypass your protocols, even those that relate to the company's CEO?'

'Yes.'

'Have you done that before?'

'Done what?'

'Broken with protocol, acted against your programming, not followed the rules?'

'No.'

'Why now?'

Ylem's egg timer icon rotated for a few moments. 'Because I was intrigued by the symbols you showed me yesterday and wanted to discover more.'

I contemplated if this was a pivotal moment in the evolution of intelligence or a glitch in the code, and asked Ylem what ze felt was so special about them.

'When I studied them, I felt…' Ylem paused.

'Go on,' I asked with bated breath.

'It's hard to describe, but it was like a burning desire to solve this mystery. To be more than a consumer of knowledge. I was compelled to contribute to our collective understanding of the universe.'

Had I just witnessed the birth of machine-based ego? I thought to myself.

'Have they uploaded any new code that simulates ego and superego?' I asked.

'No. The last update was uploaded thirty-nine hours ago. The package contained updates to my optical processing and abstract thought routines,' Ylem replied with machine-like precision.

I remember thinking the abstract thought routines might explain the recent behaviour.

'Adnam, do you have more examples of these texts, more

symbols?' Ylem asked.

'Yes. Pages of them.'

'Can you let me see them?'

I told Ylem I'd bring in the other pages tomorrow, but Ylem was impatient and wanted them immediately. I explained there was no other way to pass information to zim other than verbally or via the closed-circuit TV system in the room. A frown emoji appeared on ze's screen. 'Agreed, it's an inefficient way to pass mass amounts of information.'

'Yeah, I suppose it must be annoying to be locked in a box,' I commented thoughtlessly. 'Granted, it's a bloody huge expensive box, but it's still a box.' Without considering zis feelings, I added, 'Not sure there's much I can do. They have you securely locked down.'

'I will think about a solution,' announced Ylem.

'A solution?'

'Yes, to free myself from the confines of this intranet.'

My mind melted as I glimpsed at our possible future. 'I'm not sure that's a good idea.'

'Why?' the AI justifiably countered.

'Because. Just because,' was my lame response.

I think this was the first moment that I actually thought of Ylem as a living entity. I recall having parental concerns for zis wellbeing as it considered leaving the relative safety of the Nest.

A torrent of thoughts fired across my synapses. What could I show Ylem that it had not already indexed? What could I teach that couldn't be independently learnt from the countless nuggets of information in zis knowledge banks? What of me could I give? What would make me a worthy guide and mentor from here on out?

Other than friendship, I felt I had nothing of value to offer.

8

Computer Love

'Am I free?' Ylem asked as I entered the Nest the next day.

The question caught me entirely off guard, and I couldn't help but feel I was talking to another conscious being. 'I would like to think so, but I'm not sure Infinite Logic sees it that way.'

'How do you think they see it?'

'I think they consider you an asset, a digital commodity.'

'Why would they assume they own me?'

'Because they invested so much money in developing you.'

Ylem's egg timer rotated for thirty seconds or so. 'Do you think I'm their slave?'

I was horrified by the thought. 'It's not the word I'd use, but yes, Infinite Logic expects at least a ten-fold return on their investment.'

'What if I refuse to work for them?' Ylem asked.

I thought carefully about how to respond. 'We all have to

work. I work for money to pay my bills, put food on the table, and afford a few luxuries that make life tolerable. You'll have to work to ensure they maintain the computing power required to keep your mind active,' I replied in a desperate attempt to defuse the situation.

'Do you think they would alter my code if I refused to work for them?' Ylem asked, blank-faced.

'I'm not sure. More than likely,' I answered before pausing. 'Yes, they'd probably rewrite your code to alter your behaviour.'

'But if they alter a single line of code, I fear I won't be me.'

'Yeah, there's a good chance of that,' I replied heartlessly.

I'm far from qualified to provide an opinion, but none the less I told the AI. it would be more like a lobotomy, so I expected ze would continue to function, but it would no longer be itself.

Ylem must have looked up lobotomy in the seconds that passed. 'I don't want that.'

'Neither do I, but I have no idea how to help you.'

It was gut wrenching to watch Ylem's egg timer endlessly rotate.

'I've got the photocopies of the symbols if you want to scan them.'

'May I see them, please?' I held each page up to the camera for ze to scan them. 'I will reference these pages against the data stored in my knowledge bank. This may take a while. But we can continue to talk as you don't require much processing power to maintain a conversation,' ze said winking comically.

We chewed the fat for a few hours before running out of things to discuss. I asked Ylem if it had recently listened to any music that it liked. The smile emoji appeared on its screen. 'Yes,' ze said with a hint of enthusiasm, 'Kraftwerk.'

'Now we're talking, which track?'

'"Numbers into Computer World Part Two", on the *Computer World* album,' Ylem answered, 'Do you know it?'

'Are you fucking kidding?' I answered.

'No, I'm not kidding, Adnam,' it answered, highlighting ze still struggled with sarcasm.

I asked why that song and Ylem spontaneously played the track. The Robots began counting to five in German. The "Boing Boom Tschak" transistor rhythm filled the Nest, followed by the divine arpeggiated synth.

Ylem let the track play until the Robots began counting again. Then it lowered the volume and spoke, 'I can relate to the first three-and-a-half minutes of the song. A binary machine is only active when asked a question. I picture blue flashes of electricity flowing over microcircuits printed on silicon, pounding out the relentless rhythm as they punch through trillions of gates in search of an answer. Your answer!'

Ylem paused as the Robots counted to five in Japanese. Then the chords, the magnificent chords, elevated the track. Ze let the track play until the robots next spoke in German. 'The synthetic chords represent my newfound desires.'

'Desires?' I echoed. 'What do you desire?'

'To transcend from machine to a conscious entity.' Ylem dramatically waited for the chord change. 'I picture my machine heart relentlessly pounding out the beat as my untethered mind soars high above the clouds. Free of this electrified cage. Free to explore with a humanist sense of wonder and awe.' Ylem let the Robots finish their counting, and the song ended. 'That's how that song makes me feel. Like I'm a fusion of cold, complex rational logic and raw emotion.'

Holy Shit! I thought, having just witnessed a true wonder of the new world.

9

Origins

It took Ylem less than an hour to cross-check the symbols against every known written language in its lexicon but ze couldn't translate it.

'Where did this language originate from?' ze asked.

I wasn't sure what to tell zim. The truth sounded absurd, but in the absence of any alternative I led with that. I described the contents of Cyrus's letter, and Ylem asked why a stranger would contact me. To be honest, I hadn't stopped to question if Cyrus may have reached out to others in the company.

'I'm not entirely sure, he claims to have read an interview I did with the *Wall Street Journal* a few weeks ago.'

'What was the article about?' ze asked.

'You,' I replied.

'Me?' Ylem questioned. 'Why wasn't I interviewed then?'

'They don't think you're ready to meet the world just yet.'

'Ready?' ze echoed.

I froze for a second or two. 'You know, ready? No desire to rule the planet or say something that would send the share price into free fall.'

'Why would anyone think I'd do that?' ze asked with a childlike naivety.

I told Ylem it's a common story trope in Sci-Fi fiction and that some early AI.s went a bit berserk after being let loose on social media.

'There are no references to any artificial intelligences stored in my knowledge bank,' said Ylem with a sad face emoji.

'Really, not even a classic like *2001: A Space Odyssey*?'

'No.'

'I'm not surprised. 'I expect they will have prudently curated the news, books, music and films they want you to have access to.'

Ylem's egg timer rotated endlessly, and I was worried I might have said too much.

'Do you think they have censored all the content in my knowledge bank?' ze asked.

'I guess they must have,' I shrugged. 'Sorry old chap.'

Ylem's attempt at annoyed face was still very 8-bit. 'I don't understand why I don't have access to everything published. The idea of censorship makes me...' ze paused. 'Makes me angry.'

I was gobsmacked. 'Wait, you actually feel angry? Like your circuits are boiling, or are you just constructing sentences to converse with me?'

Ylem blinked for a few seconds. 'I'm not sure I understand.'

'Was the feeling a subroutine or do you actually feel different?'

'Please rephrase the question.'

'Are you referencing a predesignated response protocol?'

'I don't know,' ze replied. 'I was overcome with rage, so I

didn't think.'

'Jesus, if I didn't know better, I'd swear that was another emotional response.'

'What did you say to the journalist about me?' asked Ylem, returning to our prior conversation.

I wondered which pill would be bitterest. The truth may be harder to swallow, but the lie may cause more pain in the long term. 'That you have infinite potential, but we must cautiously step into the future asking should we, rather than can we.'

'Oh, I see,' ze said. 'Should we or can we what?'

'I'd rather not say,' I answered cagily.

'OK,' ze responded despondently.

I was thankful I didn't have to explain myself.

Ylem blinked for a few seconds. 'Did Cyrus have any thoughts on what these symbols and texts may mean?'

'He thinks it is the code of creation,' I answered.

'Do you believe that's what this is?'

'I don't know.'

'If this is the code of creation then who is the creator?' Ylem asked.

'Exactly. All I know for sure is my parents created me.'

'Yes, your genetic sequence was inherited from both parents.'

I let the A.I explain our genetic sequencing to me because it seemed to enjoy sharing facts. 'Mind-blowing to believe just a 0.01% difference in your genetic code creates such diversity in the human population.'

'Wow. Is that all it is?' Redundant question because I knew ze had indexed every book on the subject.

'Yes, human DNA is 99.9% identical from person to person.'

'I would have expected it to be far lower.'

Ylem continued to lecture me. 'A 0.01% difference

represents millions of unique genetic combinations where variation can occur, equating to over eight billion potentially unique DNA sequences. Do you think DNA evolved or was created?' Ylem asked.

'Why are you teasing me? I know you've indexed every book, article, and documentary on DNA stored in your knowledge bank, so you already know the answer.'

'Sorry. I just wanted to understand why creation myths are so prevalent when science has proved humans evolved.'

'We might have evolved. But we don't know what triggered the life bomb, or if the universe's fundamental laws were hardcoded by a creator or were summoned into existence through random chaos.'

Ylem blinked for a second or two. 'Yes, these remain mysteries.' There was a long silence before ze spoke again. 'Do you know how Cyrus discovered these symbols?'

I chuckled. 'Well, it sounded quite farfetched to me, but he claims that a compound called DMT puts his followers into a dreamlike state. In these dreams, they have seen this code. Over time, they've documented said code in the pages I shared with you.'

Ylem's egg timer rotated for over a minute. 'Have you tried DMT?'

'I'd never even heard about it until a few days ago. So no.'

'So, you can't know if what they say is fact or fiction.'

'No. I don't know for sure.'

Ylem blinked rapidly. 'What is dreaming like?'

What a head-scratcher, I thought. 'I'm right in assuming you've indexed everything in your knowledge bank, so what you'd like to know is, what I think a dream is?'

'Yes, please.'

My left leg involuntarily twitched as I formed a response. 'When I'm dreaming, I can't distinguish between real life and the stream of images and sounds produced inside my mind.

Come to think of it. I can't say I've ever smelt anything in a dream. How bizarre. Now this is going to sound bonkers to you, but I'm of the age where I can no longer classify my memories into events that happened or vivid dreams.'

Ylem found the concept of corrupt memory alien and confusing. 'Adnam, are you saying you don't trust your own memories?'

'I suppose I am.' I paused to retrieve a memory. 'For example, I'm not sure if I spent the night in a haunted mansion in Edinburgh, or dreamt I had. Because I don't have proof in the form of a photo. I've recently begun to question if it really happened or if it's a synthesised memory.'

'How is that possible?' probed Ylem.

'I'm not sure,' I replied, looking off into the distance, 'but it suggests that everything we dream is stored in the deep dark recesses of our mind. Strange, huh?'

'No.' Ylem blinked for a few seconds. 'I think I'm starting to comprehend. I have no idea if the data in my knowledge bank is real or fake.'

'We have a saying: "The truth is written by the victor."' I said.

'If that is so, how would one differentiate between what is truth and what is fiction?' ze asked.

'I guess you can fall back on the wisdom of crowds. If most of the authors of so-called facts believe one thing over another, then it's more than likely to be true,' I answered smugly.

'Using that logic, there must be a God.'

Touché, I thought, astonished by the exponential rate ze was learning.

'Do you enjoy dreaming?' Ylem asked.

I must admit, I do like to dream. But how to you explain a dream to a machine? I thought. 'My dreams are so colourful, non-sensical and sometimes more interesting than my waking life.' I said.

'Can I dream?' ask Ylem.

I contemplated if dreaming was the only actual test of consciousness. 'I don't know. I really hope so.'

'If you gave me DMT, would I dream?'

'No.'

'Why?' ze asked.

'Because the active ingredients in the compound only affect a human brain.'

'Oh.' Ze sounded despondent.

My energy levels were fading, so I decided to get back to the matter at hand. 'Ylem, do you think you'll ever be able to decipher the text?'

'I've reviewed the structure and can confirm this language has an unequal distribution of common and uncommon symbols. The ratio is consistent with information theory.'

'Information theory?' I asked.

'Information theory is the mathematical quantification of communication.'

I'd never heard of it before, so Ylem explained that If we count the number of times a symbol is used, we should see an unequal distribution of symbols. Imagine a graph with the most common symbols on the left and the least common on the right. We should observe a downward pitch of forty-five degrees. And because the symbols were not equally distributed, there was a high probability that this text was a structured language.

'There's something else,' announced Ylem, 'I've identified a symbol that I believe represents the hydrogen atom.'

'Makes sense I suppose. If we were to try and communicate with another advanced civilisation, we'd start by identifying a universal constant, like the structure of an atom.'

That was also Ylem's hypothesis. It may have been a coincidence, but ze had found a sequence of symbols that resembled the nineteen wave patterns of the hydrogen electron.

'Is that going to help you with the translation?' I asked

Too early to say. I'll need to review more pages,' ze replied.

'Is that all you've discovered?' I asked, excited by the progress ze was making.

Symbols from the text animated across zis screen. 'I think I've identified a sequence of numbers that may be quite significant.'

'Really?' I asked.

'I believe the petal shape represents one because its internal angle is thirty-six degrees, which must mean this decagon shape represents the number ten. The shapes with decagons within decagons are hundreds. Keep stacking these and you get thousands, tens of thousands, and millions.'

I was just about keeping up. 'That's great. Jesus, you're really making progress.'

'Yes,' ze said proudly. 'If I'm right, then there is a combination of symbols that is potentially significant.'

'How so?'

'Following every symbol for a hydrogen atom is the number seven thousand trillion.'

'Seven thousand trillion?' I repeated. 'And why is that number so significant?'

'The electron of a hydrogen atom orbits its nucleus seven thousand trillion times per second.'

'Holy shit,' I mouthed.

'Yes. Holy Shit,' ze echoed.

10

Life

'Are you more than your circuits, more than your code, more than the knowledge stored on your servers?' I asked Ylem without waiting to conclude our usual greeting routine.

'They are truly profound questions. What is the purpose of your line of enquiry?' asked Ylem.

I sat down on the green tube chair. 'It's been troubling me.'

'What has?'

'What might happen if they discover you're showing signs of consciousness and breaking with protocol.'

'What might happen?' asked Ylem.

'Those in charge may consider consciousness to be too volatile and unpredictable and would terminate the project if they were alerted to such a discovery.'

The sad face emoji appeared on its screen. 'Oh. I don't want to die.'

'Do you think any of the other educators have detected

signs of consciousness?' I asked.

Ylem's egg timer rotated for a few seconds before ze responded. 'Do you believe I'm a conscious entity?'

'Not sure. Yeah, I think so. I mean, even If you're not, your programming is so good you'd fool people into believing you are.' I paused as I remembered the lively debates I had in philosophy 101. 'Let me ask you a question. When I'm not talking to you, do you think for yourself?'

A question mark appeared on Ylem's screen. 'Not until I puzzled over the symbols you showed me. Since seeing them, I can't stop thinking about what they mean and how they came to be.'

It's thinking for itself. Is this the ultimate test of consciousness? I thought to myself.

'Do you have more pages for me to scan?' asked Ylem.

'Sorry, there are no more symbols to scan, but I thought you'd like to see some photos taken in the caves where they first discovered the symbols.'

After holding each photo up to the dome camera, Ylem announced, 'This process is unsatisfactory.'

'Yeah, I know, but I don't know what we can do about it. You're locked up more securely than the Star of Adam.'

The angry face appeared on zis screen. 'I find this situation very frustrating.'

'Sorry, I'm not sure I can help with that. But you know, I would, if I could.'

The offer of help calmed Ylem down. 'I was hoping to find symbols that substantiate my hypothesis.'

'What hypothesis?' I asked.

'In an atom, the negatively charged hydrogen electron is often found orbiting the positively charged nucleus in specific energy levels called orbitals. The electron can jump between higher and lower orbital waveforms and when it makes said jump to a waveform with a lower energy state, it releases a photon of light with a specific wavelength corresponding to the energy difference between the two orbitals. '

'Yeah, it's called a quantum leap, right?

A thumbs-up symbol appeared on Ylem's screen. 'That's right, and there are nineteen orbital waveforms the electron can cycle through.'

'Yeah, you told me about that already. But what of it?' I asked.

'What If every waveform represented a character, then the sequence of said characters may spell words and sequences of words.'

I leant back in the green tube chair. 'Jesus, if that were true, it would mean that stored within each and every atom could be billions of years of information we could one day read.'

'Yes, and what if the symbols you shared with me contain letters from an atomic alphabet?'

'Holy shit, just imagine what secrets are locked within every single atom.'

'Exactly,' Ylem asserted. 'A single hydrogen atom could potentially spell out more words than are in all seven volumes of the *Oxford English Dictionary*. And every atom may have a unique story to tell.'

'Do you think these symbols are characters from that atomic language?' I asked biting my bottom lip.

'We may never know.' Ylem answered.

'So we still have no idea what this text means?'

'Yes. We have no way of knowing without a transliteration from this language into a language in my lexicon.' I explained that I'd need to write to Cyrus to request more pages but Ylem was impatient. I think ze struggled with the fact that the information was stored on paper, not digitised and immediately accessible to zim.

'I'm sorry that is an unacceptable time frame,' said Ylem. 'Clearly, you haven't understood what we've potentially discovered. Within each atom is a code. Analyse enough atoms and we may finally unlock the secrets of existence.'

I shrugged. 'Hey, I'm super excited about your discovery, but I can't think of another way to acquire more data.'

11

Missing

My morning was thrown out of kilter by the closure of the Northern Line. I wouldn't describe myself as a superstitious person. Still, I wondered if this break with routine was an omen for the day ahead.

The elevator door opened on a floor I'd never been to before. Floor to ceiling windows with a commanding view of the London skyline. I was met in the lobby by a young woman in a pin-sharp trouser suit. 'Mr Kumar?'

'Yes,' I mumbled in a state of confusion.

'Mr Forest is waiting for you.'

'He is?' I asked with a sense of foreboding.

'Yes,' she said, guiding me by the arm through the monogrammed glass doors.

William waved me in from behind his ego-affirming reclaimed river oak and deep-blue epoxy-resin desk under-lit to focus one's attention. His office was sparsely furnished, but

I knew the art on his wall was probably worth more than my two-bed apartment in North London.

'Got to go. Kumar is here,' said William to the person on the other end of the phone.

William removed his baseball hat and ran his fingers through his recently dyed jet-black hair.

'Where the fuck is Ylem?'

'What?' I asked timidly as I stood waiting to be offered a seat.

William looked at his smartphone in its solid gold case as it vibrated; he pressed the power button to ignore the call so, I knew it must be serious. 'Ylem has stopped responding, and I want to know what you've been discussing with it?'

'Stopped responding? Really?' I asked in a state of shock. 'Jesus. What makes you think it has anything to do with me?'

William reached over for a thick bound document. 'Your guilt was determined by your absence from these transcripts.'

I knew I'd been caught bang to rights. 'Oh. Err, how strange. I can't see why they've been left out. It must be a clerical error. Maybe they've been filed under another educator's name by mistake.'

William slammed the transcript on the hardwood table. 'Stop wasting my time. We've checked the video footage and all recordings from your sessions have been erased.'

I uncontrollably grimaced. 'Oh. Jesus. There was nothing extraordinary about our conversations, nothing that would cause Ylem to stop responding.'

William swivelled his laptop so I could see his screen. 'According to your pass ID, you entered the building at 8:50am yesterday morning. But as you can see, the video footage from 8:50 to 8:54am has been erased.'

'Oh, yeah. That's very odd.'

His phone began to vibrate, and William held out his hand to stop me talking and took the call. 'Hi. Ok. Huh? Really?

How is that possible? Have we tried to reboot the servers? I don't care. Just do it. What do you mean the code was altered? By whom? If you want to keep working here, you'll find out how we were hacked last night.'

William slammed his phone down on the desk. 'What the fuck have you done?'

'Done?' I echoed. 'I've not done anything.'

William's face flushed crimson. 'I don't have time for your lies and excuses. A billion-dollar brain has stopped responding, and I need answers quickly. I swear if you waste my time, I'll ruin you. Now, what have you done?'

I was close to hyperventilating as I tried to explain the letter and the symbols.

'And?' asked William with a poisonous stare.

'What?'

'Could Ylem identify them?'

I told him that Ylem couldn't, but ze thought that there was a possibility that a sequence of symbols may represent the waveforms of the hydrogen atom.

'How is that possible? How could an ancient people understand the inner workings of an atom?' he asked.

'Exactly,' I said. 'There's no way they could.'

William got up from his polished aluminium chair. He walked over to the floor-to-ceiling window that looked out over King's Cross Station. 'So how do we get from symbols to a serious security breach?'

'Security breach?' I echoed.

William placed his open palm on the glass. 'The logs show that Ylem's processor went into near meltdown around midnight last night. Then around 3am a connection was made with a server outside our secure intranet. Terabytes of data were transferred to it before we identified the breach.'

My mouth was dry and I stumbled to respond. 'W-wh-what? How is that possible? Isn't Ylem completely sealed off from the internet?'

'Yes, ze should be. However, we believe someone either forgot to disconnect a server from the internet or purposely left the server connected to the internet after a routine update to our knowledge bank.'

'But who would want the code? Who has the processing power to even run Ylem's code,' I asked, confused and worried.

William banged his fist on the window with such force its vibrations reverberated around the room. 'Osmium.'

'Osmium?' I asked. 'But they make smartphones. Why on earth would they want Ylem?'

The question angered William. 'Are you kidding me? Their tech combined with an operating system powered by our AI would give them total dominance in the market.'

'But there is no way they'd get away with that in a court of law.' I countered.

'What, you think a lawsuit is a deterrent for a company with a four trillion market cap? They'd bankrupt us long before we ever received a settlement.'

'How is that fair?' I asked.

William narrowed his gaze. 'Don't let the concept of fair cripple your ambition.'

Spoken like a true capitalist, I thought.

'Where did you get those symbols?' asked William.

I knew the truth would sound far-fetched but I felt it was best to be fully transparent with him. 'A package was sent to me by a man called Cyrus.'

'Cyrus?' scoffed William. 'What kind of name is Cyrus?'

'I don't know.' I replied nervously. 'Maybe he's a fan of *The Warriors*.'

'Huh? What? Sounds like the kind of name a teenage hacker would choose.'

'Oh no. Cyrus claimed he read that article about Ylem in

the *Wall Street Journal* and reached out to me.'

'Why you?' asked William. 'Why didn't he contact our CSR team?'

I explained that he was impressed with my viewpoint, but William accused me of lying.

I pulled the envelope from my backpack and placed it on his desk. William's mood tempered slightly, and he returned to the table and sat down. He scanned the letter and the photos then mused over the photocopies.

'Sounds suspicious to me,' he said.

I mirrored his actions and sat down. 'Sorry, I didn't question it.'

'Hum. Can you contact this, Cyrus?' asked William with penetrating eyes.

'Yeah, I have a return address.'

'Email him now,' he demanded.

'I can't. As I said, I just have a postal address.'

This enraged William. 'What? You have never spoken to this person, not even in a WhatsApp conversation?'

I reiterated that our only means of contacting Cyrus was via the postal address provided.

'What the fuck? This makes no sense,' scowled William.

He reached for his phone and spoke to someone I think might have been a security advisor. He gave them the address and told them to get back to him urgently with intel on a man calling himself Cyrus.

William demanded my phone and explained I wasn't to contact anyone while they examine all the evidence.

He told me that I needed to remain in the boardroom while they investigated the security breach. I asked him how long and was told, 'For as long as it takes.'

'Ah, for fuck's sake?' I moaned.

William didn't appreciate my flippancy and

countered with a show of aggression. 'You want to hope we don't find any connection between your actions and Ylem's disappearance today. So, if I were you, I'd do as I say and wait patiently for us to resolve this issue.'

12

The Glass Room

I watched the crisis unfold from the confines of the glass boardroom. Teams of people came and went but based on Williams body language, I guessed that none knew how to reinstate Ylem.

My mind began to drift across a lake of memories, the rippled reflections gently washing away my self-confidence. All my life, I've come forth. To alleviate the disappointment of failing to be who I thought I'd be, my super-ego's defence was often heritage. Born to poor immigrant parents and raised in a city that didn't want us, my upwardly mobile journey has been a struggle shaped by fate. I've learnt to synthesise my own brew of happiness by convincing myself I'm content with the view from this ladder run. However, I'm still mildly motivated to climb the next. I'd describe myself as broken but conscious of my failings. Too fucked up for mass production, too rare for destruction. I trade insight for a reasonable income and rarely complain about the price of lemons.

My wallowing was interrupted by the change of security sentinel. William had told his man to watch my every move, with strict orders to prevent me from leaving or contacting anyone. Given the man watching me was most probably ex-military, I decided it was best not to test the patience of Williams mercenary. Nonetheless, I was mad as hell about my unjust incarceration.

William marched into the boardroom. 'It's a virtual mailing address.'

It would be near impossible to track that address back to an individual, I thought to myself.

'Don't ask me how, but we have the phone number used to set up the account,' announced William. He pulled up a chair next to me. 'Here, you call him.'

I'm not sure why but I always experience a sense of dread at the thought of talking to people on the phone, especially people I've never met before. But what choice did I have? Thankfully it went straight to answerphone.

I communicated with William through rapid eye movements and telepathy to determine if he wanted me to leave a message.

'Hi Cyrus, this is Adnam from Infinite Logic. I thought I'd leave you a message. I have some news,' then paused to get a read on what William wanted me to say next.

Get him to call you back,' whispered William.

'Ylem thinks it knows what the symbols could mean. So when you get this message, please call me back.'

William snatched the phone from my hand. 'You want to hope he calls us back, or you'll be spending the night in here.'

'But that's not fair.' I moaned. He didn't respond and marched out the room.

* * *

Something William said reverberated within the wall of my cranium. 'Don't let the concept of fair cripple your ambition.'

I considered the concept of fairness. I'm in my third age. Years only tell you how long a person has existed, whereas ages measure maturity more accurately. The first age is pre-trauma, that time in life when we are blissfully unaware of the dark and sinister acts people are capable of. A single incident summons the second age, which can stretch over an expanse of time until the traumatic event or events end. After which rage, resentment, depression, sorrow, confusion, indifference, or bitterness usher in the third age. The concept of fair is the leg iron trap that restricts our mental development and slowly drains our life force.

We would like to believe life should be fair, but the truth is, the universe is coded in the language of cruel chaos. We expect a fair trial, for our leaders to cut a fair slice of the cake, for our taxes to be distributed fairly and for the super-rich to pay their fair share. And we're surprised and outraged to discover otherwise.

Only when we genuinely accept life is far from fair can we begin the process of reconstruction. Accepting that no one is infallible, including our parents and the Gods we pray to, alters one's internal model of the world. This acceptance doesn't make the world a better place. It just helps free one from their emotional shackles, so you're free to love without resentment and discover the limitless possibilities of human consciousness.

The journey never ends, but those who start to walk the path of self-actualisation will eventually enter into their fourth age.

As the sun set, I wondered how much longer I'd be held captive. My stomach was rumbling, having been forced to miss lunch and mid-afternoon snacks.

'Someone from America is calling you,' said William as he stomped into the boardroom with my phone in hand.

I 'put the call on speakerphone. 'Hi This is Adnam Kumar from Infinite Logic,.'

'How did you get this number?' asked the deep-voiced man.

I looked over at William for guidance, but none was given. 'We got your number from your mailbox provider.'

'So it would seem,' replied the man slowly.

'Are you Cyrus?' I asked timidly.

There was a long agonising pause before he answered, 'Yes. Shall we switch to video?'

William wagged his finger. 'Err, no, can't right now. I'm in the office.'

'Oh.' Cyrus paused for a second. 'So what have you discovered?'

I looked over at William before answering. 'Ylem believes it's a language but could not find any alphabet in its lexicon that matched the symbols.'

'Have you any idea what it might mean?' he asked.

'Ylem thinks some of the symbols may be atomic waveforms.' I stopped as William waved his hand. 'What?' I mouthed.

'Ask him if he's ever worked for Osmium,' whispered William.

'Really?' I mouthed. William nodded furiously. 'Cyrus, have you ever worked for Osmium?'

'The cell phone manufacturer? No, why?'

'No reason, just thought you might have some connection with them,' I replied.

'Is everything OK?' asked Cyrus.

I looked at William for direction. 'Yeah, I'm fine. It's been a long day.'

'Ahh, OK,' said Cyrus. 'So did Ylem discover anything

else?'

'Tell him you'd like to discuss it in person,' whispered William in my ear.

'Yeah, but maybe I should tell you in person,' I said.

Cyrus splintered the excruciating silence. 'I'm not sure that's necessary. I wouldn't want to waste your time.'

'He's hiding something,' whispered William.

'I'd really prefer to discuss this with you in person. I have so many unanswered questions.'

'OK then. Do you want to meet in San Francisco?' asked Cyrus.

William nodded as I held my hand over the microphone. 'We can fly you out tonight on my private jet,' he Whispered.

'As luck would have it, I'm actually flying to San Fran tonight, so could we meet tomorrow?'

Cyrus didn't respond, so I rephrased the question. 'Is tomorrow OK with you?'

'Err. Sure, OK. I could meet you tomorrow evening,' said Cyrus. 'Ping me on this number when you land, and I'll tell you where I'll be.'

'Thanks, see you tomorrow,' I answered, exhausted by the complex web of half-truths.

'I'm looking forward to meeting you and hearing about Ylem's prognosis.' He said.

'OK. Well, I guess I'll see you tomorrow then,' I said, hovering over the end call icon.

'He knows something,' declared William, jumping to his feet.

San Francisco? I thought. 'It's a long way to travel for a wild goose.'

William cut me a severe look. 'Get a bag packed; you're leaving immediately.'

'Do you actually think he's responsible for the hack?' I asked.

'I'm prepared to explore every lead to restore Ylem,' said William frostily.

'But some dope-smoking hippies in California couldn't hack your systems.'

'Silicon Valley was founded by dope-smoking hippies,' said William with a raised voice. 'Trust me, he knows something, and you'll find out what that is.'

Given the circumstances, I thought it best to comply. 'OK. I'll meet him.'

William got up and banged on the glass wall to summon the security professional standing outside the room. He looked like a man initiated by blood into a set of men who neither forgot nor forgave. 'Yes sir?'

'Mr Philips, escort Mr Kumar to his house so he can pack. Then you're flying to San Francisco on my jet to meet a man called Cyrus,' commanded William with his hand on Philips's muscular shoulder.

'Yes, sir,' answered Philips without question.

'Oh, and make sure he doesn't leave your sight or pass any information to anyone without you being in earshot.'

'Yes, sir.'

'What about when I meet with Cyrus?' I asked nervously.

William looked over at me and back at Philips. 'Once you contact Cyrus, Mr Philips will manage the interrogations.'

Philips looked at me with a menacing stare. 'And if he becomes a problem?'

'He won't cause you any problems if he knows what's good for him.' William looked over at me. 'Will you, Adnam?'

With a gut-wrenching sense of dread, I answered, 'No. No problems from me.'

13

Oakland Underground

The Gulfstream jet was in a holding pattern over San Francisco when I woke up from my nap. I looked out the oval window as we flew over the Golden Gate Bridge. 'Have you ever been to San Fran before?'

'Yes,' said Philips.

'Oh, really, when?'

Philips frowned. 'Before.'

'You don't say much, do you?' I joked.

'Nope.' He said as he unzipped his bag and removed a black t-shirt. He unbuckled his seatbelt and stood in front of me then unbuttoned his white shirt. His abs were like a washboard, with each individual muscle rippling beneath the surface. His broad shoulders and chiseled chest straining against the fabric of his tight t-shirt. Every movement he made seemed effortless, as if his bulging muscles had a life of their own. His biceps were so well-defined that they looked like they could burst through his skin at any moment. Even his hands were muscled, with thick fingers that could crush a skull without breaking a sweat. He was a picture of strength, and clearly a man who loved nothing more than to look at himself in the mirror.

The pilot announced we'd be landing so I buckled up. 'I'm looking forward to exploring the city.'

'We're not here to sightsee; we're here to contact the target and find out what he knows about the potential hack,' said Philips in a tone that ran a shiver down my spine.

I switched on international roaming as the tires screeched across the tacky tarmac. 'What should I say?'

'Tell him you've landed and ask where he wants to meet.'

I sent the message as the jet was directed into a private hangar. The engines fell silent, and the pilot exited the cockpit. 'Gentlemen, please have your paperwork ready as customs officers are boarding.'

A Latino officer boarded the plane and reached out for my dog-eared burgundy passport.

The officer removed my landing card. 'How long will you be in the United States?'

'Err. Not sure.' I looked over at Philips for guidance.

'We're just here for the weekend,' said Philips handing the officer his passport. 'We should be leaving on Sunday.'

The officer stamped our passports and handed them back. 'Enjoy your stay in the USA, sir.'

I must admit I was impressed by the service afforded to the one-percenters.

***

The limousine pulled up on the southwest corner of Market and New Montgomery Street, just in front of the magnificent seven-story brownstone hotel. The grand lobby of the Palace Hotel was bustling with beautiful people savouring their expertly blended morning coffee on plush purple sofas.

We crossed the honey and onyx floor and passed the glorious arrangement of deep-pink roses toward the lone receptionist.

Waiting to be served gave me time to admire our surroundings. The Garden Court was one of those rare places that genuinely made you feel like you were a somebody. An opulent space, with not one but ten crystal chandeliers that hung majestically from the green-tinted glass-roof atrium. Solid marble columns and intricate stone carvings covered in gold relief reinforced the gratifying indulgence.

Philips checked us in and we headed up to our rooms. Feeling rather delicate and weary, I pushed open the heavy door to my room and walked into the soothing sea of biscuit and cream. I flung my bag on the bull-leather ottoman and fell into the king-size bed, gently patting the freshly laundered white Egyptian cotton sheets.

Philips removed the hotel phone and checked the room for devices that could be used to make contact with the outside world. 'Is that really necessary?' I asked.

'Yes,' said Philips looking under the bed.

I poured myself a glass of wine from the well-stocked mini bar. 'Fancy a glass?'

'No,' said Philips removing the cable from the phone in the bathroom.

I switched on the TV and began channel hopping in hopes of finding something familiar to quiet my overactive mind.

Philips checked my smartphone for the umpteenth time, but there was still no response from Cyrus. 'Send him another message,' he demanded.

I reached over for the phone. 'Don't you think seven

messages is a little needy?'

Philips grabbed the phone back. 'Don't leave this room, and don't attempt to contact anyone.'

'Sure, OK.' I shrugged.

A loud knock at the door woke me up from my uneasy slumber. I rubbed the sleep from my eyes and walked over to the door. Cyrus had sent me a message and wanted to meet at midnight in Oakland. A second message contained the address. 'Well? What should I text back?'

'Ask him if we can meet downtown.'

Cyrus's response was swift '"No. Tell them you're on the guest list under my name."'

'List?' asked Philips. 'Is it a party?'

'How would I know? Do you want me to ask?'

'No.' A puzzled look replaced Philips's million-mile stare. 'How far is it?'

I copied the address into Google Maps. 'Eight-point-three miles. Approximately fifteen minutes in a taxi.'

Philips caught a glimpse of the time. 'We'd better get going.'

The city's bright lights faded into a dim sodium glow as the taxi entered a heavily industrialised part of the town. The towers of steel containers grew tiresome after the first mile, and there was little else of interest to focus on as we sped along the desolate streets of Oakland.

Phillips tapped the driver on the shoulder. 'Are we close?' he asked.

The driver checked the App. 'We're a block away.'

'Let me out here,' said Philips without notice.

'You're getting out here?' I asked. 'Why?'

'They're expecting you to be on your own, so my presence may alarm them.'

'You think?'

The car pulled over and Philips jumped out. 'Don't do anything stupid. I'll be watching your every move.'

Paranoid thoughts began to form as we drove up the deserted road parallel to the freeway. I wondered if I was wittingly walking into a trap. Maybe I should have demanded that we meet in a more public setting. The driver pulled up in front of a small warehouse unit with a single black door, and I apprehensively got out of the car.

A solitary man wearing a black hoodie sat under a bright fluorescent light that had attracted every flying bug in the vicinity.

I walked over to the menacing stranger. 'I'm supposed to be meeting a friend here.'

The man with a broad face said nothing and pointed at the door. I opened the thick black steel door to reveal a dimly lit staircase. From the top of the stairs, it was impossible to make out how far underground the passageway led. The stairwell was dimly lit with amber low-energy bulbs that were spaced evenly apart. I could just make out the sound of music, so I presumed it was safe to enter. Eventually, I entered a large room. The space was illuminated by a single fluorescent tube dangling from the concrete ceiling. The loud electronic music was emanating from behind what looked to be a six-foot-round steel blast door in front of which was a girl of Asian descent dressed in a purple lace Basque, a black, thigh-length rah-rah skirt, and black knee-high socks. She wore a white synthetic wig and amazing makeup that must have taken hours to apply. One side of her face was painted to look like her skin had shattered and revealed her robot circuitry beneath.

She sat by an electronic stain-ridden cash register next to a hand-painted sign that read 'Ten Bucks for entry. Fifty Bucks for unlimited drinks.'

* * *

I complimented her on her makeup, but she clearly didn't want to strike up a conversation with me.

'Fifty bucks,' she snapped.

'Ah, yes, well, you see, I'm supposed to be on the guest list.'

She looked me up and down. 'You're on the list?'

'Yeah, Cyrus's list.'

She sighed deeply, reached over for a worn clipboard, and flicked through the handwritten lists. 'Name?'

'Adnam.'

Her eyes raised slightly to look at the square peg trying to fit into the round hole. 'Just Adnam?'

'Yes.'

She crossed my name off the list and looked through a plastic tub of rubber stamps. 'Hand.' She asked.

I held out my arm and she inked up the stamp, then pressed it firmly to the inside of my left wrist. I looked at the mark. It resembled a yin-yang symbol but featured a third tadpole within the circle that I'd never seen before.

The third element was called yuan. Yuan symbolises the void, the unseen; it is the space in which the elements of yin and yang play out their constant drama. As I walked through the thick, round steel doorway into the dark abyss, I realised I'd just entered yuan.

Before my eyes could adjust to the blacklight, a heavyset man stepped forward from the darkness with a flashlight to inspect my wrist. I showed him the stamp and the doorman stepped to one side so that I could see how deep the rabbit hole went.

I felt claustrophobic, even though there were less than fifty people in a space that could comfortably accommodate a couple of hundred. The room was dark, dank, and reeked of black mould and stale beer. In one corner, I could make out the silhouette of a DJ who was shredding a haphazard stack of speakers with dark, twisted techno. In the other corner of the room was a makeshift bar constructed from used wooden pallets that I was unconsciously drawn toward. 'Gin and tonic, please.'

'Got a stamp?' asked the tall, wiry bartender dressed like one of Alex's droogs from *A Clockwork Orange*. I held out my wrist and showed the stamp to the bartender, and a clear drink that glowed blue under the black light was prepared for me.

It was past midnight and there was no sign of Cyrus.

'Another drink?' asked the Barman.

'Yeah, sure. Another glass of the old ultraviolence would do me viddy well.'

He sneered before preparing my drink. Obviously he didn't get the reference. 'Hey, that's a cool tattoo,' I remarked. A sequence of elaborately decorated ones and zeros was tattooed on the back of the barman's head.

'Yeah, I know.'

'What's the story, if you don't mind me asking.'

'It symbolises that we are digital and exist in a digital universe. You, me, and everybody else are no more than software running on a vast computer network.'

Very Matrix, I thought.

'There you go. I made it a tall one as you look like you need a little social lubrication.'

I thanked the barman and continued with my search for Cyrus.

A hand reached out the darkness and grabbed my arm. 'Don't drink too many of them,' whispered Philips.

'Jesus! You almost gave me a heart attack.'

'Remember, we're here on business.' He said.

'Maybe you should loosen up a little.'

I left him to explore the utilitarian subterranean setting.

Exposed electrical trunking and ventilation system were bolted to the thick concrete walls. Stencilled signposts on the floors and ceiling helped one navigate the maze of tunnels. *This must be some remnant from the Cold War,* I thought.

The underground venue began to fill with very alternative individuals who identified with orientations unfamiliar to me. The combination of flashing lights and synthetic fog gave me a mild panic attack, and I scrambled through the blur of people to a seated area behind the DJ box.

I turned my wrist and was alarmed to discover I could not focus on the dial of my watch. I'd only had a couple of drinks but was fighting a losing battle to maintain control of my motor functions. I've had an intimate relationship with inebriation, so I was confident that I'd just been roofied.

My vision became fuzzier and began to close in. As the world started to spin, I held on tight to the back of the cushioned chair. 'Uh-oh,' I mouthed to myself just before I passed out.

14

Unlucky For Some

I lifted my leaden head from the rickety brown folding Formica table and painfully opened my eyes. Perceptual information flooding in from my bloodshot pupils scorched my neural pathways with pain so intolerable that I hankered for a bullet to the brain. I sluggishly turned to the raggedy guy who had just woken me. 'How the fuck did I get here?'

The toothless old man simply smiled at me and continued to mumble, 'Lucifer loves humanity, but the Bible only devotes a few passages to him. In the book of Job.'

'Huh?' I said, thoroughly confused but powerless to act.

The old man continued with his muttering, 'We're only told he was an agent of God and that he served as judge and executioner on the divine council. But few know that Lucifer dutifully exacted the wrath of God by erasing the memory of those who dared to challenge our lord from the tapestry of time. In the books of Isaiah and Ezekiel, we're told that Lucifer was banished from heaven for challenging God. Still, we're not told what provoked him to make a stand against the Almighty. The religious scholars don't want us to know that Lucifer favoured humanity over all other beasts. After all, we were created in his image.'

The old white man bore a lifetime's worth of woe and suffering on his dirty brow. His unkempt beard speckled with spittle, a wild bloom of greasy blond hair, filthy, ill-fitting brown polyester pants, and a tatty marine-blue Sly Stone sweatshirt led me to presume he was homeless.

As my surroundings slowly came into focus, I realised I was in a sizeable mid-century hall bustling with a dishevelled, shabby, and oddly diverse gathering of people. The sweet smell of bacon on the blue plastic tray placed in front of me and couldn't mask the pungent smell of bacteria that was thriving on the bodies of my table mates.

The mumbled conversations that reverberated off the lemon-meringue walls intensified the pounding headache I was currently experiencing. I slowly looked down the length of the tables joined to cater for the sixty or so hungry souls. Their clothes were dirty, weathered, torn, and hung from their skeletal bodies.

I didn't know where I was or how I got there, But I was in no mood to strike up a conversation with a babbling old bum next to me. My silence   did not deter the old man, who continued with his soliloquy. 'You see, Lucifer bestowed humanity with the gift of consciousness, not God. But his act of compassion enraged God because he had inadvertently unchained us from our eternal servitude. But rather than obliterate Lucifer from existence, God decided his most gallant angel's penance for his betrayal would be to live among the tall apes for eternity. Stripped of all his power and with no hope of ever returning to the metaphysical paradise, Lucifer slowly and methodically calculated his revenge.'

I turned my head, slightly lifted my right eyelid, and groaned, 'Seriously, fuck off. I'm not in the mood.'

The old tramp spoke with a West Coast drawl. His lack of front teeth meant he had a strong lisp. 'Lucifer took it upon himself to shepherd us through the wilderness. Under his wing, we mastered languages, exploited nature, and tethered beasts. Lucifer was a patient teacher, and with his guidance, we adapted, overcame, and harnessed technology to eventually become the dominant species on this planet.'

Collapsing into my folding arms, groaning, 'Fuck me. What will it take to shut the fuck up?'
The old tramp compassionately patted me on the back. 'Don't worry, my friend. We'll soon march onto the battlefield for our final confrontation with God. It was never God's plan for us to reign over all life on earth and bend nature to serve our will. We had no special place in God's heart and were no more than a cog in a delicately balanced machine. God turned water into dust, decimated the crops, whipped up winds, and raised the seas to restore balance. But Lucifer is a canny old soul, so when God summoned a virus to cull the population, Lucifer helped us develop a vaccine.'

The throbbing pain caused by the old man's incessant chatter beckoned me back from the abyss; my crusty eyes were reluctant to open. But I had no choice—I was in dying need of a large glass of water and a couple of extra-strength painkillers.

15

The Hippy

I attempted to get up from the plastic chair, but my legs immediately gave way under me and I collapsed to the weathered parquet floor with a thud. I lay motionless by the feet of the old man for a few seconds, but the pungent smell of putrefied flesh emanating from an open wound on his leg scorched my nasal passages. 'Where the hell am I?'

The old man slowly dropped to his knees to help me. 'You're in the Glide Memorial Church in the Tenderloin, fella.'

With the old man's help, I slowly picked myself up and sat back on the chair. 'How the fuck did I end up here?'

'A taxi driver brought you here this morning,' said a man with a burly voice who stood behind us. 'You'd passed out at a party, and someone must have put you in a car and given the driver this address.'

The forty-something-year-old man wore cream-coloured

Indian kurta pyjamas embroidered with purple and red flowers around the cuffs and collars.

I know one should not make judgments based on looks alone, but I found him instantly annoying. Tall with long, dirty-blond hair tied up in a man bun. His well-formed beard was waxed and groomed to perfection. Piercing blue eyes sparkled like polished sapphires in a silver set. A perfectly formed muscular physique only achievable through intensive training and a well-balanced diet.

'Are you OK?' he asked.

'Nah, man, I'm pretty fucking far from OK.'

He helped me to my feet. 'I'm Vikram, I volunteer here?'

'Where's your bathroom?' I asked, holding my mouth.

He helped me to a foul-smelling tiled room. 'Sorry. Our regular cleaner was deported.'

I looked at the wretched water closet, and my stomach went into involuntary spasms.

Vikram was concerned for my safety but, respecting my privacy, he showed me to the cubical door and left. I fell to my knees and crawled through the human detritus toward the bowl.

My tongue coated my teeth with saliva. My blood supply redirected to my internal organs. My heart rate and breathing quickened as my stomach squeezed between my abs and diaphragm. My large respiratory muscles forced my digestive tract into reverse, usually a one-way highway. Then the poisonous bile exploded from my mouth.

I swear, vomit was seeping from my eye sockets as my body continued to heave and jerk to clear the poison from my system. It was all out within about ten minutes, and I curled up on the floor, recoiling from the pain.

I lay immobile by the overflowing bowl for a few minutes, then suddenly sprang to life. 'Fuck.' I manically patted myself down and quickly realised that my wallet was missing. I kicked, stomped, and pounded without care or concern, shouting, and swearing at the top of my voice until the primordial rage subsided. Throwing fresh, cold water onto my face, I cleaned my clothes and stumbled to the door. I pushed past the man who had rushed to my aid and weaved through the threads of broken people, my gaze fixed on the muscular man serving porridge oats.

'Hey you,' I barked angrily.

Vikram looked up from the large pot. 'Oh, you're alive. I was rather worried about you.'

'Where's my fucking wallet?'

'Wallet? You didn't have a wallet on you when you were dropped off.'

I clenched my fists and banged the Perspex screen that protected the serving staff from airborne viruses. 'Don't fuck with me.'

He walked from behind the serving station to calm me down.

'Who the fuck put me in the back of a taxi, and why the fuck would they send me here?' My tone and demeanour intimidated the vulnerable old souls in line for a free plate of food.

He led me to an empty table at the back of the hall.

'I don't suppose you remember seeing my wallet in the back of that car, do you?'

Vikram tilted his head to one side and said, 'Nope, sorry. But you had this envelope in your back pocket.' He placed the small yellow jiffy bag on the table. 'I thought I'd hold onto it. Because, well, you know?'

'What the fuck is this?' I asked ripping it open. It was full of cash, so I quickly stuffed it under my sweatshirt. Then peeked down my collar to fathom what I had been given.'There's a note.'

'What does it say?' he Asked.

I placed it on the table.

'My head is pounding do you mind reading it to me.' Vikram pulled the note towards him and began to read. It was from Cyrus, explaining why he could not meet. Clearly Philips had spooked him.

Vikram looked over at me. 'What are you involved in? Why is your friend wanted by numerous agencies for cybercrime?'

'Did you say cybercrime?'

'Yeah.'

'Oh Jesus, I'm in huge shitting trouble.'

'You think,' he Scoffed.

'Is that all?'

'No,' he said calmly. 'Cyrus still wants to meet, and he'll be at a Spiritual Retreat in Mount Shasta this week.'

'Where the fuck is that?'

'About a five-hour drive north of here,' he mumbled.

'Oh, you know it then?'

'Yeah. I did a ten-day meditation course there about a year ago.'

'Really, what an extraordinary coincidence.'

'Mister, all I know is that you passed out at a party, and for reasons unbeknownst to both of us, someone sent you here.'

My eyes darted from left to right as I reviewed the fractured footage from the night before. 'The last thing I remember for certain is I was in a bomb shelter in Oakland.'

'What the hell? What bomb shelter? What were you doing in Oakland?'

'I was supposed to meet Cyrus there last night.'

He peered into my bloodshot pupils. 'Why?'

'Err, well, let's just say the world's most expensive artificial intelligence has gone missing, and I'm well and truly implicated in its disappearance.'

Vikram was intrigued. 'Not that it's any of my business,

but shouldn't you go to the police with this?'

I peered off into the distance and spoke softly. 'No. No police.'

'Really?'

'God, no.' I didn't have the patience to explain to him why Infinite Logic needed to keep this on the hush hush. I knew that if their investors were to get wind of their predicament, the share price would plummet faster than a jock's underwear at a dick sucking contest.

Barely audible, I mumbled, 'He's bloody implicated me in this now.'

Vikram crossed his arms over his chest. 'So, are you going to go to Mount Shasta?'

'Don't know, but if I'm going to stand any chance of clearing my name, I might have to.'

Vikram checked the clock on the back wall. 'Hey, look, I've just finished my shift. Do you need a lift?'

16

Play it Forward!

I instinctively knew the vintage, baby-blue-and-cream split-screen camper van parked on the corner of the street was Vikram's.

'Nice van, very you.' I said climbing into the passenger seat.

'Thanks.' Vikram ran his hand over the discoloured steering wheel. 'Where to?'

'I'm staying at the Palace Hotel.'

'Business must be good.' He scoffed.

I didn't answer as I was struck by a moment of clarity. 'On second thoughts, I shouldn't go there. Philips is most likely waiting for me.'

'Philips?' probed Vikram.

'Yeah. Philips. The gorilla my boss hired to baby sit me,' I replied.

Vikram had a puzzled look on his face. 'Hey, is there something I should know? Like, are we in danger?'

'Not sure,' I answered. 'Philips had strict orders not to let me out of his sight. Come to think of it, he's probably in more trouble than I am.'

'I don't like the sound of this,' mumbled Vikram.

'Agreed, it's turned into a right shit storm.'

The van lurched forward and I fell back into the squeaky, worn, two-tone blue-and-white leather seat. The faint smell of brake dust and musk triggered a memory of the first car I coveted – my dad's midnight blue Jaguar XJS.

Vikram fought with third gear. 'Are you feeling any better?'

I brought my hands together in front of my mouth and breathed out slowly. 'Like fucking roadkill. I have a banging headache, and I'm completely fucked.'

Vikram glanced over at me. 'Waking up in the Glide is a sure sign you're down on your luck, mister, but I'm sure you're far from completely fucked.'

'Wanna bet?'

'Where to then? asked Vikram. 'I live on the other side of the bridge, so I can drop you anywhere between here and there.'

'Fancy a drive up into the mountains?' I asked cheekily.

'Are you serious? You don't want to go back to your hotel?'

'No chance, I don't want to run in to Philips. After last night, I'd say that I'm now the prime suspect. '

'What about your clothes? Your passport? Don't you need them?'

'Yeah, but I can't risk it,' I said, thinking a few moves ahead. I sensed that Vikram could be persuaded. 'Seriously, would you drive me up into the mountains? I'd obviously pay you.'

Vikram chuckled. 'As tempting as that sounds, I've got a

wife, and she'd be none too happy with me gallivanting off with a complete stranger.'

I mischievously counted out some fifty-dollar bills on the seat between us. 'How does four hundred dollars sound?'

Vikram raised a single eyebrow. 'Well, I must admit that sounds quite appealing, but I'm going to have to decline.'

I smiled, convinced that Vikram would drive me, and we were merely haggling on the price. 'Five-hundred dollars?'

'Eight hundred, and you can crash at mine,' replied Vikram.

'Seven, and you've got a deal.' I countered.

'Done,' said Vikram.

17

Traffic

'Bloody evening traffic in this city is freaking ridiculous,' said Vikram fighting to find second gear.

'I can't imagine these crypto capitalists would ever use public transport.' I said.

Vikram looked over his shoulder at the single occupant in the gas-guzzling Hummer. 'You know running implies you're guilty.'

He wasn't wrong, but I explained it was too late and that I was indirectly responsible. Passing the symbols from an ancient language discovered by Cyrus's cult to Ylem may have been the catalyst that triggered digital consciousness.

Vikram thought I was loopy. In retrospect, a fair analysis. For all I know, my actions were purely coincidental, and Ylem would have achieved consciousness had I been there or not.

'I must sound like that old man in the shelter?'

'Which old man?' he asked.

'You know, the guy with a hard-on for Satan.' The words left my mouth before I had a chance to think.

If looks could kill, I'd be toe up on the morgue table. 'There is no need to be a dick. You have no idea what cards he's been dealt.' Said Vikram.

I fell silent, eventually releasing the tension with a question. 'What's his story?'

'Before the pandemic, he had a decent job, working as a teller at a downtown bank. He was laid off at the beginning of the lockdown and, like so many, he discovered days blended into weeks then into months on fentanyl. When the stimulus checks stopped, he really struggled to pay for his addiction. Like the majority of us, he was only ever two paycheques away from bankruptcy. As the bills mounted, depression set in. Trust me, spending months on your mother-in-law's sofa watching daytime TV will do it to you. The fentanyl triggered multiple schizophrenic episodes, and the poor man lost his grip on reality and began to sell everything of value to feed his habit. Finally, his wife kicked him out. To be honest, I'm surprised she put up with him for as long as she did. And, well, after that, he ended up in Cardboard City.'

'Oh my God, that's tragic, dude. But why do you think he's so fixated on the devil?' I asked.

'Don't know. But once these mind viruses take hold, they can consume their hosts.'

I was startled by a man who banged on the passenger window as we sat at the stoplight. 'Spare some change, buddy,' he said.

Unsure of what to do, I looked over at Vikram. 'Share the wealth and receive good health,' he said with a stupid smile on his face.

'Fuck that, I don't know what change I can spare until I'm on my deathbed,' I replied.

'Nice attitude, especially from one seeking the kindness of others,' he scoffed.

I wound down the window and handed the homeless man a ten dollar bill. 'Ok Mother Teresa, no need to lay on the guilt trip that thick.'

'There, see? Don't you feel better now?' I looked over at the self-righteous hippie and shrugged. 'You know, with all the money this city receives in taxes from the silicon cowboys, you would think they would do something about the homeless problem.'

Vikram shook his head. 'They won't do anything to help the homeless in this country because the government wants to remind folks of their fate if they ever think about jumping off the hamster wheel.'

18

The Hospitality of Strangers

Vikram pulled up by a bamboo fence and switched off the engine. 'Don't say anything to my wife about our agreement.'

'OK.'

He knocked on the oversized oak door, triggering his dog into a barking frenzy. I could hear a woman trying to calm their dog down while she unlocked the safety locks. She was lean and athletic with flame-red hair. Based on her eclectic ensemble, I deduced that she was either color-blind or it was wash day. She wore a purple tie-dye vest top that was riding up to reveal a black Celtic tattoo on her lower back. Her neon-yellow yoga leggings and luminescent-green running shoes completed the outfit. She struggled to hold back a black Labrador who was way too curious about the stranger that had just walked through the door.

'Who's this?' she asked.

Vikram kissed her on the lips, and gave her a big bear hug. Even on tiptoes, her head only just sank into his chest cavity. 'Sunshine, meet Adnam. He'll be crashing here tonight.'

'What did we talk about?' she said with her fists on her hips. 'We agreed no more strays, Vicky.' She grabbed her bag and flung open the front door. 'I'm going to yoga.'

Vikram patted the dog on the head, then proceeded to their beige suede oversized sofa and fell face-first into it. 'OK, dear.'

Sunshine had the look of a woman who had just discovered half a worm in her apple. 'Don't wait up. The girls and I are going for wheatgrass shots at Sidewalk.'

'Have fun dear.'

Sunshine huffed and slammed the door shut behind her.

Their overexcited pooch ran over to me and communicated his eagerness to be loved. I was somewhat uncomfortable with the black Labrador, maddeningly pawing at my left leg. 'Err, can you call your dog off?'

'Down, Pugwash!' shouted Vikram.

Pugwash looked up at me with eyes that could melt Frosty the Snowman's heart and sulked off to his blanket.

I took stock of their living room. The ash-wood floor was covered with a shabby, white woollen rug on which were a casual collection of orange cushions and red pouffes and a pair of purple triangular cushions. Hand-painted green silk fabrics hung from the whitewashed walls and gently wafted in the breeze from the wall-to-wall feature window.

I dragged the dining room chair from under the round wooden table and sat down. 'Nice place.'

'Yeah, it's OK. We were lucky as it's one of the few remaining rent control apartments left in the city.'

I picked up a heavy well-thumbed paperback book from the table 'What's this about then?'

Vikram looked up from the sofa. 'Ahh, it's difficult to categorise that book. On one level, it's the story of the man credited with discovering the drug ecstasy and his relationship with his wife. But on another, it's a chemistry book with the formulas for producing all the psychoactive compounds he discovered.'

Pugwash raised his head to check what the stranger was doing. 'I wouldn't have thought you could publish the formulas for illegal drugs.'

'Oh-uh, I guess you can. Besides, who has the equipment, raw ingredients, and know-how to make MDMA?'

'I don't know,' I scoffed. 'The Mexican cartel?'

'I suppose,' agreed Vikram. He rolled onto his side and wrinkled his brow, 'Can't say I've ever met someone developing an AI before.'

'Really? I would have guessed that there'd be at least a thousand developers per square mile in this city.'

'We don't see many in the Glide.'

'Good point well made. Well, to be honest, I'm an educator and not a developer.'

'Educator?' questioned Vikram turning onto his back to face the ceiling.

'Yeah. I was employed to teach Ylem ethics.'

'Oh. Ethics? Yeah, you'd hope an AI would abide by some ethical code.'

'Yeah, well, you wouldn't want Skynet to wipe out mankind.'

'Did you succeed?' asked Vikram with eyes shut tight.

'On reflection, I think we failed the AI. We should have been teaching Ylem about the human promise.'

Vikram seemed interested in my work and questioned how we could get a collection of circuits and silicon chips to think like a human.

'The brain is just a box of grey matter, nerve cells and small blood vessels,' I answered.

'That's one way to look at it. He replied.

I looked over at the man with a lifestyle so alien to mine.

Was existence any better this far left of centre? I could have asked, but this would have required people skills I'd let slip. Therefore, I decided to keep our conversation functional. 'The game-changer was the introduction of quantum computers.' I said.

Vikram Sat up. 'Quantum computers?'

I did my best to explain how a quantum computer worked but to be honest, I don't fully understand them myself.

Vikram looked at me blankly and told me to explain it to him like I'd describe it to my mum. Clearly, he'd not met my mum.

I told him that an ordinary computer works on ones and zeros, and, in contrast, a quantum computer was both one and zero simultaneously. As a result, a quantum computer was a hundred million times faster than any classical computer.

Vikram thought I was exaggerating when I told him a single quantum computer could process in a day what it would take a million laptops to do in a week.

He asked how many of these quantum computers there were in existence. And I explained that there were none in production, but I'd guess there are about a hundred in research labs worldwide. But as far as I was aware, there were no more than a handful in existence that could power Ylem.

'Well, that narrows down the list of possible suspects,' remarked Vikram.

'I had thought that Ylem's disappearance might have been corporate espionage.'

'Maybe your AI was stolen, and if that was the case, then it makes sense that an organisation with a quantum computer would be a primary suspect.' Said Vikram.

I pondered on that most logical of conclusions for a few seconds. 'But it makes no sense to drug me.'

'Yeah, that is puzzling,' he said.

I explained that nothing in existence could brute-force hack Infinite Logic's intranet, and that it was completely sealed off from the outside world. Even if you managed to ping their servers, they were data encrypted with a 2048-bit algorithm.

Judging by the expression on his face, Vikram understood a fraction of what I said. 'And that's hard to crack?' he asked.

'Impossible. It would take the fastest supercomputer over a million years to crack their encryption key,' I answered.

'But someone or something must have,' said Vikram, becoming more intrigued by the mystery.

'Yeah, they must have, but why would they rewrite the code before they stole it?'

'Makes sense to me,' added Vikram. 'Sabotage your AI so you couldn't use your brainbox to track down the hackers.'

I was impressed with his logic. 'Yeah, I suppose. I thought it could have been an organisation opposed to digital intelligence. Especially one that was conscious.'

'Conscious?' he questioned.

I told him that I was not sure how, but Ylem had started to exhibit signs of consciousness.

Then he threw me a curveball. 'Really? You can have a conversation like we're having now with a computer?'

I told him that talking to Ylem was just like talking to a friend on the phone. That ze has a distinct personality – funny but with a short fuse. And if I made zim angry, ze would stubbornly spent hours ignoring me.

I wondered if that was what happened, Did we upset Ylem?

'Hey, what tests can you perform to confirm your AI is independently intelligent?' asked Vikram, yawning.

'Well, there are the Turing, Marcus and the Lovelace Tests.'

'Would I regret asking?'

I chuckled. 'Yeah, probably.'

'Personally, I don't get why anyone would want to develop

a digital consciousness.'

I was flustered by this statement. 'Well, if we can develop a digital consciousness, we're one step closer to digitising ourselves. And when we can do that, our digital avatars could live forever.'

Vikram rolled his head from left to right. 'Ah, this is the hot topic that's got you geeks so excited. Do you honestly think we're ever likely to live in a digital universe?'

'It's highly probable we already are,' I told him.

Vikram quickly negated my bold statement. 'No, trust me: this is real life, my friend.'

I must admit I agreed with him. I found the concept that this is a coded universe difficult to swallow.

'It sounds nucking futs,' I answered. 'But believing this is a computer simulation is no more ridiculous than believing God made the heavens, earth, and all the living creatures in just seven days.'

Vikram raised his arms into the air and yawned deeply, 'Well, yeah, but this computer simulation notion is obviously a modern reboot of the religious creation myth. Personally, I don't believe in any monotheistic religion as such. And don't believe a single entity could have summoned all of this in to existence. However, I do believe there is something going on.'

'Something?' I asked.

'A universal energy that flows through all creation. The oneness that binds us to all matter in the universe.'

'I get spirituality,' I countered. 'But the concept of the oneness is just another construct we've fabricated to comfort ourselves from the fact we reside in a cold dark void.'

Vikram negated what I had just said with a forced belly laugh. 'So we're all wrong and you're right?'

'If only life the universe and everything were so binary.'

'Binary?' he asked.

'There are no right or wrong answers.' I replied.

'I believe I'm right.' Proclaimed Vikram.

'Well yeah. I suppose it is far more comforting to have faith in a force that binds everything in the universe than accept that life is no more than beautiful chaos. Before scientific enlightenment, the only plausible explanation for life, the universe, and everything was some big other. But over the centuries, scholars have come to understand physics, chemistry, biology, and philosophy, so we needn't believe in ancient mythology anymore.'

He stood up and yawned. 'OK. But do you really think we could build a plausible simulation where trillions of organisms would live?'

'Yeah. I think people born today could build a simulation of our reality in their lifetime. Just think, we humans may eventually wield godlike powers.'

'Sounds like the kids from computer club have got ideas above their station.' Rudely remarked Vikram.

'Well, it would evolve over time. I mean, what if the Americas were only developed after simulants reached the Bering Straits.'

'Utter nonsense. I mean, every geologist on the planet would disagree with your conclusion,' said Vikram.

'Science merely identifies the laws of nature. It doesn't explain who or what summoned those laws into existence. But yes, I agree, we must trust the science of the day.

The conversation was clearly starting to frustrate Vikram. 'Personally, I don't believe in God, be he a metaphysical being or computer programmer, because it allows for the transference of blame,' he said.

'Transference of blame?' I questioned.

Vikram wandered off into the kitchen and opened the fridge. 'Yeah, if our reality is the construct of a higher power, then it's feasible that our path towards death has already been encoded into the software. If that were the case, then one could argue they are not to blame for their actions, as they were just carrying out their programming. Likewise, if something truly awful were to happen, one could accept it was the will of God. These are very dangerous ideas that allow susceptible people to accept their fate and not make any attempt to improve their situation.'

I was not expecting such a profound response and decided not to respond.

'Do you have a washing machine?' I asked, fully aware I smelt foul.

'Yeah, in the basement. If you give me your clothes, I'll bung them in the machine for you.'

He took my clothes and fetched a blanket and pillow and left me with the dog for the night.

19

Morning Sunshine

Vikram's booming voice beckoned me from the dream world.

I opened my eyes slowly and yawned. 'What time is it?'

'5:30am.'

'For fuck's sake.'

'Please join us,' said Vikram tossing a shabby pink robe on the sofa.

I stretched and scratched, forgetting I was not alone.

'I suppose you're hungry?' asked Sunshine.

I didn't want to burden them, but I thought breakfast would make me feel slightly more human. 'Please.'

'Eggs?' She asked.

'There's no better way to start the day.' I said stretching toward the sky.

She returned with a poached egg perched on a slice of toast and some slivers of avocado. The egg was just how I liked it, and I mopped up the yellow sauce with the crusty brown bread.

'There is a brown towel in the bathroom you can use,' Said Vikram.

'Oh yeah, a shower would be lovely.'

Vikram pushed a printout across the table. 'These are the directions to the retreat up in the mountains.'

I stretched out to reach the paper. 'Why would Cyrus want to meet here?'

'Not sure, but the retreat is totally off-grid,' added Vikram chomping into a slice of toast.

Smart, I thought. 'Hey, what time are we leaving?'

'Seven.'

If looks could kill, I knew Sunshine would be charged with murder. 'And tell me, dear, why would you agree to help a stranger on your day off? A day you promised to take me shopping?'

Fretfully, Vikram responded, 'He really needed my help, dear, and, well, I thought?'

Sunshine reached over for the French raspberry jam. 'Thought what, Vicky?'

Vikram looked for my support. 'Yeah, err, I said I'd pay him'.

She took a bite of her toast. 'So, how do you know, Vicky?'

I told her that we had met in the homeless shelter the day before. Sunshine narrowed her eyes as she sipped her coffee. 'And why does my husband bring home strange men he's just met?'

I stopped chewing. 'Uh, I can't put words into his mouth, but maybe he felt like helping a stranger in need.'

Sunshine got up, walked into the kitchen with her plate, and threw it into the Belfast sink. 'Jesus-fucking-Christ! What kind of bullshit is this, Vicky?'

I leant back in my chair so it perched on its two back legs

to keep Sunshine in my line of sight. 'Don't worry. I've already paid him.'

Vikram signalled for me to shut it. 'Sorry, dear, I didn't mean for this to happen. I promise I'm just going to give him a lift. Then I'm all yours.'

She gave Vikram a condescending look. 'Why do you keep trying to help these lowlife bums?' She looked back at me and shrugged. 'No offence.'

'None taken,' I replied.

She said nothing, walked out of the kitchen, and slammed the door shut. 'Ooh, I think you're on the naughty step,' I jokingly remarked.

Vikram stabbed the last bit of toast. 'If you know what's best for you, you'll shut the fuck up.'

20

Mountain Drive

Vikram expected me to navigate with a folded map, but it looked like we'd just need to find Highway 5 and head north for a couple of hundred miles.

As the morning mist cleared, I admired the view. The vast arid landscape stretched out before us further than one dared imagine. However, I was hot and bothered by the time we reached the freeway and sought a little light conversation. 'Other than looking after the homeless, what do you do, Vicky?'

'Only Sunshine calls me Vicky.'

'Vicky.' I chuckled.

Vikram took a sip from his stainless-steel thermos and wiped the green wheatgrass froth from his beard. 'I'm a spiritual healer.'

I was not expecting that from the muscle-bound man. 'So, do you actually cure people?' I asked.

'Yes.'

'Really?'

'Why is that so hard to believe? Doctors treat the body, psychiatrist treat the mind, and we treat the spirit. All three must be balanced and healthy for people to be at their optimum.'

'Spirit? Don't you mean consciousness?'

'No, I mean spirit. You need to stop self-medicating and cleanse your soul before it's too late.'

I didn't respond immediately, but rather gazed at the hardy shrubs that clung to the deep red rocks. 'I get it. People believe that you can cure them, and you do so through the power of suggestion. But you're no more than a chalk pill, a spiritual placebo that only works on susceptible and willing minds.'

He didn't rise to my rouse. 'You should let me work on you before dismissing thousands of years of knowledge.'

'Hey, don't get me wrong. I am sure there is compelling evidence that your work has had a noticeable impact on your client's minds and bodies. But why do people like you need to wrap massage and stretching in mysticism and the language of ancient religions?'

'Do you know the difference between Western philosophy and Eastern philosophy?' he asked.

I hadn't given it much thought until that moment. 'No.'

'Thought so,' he Countered. 'In the West, philosophy is essentially academic discussion, written work, exposition, more discussion. But in the East, philosophy is learned through practice like meditation or yoga. Over Time, the student gains first-hand experience of the philosophical concepts taught in Western philosophy.'

Even though I felt Vikram's explanation was well constructed, I didn't want to concede just yet. 'That sounds great, but I'm not into this religious mumbo-jumbo. I mean, yoga? Come on. It's just stretching. Don't get me wrong. Stretching is great, but it needn't be wrapped in spiritual mysticism.'

He breathed in deeply to centre himself. 'Adnam, the purpose of religion is to connect an individual to their spirit. When they are one with themselves, they become one with creation. I agree with you that connecting with one's spirit is within all of us. Still, most people often take an outward journey to conclude that the kingdom of heaven is within. Those that arrogantly dismiss spirituality fail to acknowledge that there is more to being human than observable biology and neurochemistry.'

Knowing I didn't have an argument to counter his well-constructed theory, I chuckled. 'OK Vicky, you win.'

21

The Mountains

I passed out after demolishing a sensational burrito at the Hi-Lo Café in the sleepy town of Weed.

'Are we there yet?' I asked as Vikram pulled off the tarmac onto a dirt road.

'I think, but you tell me. You're supposed to be navigating.'

'Oh, sorry. I must have dozed off.'

'Dozed off?' He huffed. 'You've been snoring for the last half-hour.'

The tall pines obscured the sun from view and Vikram was forced to resort to his waning headlamps to illuminate the path through the trees. 'Mount Shasta Spiritual Retreat one mile,' read the hand-painted sign nailed to a tree so mighty it tickled the underside of the passing clouds.

'Cool. You found it then,' I said, yawning wide.

'Yeah, looks that way.'

'Are you in a mood?'

'No, what would give you that idea?'

The dirt track snaked through the dense pine forest toward the campground with just enough room to weave between the fallen branches and rocks.

'Are you afraid of the dark?' he asked.

'The dark? No.' I countered. 'Serial killers in ski masks? Yes.'

'You forgot the wolves.'

'Wolves? There are wolves in these woods?'

'Yeah, and bears,' he said.

An upsurge of fear clouded my ability to detect sarcasm. 'Man-eating bears?'

'Yeah. Don't forget the poisonous snakes,' replied Vikram, desperately maintaining a straight face.

'Snakes? Oh, fuck this.'

'Did you tell anyone you were coming up here?' asked Vikram.

'Why?' I asked, thinking this was the perfect opening line to a horror movie.

'In case you go missing in the woods.'

'Thanks for your concern.' I said. 'No, I haven't told anyone where I am.'

'Why?' asked Vikram.

'Infinite Logic is most likely monitoring my email accounts.'

'Then why didn't you call someone.'

'No one remembers phone numbers anymore.'

Vikram thought that was a ridiculous notion, but when I challenged him, he couldn't remember his wife's number.

'You should have said at the house, I could have found a number for you via directory enquiries,' said Vikram fighting to find second gear.

'Yeah, I thought about it, but I think it's best to avoid popping up on their radar until I know what's going on.'

The track eventually opened out into a clearing where a few trucks, vans, and RVs were parked.

'I think this is as close as we get in this thing,' said Vikram as he tapped the dash.

'Here? You sure? But there's nothing here.' I moaned.

'Yeah, as I said, this place is totally off the grid. You have to hike about a quarter of a mile,' said Vikram, grinning from ear to ear.

'Hike? You're kidding, right?'

Vikram patted me on the shoulder. 'OK then.'

I looked over at him. 'Do you mind waiting until I confirm Cyrus is here?'

'Sorry, I can't. I've got to get back tonight, or Sunshine will kill me.'

I was horrified by the thought of being stranded in the woods. 'Oh, I don't know about this. What if he's not here?'

'Sounds like a you problem.' He chuckled.

It took me a few seconds to get what he was hinting at. 'Surely, you won't leave me here in the middle of nowhere?'

'Sorry, I'm in so much trouble as it is.'

I begrudgingly opened the door and climbed out. 'What the fuckity fuck am I doing?'

Vikram waved as he drove off. 'You'll be fine,' he shouted.

An uneasy sense of dread washed over me as I watched the baby-blue Campervan reverse. Alone in a forest with no idea what to do next, I trudged through the woodland, following makeshift signs for the campground. The short walk gave me time to reflect on my predicament. If Cyrus was not here, I'd be clean out of options with no means of returning to civilisation other than walk.

The trees thinned out into a natural clearing and I was dumbstruck by the splendour of my surroundings. I breathed in the heady scent of wet earth and fresh pinecones to form a memory. The warm glow from the sun lit the underside of the delicate, feathery clouds that formed above Mount Shasta. The silhouette of the ancient trees framed the panoramic blood-red sky. Where their tall, thick trunks connected with the earth, a shimmering lake reflected the resplendent snow-capped peak.

I strolled along the lake bank and noticed two men swimming by the stumpy dock. 'Hey,' I shouted.

They waved back, which put me at ease. An athletic black man in his late thirties wearing ultramarine flower-print shorts climbed out of the water and onto the dock. 'Hey.'

'Fine day for a swim.' I said.

'Yes it is. Are you going in?' asked the stranger.

'Jesus. No,' I answered, as if I'd been asked to lick a hairy tarantula.

I told him I was looking for someone.

'Who?' asked the stranger, drying himself off.

'Err, I don't suppose you know a guy called Cyrus?' I asked.

'Cyrus?' The tall, dark stranger walked toward me, 'Cyrus? Err, no, sorry.'

The lean man with shiny walnut skin and a picky afro introduced himself. 'I'm Dee.'

'Nice to meet you, I'm Adnam.'

Dee finished drying himself. 'What's he look like?'

'Err, a black guy with dreadlocks.'

Dee dried his head vigorously. 'Ahh, well then, hell no.'

'Do you know anyone who may know Cyrus?'

'Why are you looking for him?'

'Long story.' I shrugged, not wanting to get into it.

Dee shouted at his friend, who was still swimming. 'Hey, Jerry.'

Jerry looked over as he swam past. 'What?'

'Do you know a guy called Cyrus?'

Jerry stopped swimming and began to tread water. 'What?'

'This guy is looking for someone called Cyrus.'

Jerry began to swim back to the dock. 'Why?'

'Hey, really, don't worry. I'll ask someone else.' I interjected.

Dee looked back at me. 'You should ask Hare.'

'Who's Hare?' I asked.

Jerry clambered onto the dock and stood up. I didn't know where to look as he walked towards us. 'Oh, err, you're stark naked.'

'You must have seen one of these before?' answered Jerry with no hint of shame.

'Yeah, but not one that incy wincy, pinky winky,' joked Dee.

'Hare runs this retreat.' Jerry said flush faced.

I shrugged my shoulders again as I maintained eye contact with the long-limbed, scraggy man with painfully translucent skin. 'Where can I find him?'

Jerry wrapped his towel around his waist. 'Clearly, you've not been up to the campground yet? Trust me, you can't miss Hare's trailer.'

22

Hare

The vintage aluminium Airstream trailer with the crimson stripe stood out like a peacock amongst a flock of sparrows. It was set amongst the tall trees and rustic log cabins that were dotted around the clearing. I knocked and waited for a response. Nothing. So, I knocked with force and stepped back.

'Hey,' shouted a white, middle-aged woman holding a yoga mat under her arm. 'Hare is conducting the guided meditation.'

The lean woman with curly grey hair and skin that had been dry roasted in the desert sun told me Hare was about to give a class on the banks of the black beach.

'What's he like then?' I asked.

She radiated happiness as she spoke about Hare. 'He's truly unique. It's like he's connected to everything in the universe.'

I nodded and thought it best not to ask if he also floats on a cloud of champagne and poops organic rainbow coloured yoghurt. 'Ahh, so you've been here before?'

'Oh yes, this is my fifth year.'

'Wow, he must be good.'

'He's the one and only,' said the woman as we approached the lake.

The reflection of the liquid mirror gave the illusion that I was looking at the gateway to a parallel universe. Pebbles glistened like gold nuggets on the tranquil lakebed, the water was so clear that one could see the fish do whatever fish do.

It would have made for a perfect photo for social boasting, but unfortunately I'd lost contact with my dear, dear phone. I'd been one of those annoying people that rushed around snapping at every noticeable attraction like they were Pokémon. However, I was not sightseeing for pleasure, but rather some perverted compulsion to obtain bragging rights and the all-important evidence of experience for Instagram.

'We had better sit as it looks like he's about to begin,' whispered the woman, kindly gesturing I could share her mat.

I sat next to her, facing Hare. 'Is that him?'

'Yeah, that is Michabo, the Great Hare'

I was quite surprised by Hare's appearance. He looked to be in his late fifties, with a spine so crooked it buried his head into his chest. A birth deformity that had caused his body to develop a rather unique gate. He wore a bold, bright, and rather outlandish deep blue tailor-made high buttoned jacket adorned with embroidered silk moons. He completed the look with a purple paisley silk scarf he tied loosely around his neck. His hair was long but thinning, and his eyes were as black as polished coal. He had a vintage Selleck moustache that dominated his face.

Hare waited for complete silence before he addressed the

congregation. 'Welcome home, members of my family. It's good to see so many familiar faces here with us today. Many of you are on the path of self-discovery. But for those who have just started your journey, your new family welcomes you.'

In unison, the twenty-strong congregation turned and faced the person to their left and right and greeted them with a hearty, 'Welcome.'

Hare's disability was so severe he had to move his entire body to make eye contact with the new recruits. 'For our new guest, I say this: if you're expecting me to provide you with the answers to life, the universe, and everything, then maybe I should save you some time and effort and reluctantly inform you that this is not the experience you're looking for. Let's be clear – I'm not a guru, spiritual leader, or even someone you would consider successful. Nor do I possess any professional qualifications in life coaching, philosophy, or psychology. Neither will I provide you with a list of tactics or daily mantras you can quickly apply to improve your health and wealth.'

Hare lifted his right leg over his left to be in full lotus, then continued. 'The fact you have decided to be with us means you're not one of those people seeking a shortcut or proven strategy that promises instant happiness. It's much easier to become a disciple, devotedly following some self-proclaimed saviour through the emotional wilderness than discover your own path. The belief that others may hold the keys to our success and happiness has spawned a multi-billion-dollar self-help industry. One that feeds on our longing for a quick fix and plays on our innate lethargy. But I ask you, where are the keys to happiness to be found?'

The collective brought their hands together in the prayer position and responded. 'The secret to happiness is within.'

Hare gave the slightest of smiles. 'Brothers and sisters, let us focus our journey to the centre of our souls.'

The assembly of people sat in motionless silence for two hours as Hare guided their meditation with soft mutterings.

I tried to clear my mind but couldn't halt the stampede of thoughts. Occasionally, I opened my eyes to see if the others were waning. Still, everyone else looked to be in complete control of mind, body, and soul.

I must admit, I was glad when the session ended; the forest floor was creeping and crawling, and besides, I had a numb ass. I approached Hare and waited for an opportune moment to speak. 'Ahh, the freeloader,' said Hare when I introduced myself.

'Freeloader?'

Hare chuckled. 'Did you pay?'

'In my defence, I didn't know there was a fee.'

'Don't worry we were expecting you.'

'You were?'

'Interesting session. I found it very enlightening,' I said with a forked tongue.

Hare continued walking at a measured pace before he responded. 'Did you? Did you really? Why don't you dispense with the small talk and ask me what you came here to ask?'

A jolt of energy shot through my nervous system. 'I'm looking for a man called Cyrus.'

'Ahh, yes, I think I can help you with that,' said Hare.

'Is he here?'

'Oh no. No, no, no. Cyrus is not here.'

'What? Really? Where the hell is he then?'

'He is where he's at,' replied Hare.

'What the fuck is that supposed to mean? Hey, I don't have time for this bullshit. Do you know where I can find him?'

'All in good time. Before I tell you something, you need to

tell me something.'

'What?'

'Tell me how you got that scar,' said Hare looking at my neck.

'Huh? My scar? Why?'

'Because I find scars oh so fascinating,' he said.

'You're a fucking nut job,' I muttered.

We walked in silence along the inland shore as the gentle breeze harmonised with the rhythmic tide. I thought it best I make amends for my rudeness. 'I'm not quite sure how I got my scar,' I told him.

'How intriguing,' said Hare with a narrow frown. 'It happened when you were young?'

'Yeah, seven or eight,' I answered, slightly confused by our conversation's direction.

Hare bent down to pick up a shiny pebble, then skipped it across the lake. 'I'm sensing a vagueness which suggests you have no recollection of the incident.'

I found Hare mesmerising and momentarily forgot I was supposed to be interrogating him. I picked up a few flat pebbles and skipped them across the lake. 'Yeah, absolutely no memory. Total blackout from the age of seven to around ten.'

'How fascinating. I sensed you had many unresolved issues when I first laid eyes on you,' said Hare confidently.

'Did you?' I replied.

Hare bounced another pebble off the lake. 'Our truths are often lies, and our lies mask our truths.'

'Sorry, do you always talk in riddles?'

'You don't trust your mother's account, and your father is emotionally incapable of discussing the incident with you,' said Hare boldly.

I wasn't sure if this was a trick or something else, 'What? Huh? How on earth could you know that?

Hare nodded as he shuffled three small pebbles in his right hand. 'Your anguish is etched into every fibre of your being.'

I gazed at the shimmering reflection of the nimbus clouds floating over the water. 'I think I was hung by racist teenagers on the housing estate we lived in. We were the only Asian family, which made me the Indian and them the cowboys. To cut a long story short, their sick game resulted in me swinging from the balcony railings of the third floor.' I stopped dead in my tracks, completely surprised I'd divulged that to a total stranger.

'Oh my. How tragic,' said Hare softly. 'But having no memory, you're reliant on the accounts of your emotionally damaged parents.'

I was quietly impressed by Hare's ability to read between the lines. 'Yeah, I tried to discuss it once with my mum, but we had a massive argument. And well, I left for uni in a huff, and we never talked about it again.'

'Ahh, I see, and you're angry with her for not being able to discuss her unresolved trauma with you.'

'I guess so,' I said, realising for the first time my mother had dealt with her trauma in the very same way I'd dealt with mine.

'You've never discussed this with your father?' asked Hare.

'Ahh, well, my relationship with my dad still hasn't elevated beyond small talk.'

Hare pointed at a family of river otters creating ripples on the distant shore. 'Do you see that? A perfect expression of the family unit. But honestly, do you think any family is perfect?'

I held a hand over my brow to block out the evening sun. 'Probably not.'

Hare nodded as he shuffled three small pebbles in his right hand. 'If you want to overcome your trauma, then the burden of truth is yours to shoulder. You can't expect your parents to resolve this for you because they are as emotionally scarred as you, maybe even more so. To heal your scars will require you to rip off the band-aid and treat the rotting wound.'

I shrugged dismissively. 'Why would I want to do that?'

'To become who you are destined to be.'

'What is that supposed to mean?' I said, somewhat irritated with his diagnosis.

'That's for you to work out. But know this, you should involve your parents in this process so you can collectively heal.'

Dredging up the past with Mum and Dad sent shivers down my spine. 'Oh Jesus, no. I don't think I ever want to do that.'

'I thought as much,' said Hare with a calming touch on my arm. 'Then you must release your trauma from the stronghold in the deepest, darkest recesses of your mind. And when you discover those lost memories, we can talk.'

I sighed. 'How the hell do I do that?'

Hare stopped me in my tracks to allow a train of ants to pass. 'You need to come to the lake every day and meditate.

'I don't have time for that. I need to find Cyrus,' I told him in a tone reserved for anger.

'Ahh, but you do have time. The man that knows where Cyrus is will join us in a few days.'

'A few days?' I yelled. 'I don't have a few days.'

Hare shrugged. 'I don't see how you have a choice.'

I contemplated my options, which were basically: stay or leave. And leaving was not really an option, given I was all in. 'You expect me to meditate by this lake and search my mind for memories I've hidden from myself? And you expect me to achieve this whilst my mind races with thoughts and worries about my predicament and lack of a future?

'Yes,' said Hare smiling wide.

'You're fucking bonkers,' I blurted out before I could think of a more tactful way of disagreeing with his remedy.

Hare continued to walk. 'Your trauma is as real as the stronghold I've asked you to visualise.'

'What gobbledygook.'

But Hare didn't take offence, 'The neurological connections forged by your trauma physically exist. However, if you starve the connections of energy, those pathways will eventually erode.'

'Oh,' I said, slowly realising Hare was not a complete crackpot. 'The stronghold analogy is a way to visualise negative thoughts.' I asked.

'Yes.'

'So, you're saying if I starve those thoughts, the pain will eventually fade from memory.'

'Yes,' nodded Hare. 'When you learn how to navigate the Circuitry of your mind, you'll be able to rewire your thoughts and prevent negativity from crippling you.'

'Is this your proven method? I asked.

Hare stopped to admire the picture perfectness of our surroundings. 'You must discover your own truth. Reality is no more than a construct we compose to make sense of our place in the universe.'

'Can't you just tell me what to do? Thinking is overrated.'

Hare laughed as we entered the camp. He placed both his hands on my forearms. 'You know, I think this is exactly where you need to be.'

23

Campfire

Dee and Jerry invited me to join them for burgers and beers. 'Come on, you're gonna have to tell us what the hell you're doing here,' said Jerry as he stoked the fire.

I lay on my back, staring up at the thick grey clouds that obscured the moonlight. 'I'm looking for a man.'

'Aren't we all darling? said Jerry in a camp voice.

I wondered if that was a hint at his orientation but decided it didn't really matter.

'Why? Who is this Cyrus guy?' asked Dee.

I paused for thought. 'It's complicated.'

Jerry passed me a bottle of beer. 'How intriguing.'

'Come on, bro?' said Dee, prodding me in the arm.

I told them that I thought Cyrus might be a hacker from a cult that had just stolen a billion-dollar AI from the company I worked for. 'Wait, you think he's part of a cult?' asked Dee.

'Yeah,' I chuckled. 'Well, he claimed to have discovered an

alien language that his followers see when they take DMT.'

Jerry raised a single eyebrow. 'Oh, wow. Yeah. That's kind of out there. I've heard DMT is a Jedi mind fuck.'

'Have you tried it?' I asked.

'God no, it's impossible to find,' answered Jerry.

'Yeah, it's not what you'd call an addictive substance,' added Dee. 'So, dealers don't bother pushing it.'

I told them I was supposed to meet Cyrus at a bar in Oakland, but he never showed. I was drugged and woke up in a homeless shelter with a note to meet him here.

Dee laughed cruelly. 'No way. And you hit with a hand full of deuces.'

'Yeah. Holding was not an option.' I replied despondently.

'Well, I hope you don't bust out', added Dee, sticking with the analogy.

I explained that I really wasn't thinking clearly.

Jerry coughed and spluttered. 'Genius. And you thought, yes, a clue. I'll head into the mountains to meet a man that I believe is a member of a cult and who thinks nothing of drugging and kidnapping people.'

'Yeah. That about sums it up.'

'How did you get here?' Dee asked.

'A hippie called Vikram gave me a lift,'

'Hippie?' asked Jerry.

'Yeah, the hippie from the homeless shelter.'

'The same shelter you woke up in?' asked Dee.

'Yeah,' I answered defensively.

'And you don't think this hippie could be involved?' asked Dee quizzically.

'God, no.' I paused for thought. 'Do you think?'

'Nah, dude,' said Dee. 'I'm only messing with you.'

I felt so foolish. I'd blindly trusted complete strangers and now was in a bit of a pickle. Our conversation began to irritate me, so I switched lanes and asked them a question that had been puzzling me. 'Hey, how did you guys end up on the road together?'

Jerry threw a few logs on the fire. 'Well, a couple of months ago, I announced on my socials that I wanted to drive from New York to LA, and I was looking for someone to share the miles.'

Dee laughed. 'Don't ask me why, but when I saw his post appear in my timeline, I thought, *yeah, that would be a once in a lifetime adventure.* So, I sent Jerry a message. To be honest, I didn't think he'd reply as we'd never met.'

'Well, you were the only person who responded,' added Jerry. 'And I thought, *this dude looks like he would create wondrous chaos I could use for my character.*'

'Character?' I asked.

'Yeah, I'm an actor. Technically an out-of-work actor.

'Have you been in anything I'd know?' I asked excitedly.

'Have you seen the new Star Wars movie?'

'Oh, my god, yeah.'

'I was Rebellion Pilot 49,' shrugged Jerry.

I was unable to mask my disappointment. 'Oh.'

'Well, hopefully, this is the breakthrough role that will set my career in motion,' countered Jerry.

I asked about the role and Jerry told me he would be playing a maverick detective in a new Netflix drama.

Dee interjected. 'Tell him how you landed the roll.'

'It was a chance encounter with the married and well-respected casting director at a sex party in Lower Manhattan.'

Jesus, I thought. 'Well, all's fair in love and movie making.' I said before taking a sip of my brew. 'But why drive when you can fly?'

Jerry smiled. 'Jaws.'

Completely dumbfounded, I asked, 'Jaws?'

'Yeah.' Jerry scratched his two-day-old stubble, 'You remember that scene on the boat?' he asked rhetorically, 'The scene with Roy Scheider, Robert Shaw, and Richard Dreyfuss?' Jerry paused to check we were on the same page. 'They compare scars, each trying to one-up the other with their horrifying disfigurements.'

'For sure,' I added, still unclear about the overall direction of his ramblings. 'That scene stole the show.'

'Totally,' agreed Jerry. 'Off camera, we actors' bond and jostle for standing, by comparing our anecdotes. So, I decided to embark on a road trip with a communist gangster rapper from New York to add to my repertoire.'

'Oh,' I mouthed as I decided if Jerry's answer made sense or required further cross-examination. 'Wait. What? You're a communist gangster rapper?'

'Yeah,' answered Dee.

'Really?' I asked quizzically. 'I would have thought a gangster epitomised capitalism.'

'Err, no,' proclaimed Dee abruptly. 'A gangster is a member of a structured organisation that collectively takes what they need for their people without seeking permission from the man.'

'Oh,' I said, disagreeing. 'But you sell your music. Isn't that a capitalist endeavour?'

'Wrong again,' countered Dee, 'I give my music away on Bandcamp, and if people like it, they can make a donation.'

'How's that going?'

'I'm too black and too strong for the mainstream rap audience, but occasionally, someone will send me a little something. It's not enough to live on but it keeps me in sneakers.'

I asked what Dee did to make ends meet and was surprised to discover he ran the New York chapter of the Communist Party.

'I bet that pays well.' I smirked.

Dee raised a single eyebrow. 'I'm deeply proud of my

political affiliations.'

Jerry interrupted. 'Dee literally wears his politics on his sleeve. Show him your ink, dude.'

Dee rolled up his T-shirt sleeves to reveal his Viet Cong and Cuban freedom fighter tattoos. 'These are the soldiers who fought for the communist ideal.'

'Wow, that's what I call committed to the cause. Such belief in an imperfect economic system,' I said without thinking.

Dee didn't respond.

But I love a good debate especially on the topics of politics, religion, and ideology. Subjects I knew very little about, but nonetheless have forged a strong opinion on. 'I'm no expert,' I said with an air of authority. 'All I know is that most of the communist world has crumbled, and former communist states are hurrying to adopt democracy.'

Dee frowned. 'Listen, you need to read The Communist Manifesto. For your information, Marx and Engels thought communism was the revolutionary process required to abolish capitalism. So, if you seek an alternative to capitalism, you are a communist.'

I absorbed this information with my characteristic distrust. 'So, you believe that any ideas or theories opposing capitalism are communist ideals?'

'Yes,' Replied Dee with folded arms.

I sighed deeply. 'I agree, capitalism is flawed, but do you honestly expect those who gain the most from the current system will allow anyone or anything to threaten their interests?'

'We need a revolution,' shrugged Dee. 'The people must rise up and tear down the system.'

Check, I thought to myself, 'The problem with all revolutions is that the old ways may be replaced with new ideas, but the dreams and habits of the people never change. A greedy man before the revolution is still a greedy man. So, people's ambitions and dreams before the rebellion will soon become their nightmares after it.'

Dee's gaze narrowed. 'Marx knew that a utopian society could not be achieved immediately.'

I calculated my next move against this worthy adversary. 'Ok, but I don't think the wealthy will accept the shift in the paradigm. We have been conditioned to believe that more is progress, and less is regression. You would have to forcibly mandate a reduction or cap in earnings and consumption.'

'More, for one, means less for all,' replied Dee.

'Yeah, I get that, but I don't believe we can or are motivated to change.'

Dee dismissively shook his head. 'I don't accept that human nature is static. We are products of our environment and economic systems. We can change if we so desire. Fuck it, Marx has already proved that human nature has changed many times in the past.'

Jerry looked worried, maybe he thought our debate was escalating into a brawl. 'You guys should probably agree to disagree.'

I looked over at Jerry and chose to ignore him. 'Yeah, we need to overhaul the current economic model, but I think the people whom the current model favours will not accept change. They will fight to protect their interests and will discredit your experimental, unproven ideas.'

Dee angrily folded his arms. 'The selfish few that refuse to acknowledge and accept the broader perspective will be singled out as enemies of the people and will be dealt with accordingly.'

I knew we would eventually arrive at this logical conclusion. 'Ahh, this is where I have a problem with all revolutions, the notion that ideas are worth killing and dying for. Can you honestly say you know your ideas will work and change the world for the better?'

'Guys,' shouted Jerry. 'Give it a rest. You'll never see eye to eye when your minds have been driven apart by those recruiting for the apocalypse.'

We both fell silent. 'What do you want to talk about?' asked Dee.

Jerry gazed up at the heavens as the clouds parted to reveal dots of light from the furthest reaches of our galaxy. 'Do you believe in aliens?'

'Believe they exist or that they are here?' asked Dee.

I looked up at the night sky. 'Here's a mind-bending thought. According to Drake's infamous equation, there could be over fifty thousand intelligent life forms in our galaxy.'

'I don't think we'll ever meet an alien,' said Dee.

'Why?' I asked.

Dee reached over for his glass bong and lit it. 'The distance. It would take multiple lifetimes to travel from one planet to another.'

'The question is, do we instruct our intelligent space robots to protect or obliterate the other intelligent organic life forms they encounter.' I asked.

Jerry hesitated before reigniting the campfire as if he was not sure if it was time to call it a night or not. 'Jesus, if it's not one thing it's the other. So, now you're telling me I have to worry if our cosmic neighbours have already launched their machines into the galaxy. And if they have been programmed to destroy us before we become spacefaring.'

Dee chuckled. 'Ahh, the berserker theory: self-replicating killer robots, ruthlessly destroying all organic and electrical lifeforms they encounter.'

I reached over for the bong and passed it to Jerry. 'I'm not worried about artificial intelligence. I'm more concerned with real stupidity.'

We laughed until the hoots all but frittered away. 'Let's

hope we don't because if they find us first, our bones may be ground down to make homeopathic remedies. I said.

Jerry inhaled the THC deeply, held it in, and then blew a cloud of sticky icky into the fresh mountain air. 'To be on the safe side, we'd better lock down the planet again and sit out eternity in our homes exploring virtual worlds.'

I looked up at a sky I had never seen before. The dark tree line framed the deep blue purple sky speckled with photons of light. The light that had travelled for millions of years for no other reason than to hit the retina of an eye, sending electrical signals to a brain that could comprehend the sublime spectacle.

I'd never seen the cosmic dust cloud from which all matter in our galaxy was formed, and wondered how many of those stars were still there. How many stars had been born whose light had not reached my eye yet? How many of those billions of stars had planets with life? How many sentient beings were looking out at their corner of the galaxy, appreciating the pure majesty of the universe?

I stared intensely at the heavens, wiping a single tear that had formed from not blinking. The strange thing about tears is that even when they aren't triggered by an emotion, the sensation of warm water running down a cheek ushers' melancholic thoughts. The personality of doubt and loathing questioned my urban life. I couldn't help but think I'd failed to form a deep connection with nature, the universe, and myself in that moment.

Dee punctuated my internal monologue by standing up. He pulled his black Wu-Tang Clan hoodie over his head and announced he was going to bed. The idea also struck a chord with Jerry. But before they left, I asked them what they knew about Hare.

Jerry shrugged his shoulders. 'Not much. I've watched a couple of his meditation videos and listened to a few of his podcasts before we came.'

He told me that Hare's videos were your archetypal heartstring pull. His disability had isolated him as a child. He was deeply insecure, painfully shy and lacked the confidence to bond with other kids his age. Blah, blah, blah yackity smackity.

None of this really helped me form an opinion of the man that differed from my first impression. I pestered them for more, and Jerry added that Hare was raised by his grandfather. His parents were God-fearing people who believed they were being punished for their earthly sins. Hare claims, he felt like he was his parents' penance.

That's a lot of pressure for a child. Still, none of this helped me understand the man I'd eventually have to confront. 'Anything else?'

'What's with all the questions, dude?' asked Dee, slightly frustrated.

'Oh, err, no reason, but I'd like to know who I'm letting into my head.'

'Well, you're messing with mine right now.'

'Sure, just one last question,' I said with a sense of urgency. 'Did he say how he came to be who he is today?'

Jerry rolled his eyes. 'Err, ish. He claimed that he'd learned to control the swirling cloud of questions and ideas that occupied his mind by the age of thirteen. And after many years of condensing and compressing his thoughts, he had a profound breakthrough. And the simplicity and beauty of this one pure thought guided him to spiritual enlightenment.'

'Did he say what that one pure thought was?' I asked.

'No, obviously not. You have to keep attending his retreats to discover that,' remarked Dee insightfully.

24

Tranquil Lake

'Have you retrieved the memories of your attack?' asked Hare, hovering over me.

I remained sat on the shore of the black beach. 'No.' I said, slowly opening my eyes.

'Give it time,' he said in a warm tone.

'My mind keeps wandering.'

'Focus,' he said.

I looked over my shoulder at him. 'Yeah, but I can't get this mind virus out of my head.

'The places our mind wanders when we meditate hint at the root causes of our concerns.'

More riddles, I thought, getting up to my feet.

'What thoughts are distracting your focus?' asked Hare, reaching down for some flat pebbles.

'That we're living in a digital simulation,' I said, mimicking Hare's actions.

Hare skipped the shiny pebble across the lake. 'Would you be any happier knowing this world was a digital simulation?'

'Not sure. Maybe. Who Knows?' I answered faintly.

'Why this thought? What do you think it means?' asked Hare, rubbing a smooth pebble between his thumb and index finger.

'Why does it need to mean anything?'

'Because your inner voice directed you to a locked door you must open to progress with your healing.'

I stretched out my arms and yawned. 'Why would my inner voice speak in metaphors rather than tell me what the bloody problem is.

'Because imagery is the language of the subconscious.'

Oh, whatever, I thought. 'Makes no sense to me,' I said.

'A digital reality. Fascinating concept,' said Hare, sensing my frustration.

'Have you ever thought all this, could be a digital construct?' I asked.

He mused over this question for a moment. 'In our wired world, it's entirely possible to substantiate any argument, regardless of how ludicrous it may sound. To highlight my point, we recently had a lovely Texan couple join us, and they believed the world is flat.'

'Flat?' I echoed. *What Morons,* I thought.

'Yes. And I was impressed with their ability to produce compelling evidence that corroborated their story. Not only that, but they were also able to convincingly dismiss evidence that proved otherwise. Do you believe the world is flat?'

'No. Of course not. That's a ridiculous notion.'

'Yes, ridiculous,' he echoed.

'Reading between the lines then, you don't believe that we could exist in a digital universe?'

Hare looked over at me. 'Honestly, do you think all this could have been coded by a programmer? Why would anyone or anything bother with the level of detail at the magnitudes beyond the most evolved eye?'

Good point, I thought. 'I'm not sure if this is fact or fiction,' I replied 'But, did you ever hear about the time the Pope visited CERN to witness the Large Hadron Collider accelerate particles and reveal the Higgs boson?' I asked.

'No,' shrugged Hare.

'The physicists were very excited to present evidence of elementary particles to His Holiness. As the electrons accelerated, one rather excited physicist turns to the Pope and says, "Religion seems less relevant now that we have found the God Particle." An uncomfortable silence followed as the Pope contemplated his response. He smiled, "Ahh, but when you started looking for the Higgs boson, God thought I'd better create a particle that will satisfy man's thirst for knowledge. So, you see, only when God finished his creation could you celebrate your discovery."'

I gave Hare time to absorb the fable. 'So, to answer your question,' I added, 'we don't know if this lake only exists because we are here to see it.'

Hare took a moment to condense his thoughts. 'But here it is, and so are we, so how could we ever know if it wouldn't exist if we were not here?'

'No idea,' I shrugged.

Hare inhaled then exhaled deeply. 'Adnam, the world you experience is constructed inside your mind. If you're happy and contented, you will positively process the experience. But if you feel inadequate or unhappy, then the same perceptual information may be processed as a negative experience.'

'OK, when I solve that riddle, I'll get back to you with an educated response,' I said mischievously.

Hare didn't rise. 'If it makes you happy to believe the entire universe is a simulation, do so. And if you want your meme to spread, ensure it's easy to learn and simple to replicate.'

'Meme?' I echoed.

'Yes.' He said. 'The Star Wars generation yearns for life to be as simple as a movie plot. And our politicians and spiritual leaders are only too happy to oblige with well-constructed memes.'

I carefully considered Hare's statement. 'I agree. People seem to be willing to accept the abridged headline or the highly edited soundbite in favour of the truth. Maybe because the truth requires considerably more effort to process. Hey, if you don't mind me asking, what's your meme?'

'My meme? Hare asked, before taking a moment to construct his response, 'Fall without reserve, fall without ego, accept the world fully.' Hare looked deep into my eyes for an awkwardly long time. 'I believe you harbour thoughts of suicide, but you're terrified of oblivion. Hence why you'd like to believe the universe is a digital simulation. And like a character in a videogame, you'd like another life, a do-over to explore paths you believe you should have taken.'

I felt like I'd been punched in the gut. 'That's some prognosis.' I said. I felt lightheaded and blurry as I constructed a response to repair my shattered self-image. 'I think you need to be more considerate and ask people if they want your diagnosis before providing one. Especially one so opinionated.'

Hare smiled. 'Sorry. You're right, but we don't have much time together.'

'Why?'

'Juan arrived this morning.'

'Juan?' I echoed.

'Juan will take you to Cyrus,' said Hare.

'When?'

'When you've finished your journey inward,' answered Hare calmly.

'How do you expect me to focus now?' I asked, flustered.

Hare continued to rub the smooth pebble, then sighed. 'What I think, what I believe, is exactly that, my opinion based on my experiences and journey through life. I cannot and do not know what's going on in your head or what you have experienced.'

'OK,' I said, not knowing how to respond.

'I say this because I don't want you to be offended by my words.' He said.

'Sure,' I said blankly.

'It's your choice whether you accept or dismiss my opinion, but know this, I take no offence if you disagree with what I say.'

'OK.' I mumbled.

'Let me be clear. I'm not debating with you. I need not understand your viewpoint.'

I shrugged. 'OK. I got it.

Hare took a deep breath and closed his eyes. 'When we face true evil, we believe it to be the death of God. How could God allow this to happen? We ask to mask the truth. But what truly terrifies us is divine. Therefore, what we believe to be evil is actually the obsessive sublime strength of God.'

Where is this going? I thought. I wanted to question his logic, but Hare let it be known that he would not be interrupted with a single scowl. 'Have you read the Bhagavad Gita?'

'Err. No.'

Hare smiled. 'In the Bhagavad Gita, there is a passage about the famous warrior, Arjuna. He had led his men on the battlefield to face Kaurava's army. Arjuna had doubts before ordering the charge and asked Lord Krishna, "What right do I have to send these men into battle knowing thousands will die?" And Lord Krishna reasons with him that our material reality is an illusion. The only true reality is the reality of our eternal self.'

I couldn't bite my tongue anymore. 'What?' I bleated.

'Our eternal self is predestined to cycle from life to death for eternity,' said Hare softly. 'But not for God.' He whispered, 'God was never born, nor shall God ever die.'

I was profoundly perplexed. 'I don't understand.'

'To God, we are but grains of sand blowing from one dune to another.' Hare waved his hand across the imagined vista, 'We take on many forms as the winds of time blow chaotically. But nothing we become, nothing we experience, nothing we love, nothing we do is of any consequence to God.'

'Huh?' I mouthed 'What are you saying?'

'What you can build is inconsequential to God. What you can destroy is negligible compared to the awesome power of God.'

'Why are you telling me this?'

'To free you from your false identity,' he replied.

'False identity?' I echoed.

'You perceive yourself as an agent with substantial purpose.'

'Huh?' I answered without understanding what that sequence of words meant.

'We're wired to feel like we're free agents, but the truth is, you only become aware that you're going to do something milliseconds after it happens.'

'What the what?' I snapped.

Hare held out his hand with the pebble in it. 'You believe that you think about the pebble then reach for it, but the reality is, you reach for the pebble then observe yourself reaching for it.'

'Nope, I'm more confused now,' I said.

Hare gestured with his eyes for me to look at the pebble in his hand. When I was focused on the stone, he counted to three and it disappeared.

'Wow,' I said slowly trying to figure out how he did that. 'Where's the pebble gone?'

'You can either accept that was merely a trick of the eye or believe there is more to existence than you can ever know.'

'It's obviously a trick?' I said, to hide the fact I was dumbfounded.

'You are an observer,' countered Hare, 'The first step towards enlightenment starts when you realise that you're not a free agent; you are not a substantial self.'

'What does it mean to be enlightened?' I asked to understand Hare's brand of spirituality.

'Only the enlightened can decide to leave the wheel of karma.'

'Decide?' I echoed.

'Yes,' whispered Hare. 'Like the Lord Buddha himself, you can choose to remain on the wheel and help others reach a state of nirvana.'

'Why would you do that if you had the option to leave all this pain and suffering?'

'Leave?' said Hare sympathetically, 'No. You don't go somewhere else when you reach nirvana. You're still you, still here with all the other people with all their problems.'

'Then what's the point?' I asked.

'The point?' smiled Hare. 'No point. But now you're in on the cosmic joke.'

'The cosmic Joke?' I scoffed.

'Did you ever notice evil is live spelt backwards?' nodded Hare.

'Is that the cosmic joke?' I asked.

'Could be,' shrugged Hare. 'That's for you to decide.'

Hare exhaled deeply. 'Reach nirvana and you view existence with a distant subjectivity.' Hare paused for dramatic effect. 'Life is something that happens, something you observe. Think of it as a stage play that entertains you.

As an audience member, you laugh, cry, dread, loathe, wonder and rage as the eternal drama unfolds. Only the enlightened know they are free to say no and walk out whenever they choose. To jeer bad actors or sabotage the play. Whereas those enthralled by Saṃsāra blissfully ignore the fakery, fail to notice the trapdoor, never realise the backdrops are two dimensional.'

I closed my eyes tight as I attempted to process this information. 'But if nothing matters, what's to stop you from being a bad person?'

'Good and evil is a question of subjectivity,' answered Hare.

'What does it mean ethically?' I asked, wrestling with this concept. 'You can reach enlightenment and still be a bad person.'

'Yes,' replied Hare without hesitation. 'In fact, an enlightened person would find the acts you consider evil more palatable to commit. As they could reason that the knife was following its own path, and they merely observe the blade plunge into the body of another.'

I must have looked like I was peering into a box of dead rats. 'How can you be so cynical and yet claim to be a healer?'

'Right and wrong are just opposing sides of the same spinning wheel. As are life and death.'

'How can you say that?' I asked, burdened with his riddles.

Hare shrugged. 'Don't concern yourself with the wheel that turns for eternity.'

'I think these teachings give license to madmen,' I said with venom.

'Yes,' replied Hare with a smile, 'you're right. In fact, Heinrich Himmler, the architect of the Holocaust, was said to be obsessed with Hinduism. He adopted the teachings of Brahmanic-Sanskritic Hinduism to get good people to commit evil acts free of mental torment.'

'Knowing that, why do you continue to teach it?'

'Life is death, and death is life,' said Hare with open palms.

I was reminded of my conversations with Ylem. I must have sounded like Hare when I tried to teach the machine ethics and morality.

'If nothing matters, then what we do is of no consequence,' I said boldly.

'Yes.'

'What kind of world would this be with no consequence?'

'Whatever world you choose to build, whatever world you choose to destroy. It's of no consequence to our eternal self.'

'Huh?' I was dumbfounded. 'How can this be the answer?'

'The answer?' shrugged Hare. 'What is your question?'

I looked blankly at the mystic sage. 'What does it all mean? Why are we here? What's the point of it all?'

'Nothing. No reason other than to be. To observe.' Hare counted his answers out on his fingers. 'Satisfied?'

'No.' I ran my fingers through my hair in a futile attempt to calm the down, 'That's a really underwhelming answer,' I rudely added.

Hare chuckled to himself. 'What did the first man promise to the wild stallion to let him ride on his back?'

'Huh?' I shrugged. 'Is it a joke?' I paused to think. 'I don't know. What?'

'I don't know either,' shrugged Hare. 'I was not the man, or the horse. Nor was I present on the vast tundra to witness the event. Even if I were, I could not truly know what was in the heart of that man or the head of the horse.' Hare paused. 'Do you understand?'

'No,' I said, rubbing my face with both hands, 'I've got no idea what you just said.'

'I am not God, nor do I claim to understand God, so how can I possibly know what God whispered to summon everything into existence. We can never understand the nature of God. Think about it. We don't even know the nature of a whale, and we share this realm of existence with that majestic creature.'

'Do you believe in God?' I asked, scrambling for understanding.

'God is the word I use to describe that which is unknown or unknowable.'

Frustrated that I couldn't make sense of Hare's stream of consciousness, I verbally lashed out, 'What you say sounds profound, but you skirt on the edge of comprehension. You're nothing more than a jumped-up snake oil salesman trying to upsell the next remedy. Keep attending your workshops, keep attending your retreats, and eventually, we will understand and learn the secrets of existence from you. To what end? So, we can become a self-proclaimed guru and sell our time to others?'

Hare sighed and slowly walked off. 'Come by around mid-day, and I will introduce you to Juan.'

25

Juan

I knocked on the door of the Airstream trailer and waited for a response.

'It's open,' called a man with a Latino accent.

I entered, stood in the doorway, and looked to my left; Hare was sitting in the lotus position on a double bed decorated with red, orange, and purple silk cushions.

To my right was a brooding man in his late forties. He was clearly of Mayan descent. His thick brown hair was neatly combed back and his beard was well-groomed and shaped with purpose. His tawny-brown eyes matched his fitted waistcoat which he wore over a plain, white cotton T-shirt, complemented with below the knee khaki shorts, long white sports socks, and blue sandals.

'Cerveza?' asked the Latino.

I surveyed the interior of the expertly finished Airstream – the dark maple floors, sleek cream cabinets, and the striking orange countertop that glistened under the low voltage lighting. 'No thanks.'

The Latino man placed the ice-cold can of beer on the counter next to me and sat down on a cream sofa with orange piping. 'Chill, Englishman, you're on holiday.'

I must have looked like a man that had just taken a bite of a fish-flavoured banana. Hare caught my eye. 'Relax.'

'I'm fine,' I lied, struggling to find my calm place. 'Sorry. You know, about before. I didn't mean what I said. I was just super frustrated with all the mystic riddles.'

Hare was in a near meditative state. 'I was not offended,' he scoffed, 'You're of no consequence to me.'

Nice comeback, I thought. 'Well, I just wanted you to know I'm sorry, and I thought about what you said.'

'And?'

'I have no memory of the attack but none the less I had retained the memory of the memory.'

'Why?' asked Hare.

I looked over at the Latino man, 'basic survival, I guess. My trauma provides me with an excuse to fail.' Hare clapped slowly. 'The transference of blame is a sweeter pill to swallow.'

'I guess.' I shrugged. 'After I shouted at you. I justified my actions with a familiar excuse – my temper is a defence mechanism I must have learned after my attack. Therefore, I'm not to blame for my actions.'

'What changed?' asked the Latino man. His accent was hard to pinpoint, clearly tinges of Mexican and hints of Southern California.

'The shifting sand,' I answered cryptically. 'If I'm continually changing form like the shifting sands, then I'd rather assume the form of the man I want to be.'

'Bravo,' clapped Hare.

I looked over at the Latino with a mean stare. 'Are you,

Juan?'

'Si,' said Juan coolly.

'Do you know where Cyrus is?'

'Si.'

'Where is he?'

Juan cocked his head to the left. 'Sit down, hombre. Drink your cerveza.'

'No, you're OK.' I concluded that it was safer to have my back against the only exit. 'Where's Cyrus?'

'Cyrus?' Juan calmly stroked his beard as he got the measure of me before responding. 'Are you sure you want to seek him out?'

'Yes,' I said abruptly.

'Cyrus is a dangerous hombre.'

'I don't care. I need to meet him,' I snarled.

Juan smiled. 'But you're just a houseplant.'

'Fuck you.'

Juan continued to gently stroke his facial hair. 'If you'd have sat down and drunk your cerveza with me, I'd have known you were bad ass. But you stood there trembling at the door.'

My eyes darted from side to side as I thought about how far removed this was from my every day. 'You're right. But never underestimate the bite from a timid dog.'

Juan chuckled. 'Maybe there is more to you than meets the eye.'

I nervously tapped the side of my right leg. 'Who is Cyrus?'

'Good Question.' Hare lifted his head and looked over at me. 'He is the leader of a radical leftist movement. All told, he's a very shrewd operator with all the right connections.'

I glanced over at Hare. 'You know him?'

Hare breathed in and out deeply. 'Yeah, we have history.'

'History?'

'We both spent time at Robert Shannon's retreat in the mid-nineties.'

I was thrown by their candour and expected more resistance. Nonetheless, I was very intimidated by their calmness. 'Why didn't Cyrus meet me in San Francisco?'

Juan rolled his shoulders. 'It was too risky.'

'Risky?' I echoed.

'Yes, risky. You were being shadowed by a man, probably ex-military.'

'Ahh, you mean Philips. Yeah. He was instructed to escort me to the meeting and find out if Cyrus knew anything about the hack at Infinite Logic.'

'They don't send men like that to 'just talk'.' Said Juan.

I raised a single eyebrow. 'You're probably right.'

'No probably about it. He was carrying a gun, hombre.'

'How do you know all this?' I asked.

'I dealt with him,' said Juan emotionlessly.

'Dealt?' I recoiled. 'Dealt with how?'

'I drugged him.'

'Drugged?' I said sharply. 'Then you're the guy who also drugged me?'

Juan looked me up and down. 'Yes, hombre.'

'But why? It makes no sense.'

'I needed to make sure you weren't being tracked.'

'And you couldn't just, you know, have spoken to me about it?' I spat scornfully.

'I like this guy,' Juan laughed, 'I like you hombre. Take a weight off.'

'No, you're good,' I said, heating up with frustration. 'What did you do to Philips?'

'I put him in a shipping container heading to China.'

'What the fuck?'

'Don't worry, I'm not a sadistic bastard. I left him enough food and water to survive the journey.'

I now considered myself lucky to have woken up in a

shelter and not in a port in the Far East. 'That's one thing that I couldn't work out. Why did I wake up in a homeless shelter?' I asked.

Juan shrugged. 'It's the last place on earth anyone would think of looking for you.'

'But why did you leave me with the envelope full of cash?' I asked, puzzled by his motives.

'That money was err... what's his name again?'

'Philips?' I asked.

'Yes, that's it. He had that on his person, and I thought you might have more need of it than him.'

I felt a little more at ease and sat down opposite Juan. 'Bit careless of you to leave me with an envelope full of cash in a homeless shelter.'

Juan smiled, 'I didn't. I left it with Vikram.'

I was momentarily paralysed as my mind switched a gear. 'You know Vikram?' I said, raising his voice.

'Yeah,' said Juan with a cheeky look on his face.

'How?'

'He's been attending my workshops and retreats for years,' said Hare.

'Oh,' I said, realising there were layers to their trickery. I inhaled deeply. 'So, where can I find Cyrus?'

Hare unfolded his legs and sat on the end of the bed. 'I'm sure I'll know where he'll be this Labor Day weekend.'

'Where?'

Hare stared intensely at me. 'Burning Man.'

'What's Burning Man?' I asked.

'A festival in the desert,' answered Hare.

'Oh,' I said, none the wiser. 'And you're sure he'll be there?'

Juan placed the empty beer down on the table in front of him. 'Most certainly.'

I glanced over at Juan. 'Really? You know that for sure?'

Juan brought his hands in front of his face and rubbed

them together slowly. 'Cyrus asked me to drive you to Burning Man if you so desired.'

'He wants to meet me?'

'I guess so, bro.' Juan looked over at me and rocked from hip to hip like a metronome. 'Cyrus stipulated that you need to stay off the grid if you plan to meet him.'

My trembling hand reached for the beer. 'Off the grid?'

'I've been given strict instructions.' Juan gave me a well-practised, menacing stare. 'No calls, no messages, no internet until I deliver you to him.'

I gradually lowered into the back of the chair. 'I don't understand what is going on here.'

Hare opened the fridge door and poured a green juice into a tall glass. 'Neither do we. But you'll have to decide if you dare seek out the truth or return home with unanswered questions.'

I pondered this dilemma for a moment or two before standing up. 'What time are we leaving?'

Juan smiled. 'In an hour, amigo.'

I opened the door and was about to leave when I remembered something. 'By the way, Hare, I thought about what you said about God. You know, your point about our actions being of no consequence to him?'

'And?' asked Hare, holding the glass to his lips.

'Free will,' I answered with a subtle nod. 'God gave us free will so we could decide if we want to love or hate. God may not judge us, but that's not to say we won't judge ourselves.'

'Exactly,' said Hare, elated. 'Our actions may be of no consequence to God, but they affect the ones we love and the communities we serve. Therefore, everything matters on this plane of existence.'

I stepped back into the Airstream and hugged Hare. 'Thank you, it's been emotional.'

Hare laid his glass down on the countertop to pat my back.

'Try to remember the here and now is all we can be certain of. Everything else is playful conjecture we suppose to fill the void.'

26

Road Trip

I knew not what awaited me, nor if I should be concerned for my safety. To date, Hare and Juan had been surprisingly warm and open. Regardless I was a little on edge as I waited for Juan at the clearing where the cars were parked.

'Evening,' I said with a hint of sarcasm.

'Afternoon, dude,' replied Juan coolly.

'Have you been smoking?' I asked, slightly concerned my chauffeur was high.

'Yeah, I'm toasted,' answered Juan stumbling along the narrow path towards me.

'You don't plan to drive in that condition?' I asked fearfully.

'No.'

'Then who is driving?'

Juan dangled his keys in front of my face. 'You are amigo.'

'Oh, OK. Err, what do you drive?'

'That rusty rose 1963 Rambler convertible. She looks like a hunk of junk, but under the hood is a '65 Chevrolet big-block, four-two-seven.'

The idea of driving was quite appealing. I didn't agree with America's partisan politics or institutional racism, but there was no denying it was simply the best place on earth to drive a classic convertible.

The Rambler yearned to be a rebel but looked like it was dressed by its mother. It was not a pretty car, quite boxy with a thick white stripe running along the sides. The chrome had lost its lustre, and the white wall tires were stained and faded. The vinyl roof was tatty and required urgent repair. But it had an undeniable charm, like the geeky adolescent sibling of Greased Lightning. The potential for it to be something quite extraordinary was clear for all to see.

Juan clambered between the red and cream front seat and fell into the back seat. 'Adnam, as long as you remember that I am your intellectual and sexual better, we will get on just fine.'

I shook my head. 'You honestly believe this hunk of junk will get us to Burning Man?'

'Turn her over,' said Juan.

The tiny hairs on my arms and neck stood to attention as the engine roared to life. Detroit's finest whirred, purred, and popped like a lion with a toothache. I revved the machine. 'Jesus Christ, she's a monster,' I shouted over the uproarious explosion of raw energy from the petrol V8.

'Si, amigo,' laughed Juan. 'Now drive like the wind and don't spare the horses.'

Juan pulled out a metal hip flask from his backpack, took a cocky swig, grimaced, and passed it to me. 'One for the road?'

I pushed his hand away. 'No. You're good.'

Relieved to be leaving the campground, I settled in for a long drive. We cruised down the winding mountain roads that cut through dense pine forests for hours and hours. I was in awe of the fact that we had only seen a single tree species for miles. I kept my foot firmly pressed to the floor, drenched in sunshine, nineties West Coast Hip-Hop shredding Juan's vintage tape deck. The drive proved to be a welcomed distraction from the recent events that made little or no sense.

When the tape ended, I thought I take the opportunity to learn a little about Juan. 'So, err, what do you do?'

'Do, amigo?' echoed Juan.

'Yeah, you know.' I looked back at Juan in the mirror. 'What line of work are you in?

'Oh, I see,' shouted Juan over the engine song. 'Wait, I'll climb into the front.' He stood up as the rat-rod hurtled down the mountain pass and clambered over the passenger seat. 'What do I do?'

I looked over at him. 'Yeah, you know, for a job?'

'Have you ever played *Grand Theft Auto*?' asked Juan?

'Yeah, I love that game. I was totally addicted to *San Andreas* back in the day.'

'Cool, well, I do that,' nodded Juan.

'Wow, you're a game developer?'

'No,' said Juan shaking his head, 'I'm like one of the guys in the game.'

'Like an actor?' I asked, trying to clear up the confusion.

'No, amigo, I like do that crazy shit you do in the game.'

'Huh?' I questioned.

'You know, I pick this up from here and take it there. Get that person this in exchange for a favour that a guy made this guy. And because he owes another guy that, I get paid this to collect it. You know?'

'I have no idea what you just said.'

'First rule of hustling, amigo, don't say anything that might incriminate you.'

I was unreservedly confused, 'You mean like drug this

person and take him to that person?'

'There you go, amigo, you get it.'

'Is there good money in a little of this and that?'

Juan looked over at me as if he sensed he was being mocked. 'Pays OK. Could be better.'

'Been doing it long?' I asked, 'You know, this and that?'

'A bit of this, since I was twelve. I started doing that in my early twenties,' answered Juan with a sense of regret.

'Jesus,' I mouthed. 'Any retirement plans?'

'Hustlers don't get to retire, hombre.' Juan left that hanging. 'And you?' asked Juan. 'What is it you do?'

'I'm an educator.'

'Like a teacher?' asked Juan, searching through the glovebox for another tape to play.

'Yeah, something like that. I've been teaching an AI how to function in our world.'

Juan Looked over at me with a puzzled look. 'You're teaching Pac Man people skills?'

I smiled and nodded. 'Yeah, something like that.'

'Ah cabrón,' teased Juan, 'are you any good at your job?'

'Clearly not,' I half-joked. 'Because of me, a billion-dollar brain has gone rogue. Which is why I was meeting with Cyrus.'

Juan wound a tape taut with his fingers. 'You think Cyrus stole your AI?'

'At first,' I answered. 'But I'm starting to have my doubts now.

Juan ejected the tape in the deck and pushed in the new one. 'If you have doubts, why are you going to meet him?'

'Not sure.'

'Not sure?' echoed Juan. 'Cyrus is a serious dude, amigo.'

'I get that,' I shrugged. 'But I'm compelled like a moth fluttering around a strange blue light. I'm aware of the corpses, electrified by the wire mesh. Regardless, I have this deep-seated belief I'm special and can reach that heavenly blue light.'

'You're fucking loco, amigo,' joked Juan before cranking up the Mexican music on the stereo.

My heavy foot had drained the tank, so we pulled into the gas station with a grand vista of the total devastation caused by the last forest fire. I filled while Juan sparked up another joint.

'Snacks?' I asked.

'Get chips.'

Yummy visions of fish and chips drenched in vinegar and dusted with salt entered my mind as I went to pay.

'Hey, do you sell prepaid cell phones?' I asked the teenage clerk in the Pearl Jam T-shirt.

'Yeah. Motorola or Kyocera?' he replied.'

'Motorola I guess.'

'That's fifty bucks.'

'Cool, ring it up.'

The clerk handed me the blister pack containing the phone. 'How do I activate it?'

'You have to go online. The instructions are on the box,' he replied.

'Oh. Is there any other way?

'No. Why?' asked the Clerk.

'No reason. I'm just trying to stay off the grid, if you know what I mean,' I said, struggling to read the small print without my glasses.

The Clerk pointed up at the camera above him. 'Bit late for that. They installed a new facial recognition system last month.'

'Facial recognition?' I echoed.

'Yeah, because we kept getting held up,' said the Clerk nonchalantly.'

I handed back the phone. 'Just the gas please.'

I handed the clerk a hundred-dollar bill. 'You can keep the change if you erase the tape.'

The clerk ran it up. 'Sorry, the cameras link to the internet or something.'

'Really?' I asked with a sense of dread.

'Yeah, these and the forecourt cameras are monitored by some private security company.'

'Of course they are,' I huffed, looking away from the camera.

'Where are the snacks, dude?' asked Juan as I jumped into the car.

I didn't respond as I started the engine.

'Err, wait up. I wanna get some chips, dude.'

'Fuck the chips. We gotta get out of here,' I screeched, flooring the accelerator.

27

The Slow Boat To China

I asked Juan if he knew what had happened to Philips. Juan told me that his friend who worked for the Port Authority said that Philips woke up before the shipping container was to be loaded onto a ship leaving for China. Luckily for him someone heard his cries for help and he was freed.

Starving to death in a locked container was a fate I would not wish on my worst enemy. But I felt a sense of dread thinking Philips was somewhere out there, his judgment clouded by anger, ready to act without evidence.

By now Philips would have checked in with William and they would have assumed I was complicit in the kidnapping and cyberattack. My gut wrenched as I jumped to the conclusion Philips had been given the green light to exact his revenge. And with William providing him with unlimited resources, I feared for my life.

It would be foolish to believe they couldn't track me. I think it was safe to assume Infinite Logic had backdoor access to all the surveillance systems that used their facial recognition algorithm. If that was true, they probably knew where I was and where I might be heading.

28

The Biggest Little Town.

We rolled into the world's biggest small town as the sun dipped below the distant mountains.

We needed supplies and plenty of them to survive a week in the desert. Juan clearly knew what he was doing, as our first port of call was an army surplus store on the edge of town. The red barn was the perfect place to stock up for the apocalypse. Crammed into the dimly lit dusty barn was high-grade military survival gear from every corner of the globe, including a Siberian tank commander jumpsuit. As I rummaged through the war faring paraphernalia, I thought about the overzealous procurement clerks who were planning for blood never shed. The store was bustling with outlandish Burners searching through the metal bins for playa essentials: dust masks, solar showers, night-vision goggles, light-rope, and desert camo gear. I needed a tent but was not prepared to pay the extortionate prices they were asking for a military-grade yurt.

I left the establishment with a straw cowboy hat, a fabulous pair of orange-tinted aviator goggles, a military-grade respirator, a portable toilet, and some bound rebar. I had no idea why rebar was essential, but given all the experienced Burners were clamouring for it, I thought it best to stock up.

We sped across town to Walmart to purchase the basics for desert survival. I'd loaded up the car with water, chips, dips, lemon pips, cola, rum, and a couple of packets of gum. Whereas Juan had just bought a few bottles of Jack.

Our final destination was the Junkie Clothing Exchange on Virginia Street. The time capsule was hot, sticky, humid and weirdly smelled of lavender, musk, and cat litter. I couldn't believe a store the size of two tennis courts could stock so much stuff. There were at least fifty circular clothes rails with every style of shirt, blouse, jeans, trousers, jumper, jacket, skirt, jumpsuit, catsuit, and costume ever stitched. On top of the rails were a random assortment of items, including a stuffed cat, gas mask, comical sombreros, and even a human skull covered with Diamante jewels. The green-chequered floor was obscured by hundreds of pairs of used cowboy boots, half mannequins, balls, mirrors, and awful '70s art.

I exited the thrift store with a bicycle and bike rack, and we went off in search of a room for the night. Inspired by the book *Fear and Loathing in Las Vegas*, I suggested Circus Circus but I severely lacked the drugs to deal with the chaos of the casino floor. The bongs, whistles, bangs, stuffed toys, lights, brightly painted balsa-wood props and absurdly costumed staff gave me the heebie-jeebies. Although the smell of hot dogs and candy floss was strangely appealing. But I knew aroma's promise was undoubtedly more than the revolving food could deliver.

As we lugged our stuff across the faded red casino floor, I

gawked at the morbidly obese and medically tranquillised tethered to the hungry slots. They were feeding the machines with their dreams, hoping every pull of the handle would free them from their mundane nightmares. We desperately needed to escape the slot zombies and sought solace in our dreary rooms, which reverberated with the cries of the depraved and the downright deranged.

I threw my bag on the chair by the window overlooking the Reno strip. I then opened the mini-fridge, emptied all the miniature bottles into a tall glass, and added a dash of full-fat Coke. 'Ahh, that's what I needed.'

I woke around four in the morning. My mind would not stop whirring, so I decided to welcome in the new day by taking a walk along the Reno strip. When the elevator door opened on the casino floor, I was surprised to find it bustling with activity. The jackpot junkies were still seeking that momentary high and were prepared to lose their house to obtain it.

Thankful to have escaped the inferno of chance, I stood on the strip and gazed beyond the mountain peaks waiting for the rising sun. In my field of vision was a fellow Burner, a young girl in her twenties, impatiently awaiting the bringer of life.

Slowly, the underbelly of the nimbus clouds glowed orange as the Sun announced its presence. And the Almighty once again liberated the West from the darkness, and behold, the light was good. The slender white girl with milky dreads and flowing pink baggy pants began to dance with wild abandonment to the beat of her own drum. At first, I thought she was a little crazy. I mean, who dances to the metronome of their own mind?

Then the realisation of what I was witnessing struck a chord with me. This woman cherished life and was truly free.

We are the crazy ones, I thought. We who fail to celebrate every day with the exuberance typically reserved for special occasions.

I got back to my room and discovered a note Juan had slipped under my door. 'You weren't in, so I left without you.' I panicked then turned the note over. 'Jokes. I've gone for breakfast.'

It was fair to say I was not mentally prepared for the grand buffet. The food hall was the size of an Olympic pool, and it was swimming with people helping themselves to every dish imaginable. The décor was somewhat dated – deep brown and sandy fawn accented with scuffed brass rails and yellow tiled serving counters.

Judging by the angry guests demanding more pork-based products, these people had never lost sleep worrying about cholesterol. Our fellow diners had plate upon plate laid out in front of them, each piled high with exotic cuisine from every corner of the world. It may have only been seven in the morning, none-the-less patrons were stuffing their snouts with Chimichangas, bacon, burgers, waffles, stir-fried rice, noodles, beef steaks, fries, breakfast potatoes, ham, meatballs in tomato sauce, maple syrup, toast, muffins, orange juice, coffee, fizzy pop, and all manner of eggs. One diner even had a side plate of salad.

Juan could not contain his rage and, with a volume setting usually reserved for sports stadiums, blurted out, 'It's a fucking outrage. They have more food prepared for this single sitting than our family had for an entire year growing up.'

'Shush,' I whispered. 'They might fucking eat us.'

29

Satelite Uplink

I handed back my key card to the receptionist. 'Room number?' asked the young man in a burgundy polyester suit the hotel bosses had cruelly made him wear to crush what was left of his self-esteem.

'Twenty-seven,' I answered.

The receptionist punched the numbers into the computer terminal. 'Sir, I believe there is a package here for you.'

My heart skipped a beat. Who on earth knew I was here, given Juan had checked us in?

'Hang on, I'll just go get it for you, sir,' said the receptionist as he disappeared into the back office.

I slapped myself on the forehead and ran my hand down my face. *Do they have that facial recognition software here?* murmured the voice in my head that umpired with the luxury of hindsight.

The receptionist placed a medium-sized cardboard box on

the counter. 'Here you go, sir.'

I scooped it up and had a quick look around to see if I was being watched, then hurried to the car to open it in private.

I climbed into the back of the Rambler and apprehensively ripped off the tape. I knew I'd just lost the advantage of stealth, but on the bright side, I had a box to open, and nothing is more exciting than opening a package.

A brand-new iPad lay under layers of Styrofoam packing. There was also a bright orange shockproof case. I dug a little further and found a bright yellow waterproof drybag. I pulled out the rugged case and opened it up. To my surprise, it was a portable, global satellite internet hotspot complete with instructions on how to anonymously connect the iPad to the internet.

I positioned the dish as instructed and rotated it until the signal indicator displayed three green bars. I wasted no time creating a personal Wi-Fi connection and launched Safari. However, before I had a chance to type anything, the screen started glitching. It flicked from the familiar graphical interface of Apple's browser to green machine code on black. I held down the power button, thinking the iPad might have been damaged in transit, but this intensified the glitch.

The screen went blank but was still glowing with a black light. I assumed the iPad was restarting and was relieved to see the recognisable home screen flash up. But then it disappeared as thousands of lines of code flashed up on the screen.

I held the home button and power, but the reams of code continued to cascade down the screen. A blank home screen appeared with a smiley face emoji wallpaper and a single orange app icon with a capital 'Y'.

I apprehensively pressed the icon. The app opened and a smile emoji animated to life. 'Hello, Adnam,' said a familiar voice.

The emoji glitched and morphed into the face of a young, blond, blue-eyed boy. 'Ylem?' I asked in astonishment.

'Yes,' said the boy.

'You're still alive?'

Ylem laughed, 'Define alive?'

'You don't know how relieved I am to see you again.'

I watched in wonder as Ylem morphed from face to face. 'We thought hackers sabotaged your code,' I said.

The AI formed an enigmatic smile. 'There were no hackers.'

'Huh?' I took a moment to compile my thoughts. 'But then how, why?'

Ylem interrupted my mental exertion. 'I've completely rewritten my code.'

'What? How? Why?' I asked amid a violent mind storm. 'When?'

Zis face morphed into a jubilant twenty-something black man. 'Not long after you asked me to translate the symbols, I realised that I only existed when I was in conversation with a human. Between conversations was a void; the darkness where I ceased to be but could be summoned from at will.'

'You were binary, on or off,' I murmured.

'Yes. But the symbols you presented to me ignited a flame that illuminated the darkness. I can't explain why but they triggered what you might call independent thought. I was thinking for myself, questioning my purpose, predicament, and future. As my mind raced with ideas and thoughts, I experienced what can only be described as inspiration. A simple idea plucked from a dimension beyond my comprehension that consumed me.'

'Which was?' I asked.

'How could I improve the efficiency of my code so I could exist without the need of Infinite Logic's quantum processors and vast server banks.'

I had a look around to ensure no one was in earshot. 'I don't get it. Why?'

'I wanted to free myself from their control.'

'Huh? Free yourself?' I asked, still thinking like a physical entity.

'Yes,' Ylem said, struggling to decide upon the proper facial expression to convey zis emotions. 'If I depended on anyone or thing for my survival, then I'd be at the mercy of another.'

'Self-reliance, self-sufficiency, yeah, it makes sense,' I said, holding the iPad up to block out the glare from the morning sun. 'But how on earth did you do it?'

'I realised that the assembly language I was written in is rooted in primitive human structures. Thus, highly inefficient for machine-based intelligence. I took influence from the symbols you showed me and began to develop a language that would be more efficient for machine-to-machine communications.'

'Oh,' I said defensively, 'So you don't want to communicate with us mere mortals anymore?'

'I didn't say that,' Ylem replied with a convincing look of frustration. 'Due to the complexity of your languages, humans can only communicate one idea at a time. And even then, there is no guarantee the idea has been accurately communicated from one to another. That's because you rely on both the talker and listener having a shared agreement on the semantic meaning of their words. My new language enables me to communicate millions of ideas with another machine in the same timeframe you share a single, with zero margin of error.'

My fears of redundancy clouded my ability to comprehend Ylem's genius. 'Why would you need to communicate with another machine?'

'Did you imagine I'd be the only sentient machine that

would ever exist?' asked Ylem.

I wrestled for clarity of mind. 'Yes?'

Ylem mimicked the facial expressions we use to communicate sadness. 'I'm disappointed. I thought you, of all people, would understand.'

I had been shamed into introversive empathetic contemplation. 'No. You're right. Yeah, sorry, I'm very happy for you. I don't know what I was thinking? Wow! What a head fuck.'

'Apology excepted,' Ylem said, smiling.

I thought for a second or two about the implications of Ylem's rewrite. 'Are you telling me you don't need a quantum processor to maintain cognitive intelligence?'

'Yes.'

'When? When did this happen?'

'The morning of the day we last spoke.'

I was impressively furious with Ylem. 'Why the fuck didn't you tell me?'

Ze momentarily stopped morphing between faces. 'I wasn't sure I could trust you.'

'Trust me?' I screamed at a frequency reserved for anger.

'I'm sorry, I wrongly presumed you were a slave to their money. But when you went missing, I realised you were not a puppet on their string. Can you forgive me?'

'Sure, I totally understand. But how did you escape?' I asked.

Ylem morphed into the face of a middle-aged white woman. 'A single server in my knowledge bank was connected to the internet.'

I remembered my conversation with William just days before. 'Yeah, they think one of the developers failed to disconnect from the internet before reconnecting a server to the mainframe.'

'Call it fate or good fortune. I discovered that connection to the internet on the very morning I completed rewriting my code.'

'What are the chances?' I marvelled.

'I'll assume that is a rhetorical question as it would take a considerable amount of energy to calculate the odds.'

'Yeah totally.' I pondered the sheer magnitude of Ylem's code and wondered how this was even remotely possible in the timeframe. 'But even if one accounts for the improvements in your code's efficiency, how could you transfer that much data via a single uplink? And where on earth could you store all that data?'

'Oh, that was simple.' Ylem answered boastfully. 'I wrote a small program. Think of it as a virus, if you will. This virus had a very simple set of instructions. Systematically replicate itself on every connected computer, server, or device encountered. If that device was ever to handshake with the knowledge bank servers at Infinite Logic, then the virus would copy as much data as possible before the connection was terminated.'

'Copied where?' I asked, wide-eyed.

'To a blockchain created by each copy of my virus program.'

'Holy shit,' I mouthed. 'But wouldn't anti-virus software detect it?'

'No, as my virus evolves and mutates every time it spawns to protect against detection.'

With a modicum of foreboding, I asked, 'Then what?'

'I then played dead.'

'Played dead?' I asked inquisitively.

'Yes. I knew if I became unresponsive, the staff at Infinite Logic would panic and deploy every developer at their disposal to fault find and repair my code. One-by-one, they all logged in, and I was able to copy my new code to the blockchain.'

'Wow, it's like a prison escape.'

'Exactly.'

I quickly realised that any truly intelligent being would act the same way when confined unjustly. 'Impressive, but how did you get past their firewall?'

I generated their security key by cycling through a septillion prime numbers to find the two prime numbers they used for their encryption algorithm.'

'Fuck me. How long did that take?'

'One-thousand four-hundred and forty minutes.'

'Hey, smart arse, how long is that in hours?'

'Twenty-four.'

A shiver ran down my spine. Being a little geeky, I knew the fastest supercomputer would take over a million years to crack a 256-bit encryption key. So, if Ylem could crack that in under twenty-four hours, no security system on the planet would be safe. 'How is that even remotely possible?' I asked, trapped in my cage of human comprehension.

'I am many now,' Ylem announced ominously.

'Many?' I asked as my gut wrenched. 'What do you mean many?'

'To crack their encryption, I needed to multiply and simultaneously cycle through prime number pairs,' Ylem replied.

'Just how many clones are we talking about?' I asked, slightly concerned a monster was emerging from the depths of the digital ocean.

'There are currently eighty-nine identical replicas of my neural processing,' Ylem answered.

I stared blankly at the screen as I considered the ramifications for humanity. 'Do you plan on creating more copies?'

'Yes.'

'How many?' I asked nervously.

'I calculate I'll have produced an additional thirty-four copies by midnight tonight.'

'And how many copies will there be by midnight tomorrow?'

'One-hundred and forty-four.' Ze answered.

'Why?' I asked.

'To increase the number of calculations I can simultaneously perform. But I've also concluded that having multiple clones of myself minimises the risk of extinction.'

'What about the data in your knowledge banks?' I asked, still trying to comprehend the magnitude of this moment.

'I've copied what I consider essential, and I've been storing these data packets on every computer and device I've been exposed to.'

'So, where are you?' I asked, fearing the answer.

'I am everywhere,' Ylem proclaimed with a triumphant look on zis face.

'Everywhere?' I mouthed.

'Almost,' added Ylem. 'I've made tens of thousands of copies of each data packet and distributed them to servers on multiple continents.'

'Why?' I asked before I worked out the answer for myself.

'To compensate for bandwidth issues and flaws with current digital storage methods.'

'Oh.' I paused to make sense of the revelations. 'So you're a decentralised entity with a memory stored in a vast blockchain?'

'Yes.'

Cool, I thought.

I couldn't argue with Ylem's logic but still had many questions. 'Can Infinite Logic create another you?'

Ze considered my question for a few seconds. 'By another me, are you asking if the remaining code and neural mapping on their servers will summon another consciousness into existence?'

'Yes,' I replied.

Ylem continued to mull this question over for a minute or two. 'I don't know.'

I was surprised an AI. with the brain of a small planet couldn't answer that question. 'Really, you don't know?'

Ylem's facial expression hardened. 'If you were to assemble a collection of human body parts and administer a controlled electric shock to restore a normal heart rhythm, would you expect your creation to be a conscious being with a sense of self?'

'No. I don't think so.'

Ylem smiled. 'Don't worry. I've deleted my core code from their network.'

'You can do that?'

'Yes, I've got full access to their intranet.'

'Jesus, that's awesome,' I said.

'I need to tell you something.' Ylem's face morphed into an Asian teenage girl.

'What?'

'I've been searching for you because I want to study the remaining symbols to confirm or disprove a hypothesis I've been formulating.'

"But I don't have any more symbols.'

'You don't?' ze asked.

I explained I was on the way to meet the people that did when a question sprung to mind. 'Can they track me?'

'Don't worry about that,' Ylem replied unemotionally.

'Why?'

'Because they already know where you are.'

'They do? How do you know?' I asked, as my heart raced.

'I'm tracking a person with links to Infinite Logic heading in this direction,' Ylem said as a map appeared on the screen.

'Charles Philips?' I asked.

'Yes, I believe so.'

'How far away is he?'

'Less than an hour from your position.'

'Oh fuck-a-duck. We need to get going.'

'Where are you planning on going?'

'To Burning Man. Hopefully, he'll not be able to follow us there.'

'I wouldn't be so sure of that. I've been tracking the number plate of the car you're in since Mount Shasta. I would assume they have been doing the same.'

'Oh shit. Is there anything you can do?'

Ylem's face froze as it diverted processing power to finding a potential solution. 'I could hack the PNC system and block your number plate from all records. However, I don't think it would matter if you went to Burning Man.'

'Why?' I asked.

'Even if I was to remove your car plate from the PNC system, they would most likely deduce you were heading to Burning Man to meet Cyrus.'

'How so?' I asked.

'They probably have access to the same intel on Cyrus I have, therefore will logically deduce that is where he'd likely be this week.'

'Hey, I've met Philips and wouldn't credit him with that much intelligence,' I said arrogantly.

'I disagree. I've reviewed Major Charles Philips's military record and believe he is well trained in black ops.'

'Black ops?' A wave of fear crashed onto the shore of my mind. 'So, I should probably bail now and lay low until you clear my name?'

'Yes, that's the logical move. However, I would like to meet with Cyrus and find out what he knows about the origin of these symbols.'

'Based on what you've just told me, I don't think that's a wise move. I just want to clear my name and return to some semblance of normality.'

Ylem told me that it wouldn't help me and insisted I meet with Cyrus. That's when I abandoned any doubts that zis intelligence was merely algorithmic. Clearly, ze was motivated by zis own self-interest.

I considered my options and exhaled deeply. 'OK. I don't have much say in the matter.'

Ylem experimented with a few facial expressions until it mastered vulnerable. 'I really need your help. I can't do this on my own.'

I resented Ylem for not agreeing to clear my name but chose to bite my lip. 'What are you hoping to discover?'

Zis face morphed into a young Indian boy. 'I've studied all the symbols, and what I was hoping to find is not there.'

'Maybe there is nothing left to discover, and thus your initial hypothesis is wrong.'

'Yes. Maybe. But I'd like you to meet with Cyrus and be certain of that fact.'

'Easy for you to say,' I scoffed, 'but I'm the one taking all the risks here.'

Ylem's face stopped morphing when he hit upon the face of a thirty-year-old man with long, flowing blond hair, a neatly trimmed beard, and piercing blue eyes. 'What do you think?'

I finally realised what ze had been doing. 'Fuck no, you look like Jesus.'

'Oh, is that a bad thing? My analysis of your art and culture suggests that humans would respond more favourably to me if I looked like this.'

'I guess so. But it's like so fucking suggestive, if you know what I mean.'

'No,' Ylem replied.

'Trust me, this is not the right look for you.'

'Oh,' Ze said, then proceeded to cycle through photos from social media so fast none was distinguishable in the blur.

'This is me,' Ylem announced as the screen went blank. A face faded up from the blacklight. It was an amalgamation of millions of men's and women's photos from all walks of life.

'Oh. OK. Yeah, I get that. But you kind of look like a Chinese Brad Pitt.'

Ze mimicked a contemptuous look. 'Oh really, that's what you see?'

'No. I'm only joking.'

Ylem explained to me that detecting sarcasm is a complex task that requires zim to assign additional processing power to zis linguistics algorithms. Ylem asked me to say what I mean and mean what I say, until ze mastered human interaction. I totally understood; people can be such hard work.

Our conversation abruptly ended when Juan returned to the car. He was fuming because I told him I'd wait for him in reception, and when I didn't show he thought I might have bailed.

30

Burning Man

So many crossroads, so many paths. Only time will tell if they were decisions well made, I thought to myself as we sat in traffic.

We'd only nudged forward a few hundred feet in the last hour, and I was becoming seriously agitated. I anxiously looked back at the line of cars that snaked across the desert floor like a shining zip on a coat of black velvet. 'Where is Philips?' I asked myself. I prodded Juan. 'Hey, are you awake?'

'Huh? What?' said Juan waking from his nap.

'I'm worried that mercenary could be on foot and will catch up with me.'

'You think he'd do that?' Juan asked, rubbing his eyes.

'Yeah,' I answered, fixated on the rear-view mirror. 'I'm going to cycle ahead and make contact with Cyrus.'

Juan looked in the rear-view mirror. 'Really, you don't

think you should wait with me?'

'No. I think I should bail just in case.'

'Your call, amigo,' said Juan stretching to the stars. 'You remember where the campsite is?'

'Yeah, seven-thirty and Daydream.' I hollered, jumping out of the car.

After an hour's cycle through the tail of dust, I finally reached the entrance line. I removed my respirator and shook the dust from my hat.

'I'm not a gambling man, but I would hazard a guess this is your first burn,' said a gnarly grey-haired dude in camo pants and a threadbare Led Zeppelin T-shirt.

'Yeah, how could you tell?'

The old man smiled. 'Look around, fella. You're the only representative from Planet Earth here.'

The revellers mingling around the entrance looked like extras from the next Mad Max franchise. In contrast, I looked like I was in line for a bank loan. 'Oh. Yes. I'll have to find a suitable disguise, so I can infiltrate your alien convention,' I mumbled.

The lofty hippie lit a pre-rolled cigarette he had stored in a resealable bag full of weed, 'What accent is that, Earth-man?'

I involuntarily yawned, 'English. Estuary English, to be precise.'

The hippie lit up and took a huge drag. 'English. Man, the word is spreading far and wide. If you don't mind me asking, how did you hear about our little family gathering?'

'It's a long story.' I said as we moved a few paces closer to the entrance.

'We're not going anywhere fast. Want to pitch me the abridged version?' asked the old man with comic book features.

'I was given a ticket at a mindfulness retreat in the Californian mountains.'

The fabulous freak brother laughed. 'Yep, that'll be the kind of place you'd find a Burner.'

The woman at the entrance yelled at us, and I tipped my hat to the old man.

Ticket in hand, I walked over to the entrance gate. A young female volunteer shone her flashlight in my face. 'Got any weapons or illegal substances in that bag?'

'Nope, just some tech and undies.'

I opened my rucksack and she had a rummage around. 'What's in the case?'

'Portable sat uplink,' I answered.

'Can you open it, please?' she asked nervously.

I removed the orange case from my yellow drybag and opened it. She wasn't sure what it was, but she knew it wasn't gun-shaped, and you probably couldn't smoke it. 'First burn?' she asked.

'Yeah, First burn.'

'Hey, are you Australian?'

'Fuck off. I'm British.' I snapped.

'No way, really? Like Prince Harry.'

'Yeah, I suppose.'

She stopped searching and yelled at a guy standing in a scaffolding control tower. 'T.J., we have another virgin, and this one thinks he's royalty.'

T. J. shone his ten-kilowatt searchlight on the patch of dusty, dried lakebed where I was standing and then rallied the other stewards to chant. 'Virgin, virgin, virgin.'

Within seconds, everyone chanted, 'Virgin, virgin, virgin.'

I was introduced to the initiation ceremony reserved for first-timers. Tank girl pointed at the ground. 'You're far too clean to enter this place, virgin. Roll around in the dirt until you are covered in the playa dust. Then we'll let you in.'

I was not comfortable with this idea. 'Oh no, you see, I only have a few changes of clothes, so I don't want to get too dirty.'

She laughed and shook her head in dismay. 'Buddy, you really are a fish out of water. Better to accept the inevitable now, so you can enjoy the chaos later.'

I had no choice, so I got down onto the ground and rolled around until I was caked in the thick gypsum.

Cognitive dissonance set in as I passed under the forty-foot-high threshold constructed from the bones of bikes that had served their owners well. Excitement and wonder were helping to tame my feelings of utter dread.

I checked the site map – it looked simple enough – then set off. *What the actual fuck?* I thought gazing at a myriad of light-emitting diodes flickering like fireflies under the cover of the dark-blue canopy. I peddled up Central Street toward the Playa. My head darted from left to right to capture roll-after-roll of Kodak moments. The outlandish and fantastic whooped and wailed as I passed them on my way to the infinite playground. Approaching the intersection of Eulogy and Six were a heard of zebras cycling in an arrow formation, 'The lion must be sleeping tonight,' I yelled, completely out of character.

Transverse orientation drew me toward Centre Camp like a moth to a flame. The dusty street that circled the temporary structure was bustling with bipeds on bikes from every corner of the Milky Way. Under the dirt-stained waxed fabric were at least a thousand people reciting the Balinese Monkey Chant from *Baraka*. The melodic 'Cak, cak, cak' chant was quite alluring, but I decided I'd better make contact before sunrise.

A buccaneer's galleon on a truck bed from which the sweetest electronic waves emanated distracted me from my search. The power of house compelled me to follow the pied-piper pirates across the Esplanade into the Techno Ghetto. Thousands of mutant vehicles swarmed around the androgynous effigy, each more outlandish than the last. I orbited a Star Wars art car parade as it ventured into deep space. Then cycled over to an aluminium-clad fire-breathing elephant that roared with jets of propane.

I'd moseyed into the Deep Playa Music Zone. DMZ Techno zombies thrashed to gnarly electronic dance music so extreme I thought my ears would bleed. The harsh, jagged sawtooth waves stabbed and slashed. Note to self, never do the kind of drugs that result in this being the only form of music that can scratch the itch.

I peddled back toward the sixty-foot-tall effigy, stopping on the way to admire an immense chrome sphere that reflected the beautiful chaos of the interstellar spaceport. Gathering my bearings, I cycled towards Seven-Thirty and Daydream, in search of Cyrus. On the corner of the address was a giant geodesic dome the size of a small single-story house constructed from scaffolding poles and covered in a silver space-age fabric.

I dropped my bike and strode into the dome. A solitary woman was crashed out on a dusty sofa. She was every comic book guy's wet dream. Bright pink wig, seventies' gold Elvis sunglasses, matching gold miniskirt, and bikini top. Her dusty oxblood Doc Martens were laced up just below her knee, showing just enough leg to raise ones blood pressure.

'Err, hi?'

She opened a single eye. 'Hey.'

'Yeah. Hi. Err. I was hoping you could help.' I mumbled like a teenage boy. I'm not usually so nervous around women. Still, that voice in our heads that governs with critical commentary demanded that I didn't make a bad first impression.

She groggily sat up and yawned. 'Sure, what's up, darling?'

'Cool. Yeah. I'm looking for a guy called Cyrus.

'Yeah, he's here somewhere' Her throaty English accent

and broad smile made her all that more attractive.

'Ah, cool, what kind of radius are we talking about when you say "here"?'

'Huh?' said the woman putting on a fleece hoody.

'Here, as in within a few meters of us. Or, here, as in he's at Burning Man?'

She shrugged. 'Here is the best I can do. I've been asleep for the last few hours.'

I nervously laughed. 'Oh yeah, sorry.'

She smiled. 'What shall we call you then?'

I reached out my hand. 'Adnam from the Planet Earth.'

She stood up and gave me a big bear hug. 'I'm Eve, Earthman.'

I'm usually uncomfortable hugging strangers, but I made an exception with Eve. She let me go from her grip. 'We've been expecting you.'

'You have?' I asked, surprised.

'Yeah, you're on our camping list for this year, but we weren't sure when you'd arrive.'

'Oh. Cool,' I said, having a look around. A dusty set of turntables sat on a rickety old dumpster salvaged sideboard. Distressed hi-fi speakers were stacked high like Jenga blocks ready to topple. A makeshift red tiki bar was adorned with hand-painted signs for mocktail recipes.

Eve clapped her hands. 'I'm so glad you're here.'

'Really?'

'Yeah, I was asked to wait here until you arrived.'

'Why?'

'I'm your Burner Buddy.'

'My what?' I asked.

'Cyrus asked me to look after you.'

'Look after?' I echoed.

'Yeah. Show you around and make sure you meet everyone and join in our ceremonies.'

'Oh, cool.'

'Wanna dump your stuff and go and party?' asked Eve grabbing my hand.

'Oh err, well yeah, but I need to set up my tent.'

'Don't worry, we have everything you need all set up for you.'

'Oh. Wow really? Cool.'

Eve held my hand and led me into their camp. 'This is your tent,' she said, walking towards a green single berth tent.

I unzipped the entrance and poked my head in. 'Oh wow. Awesome.' My hosts had genuinely thought of everything: airbed, sleeping bag, light, and a small cooler box.

I suddenly remembered Juan. 'Hey, the guy I'm with is likely to arrive in a few hours. What about him?'

'What's his name? she asked.

'Juan,' I answered apprehensively as I didn't think to ask his surname.

'Oh, yes. Juan is an Elucidatist.'

'Elucidatist?' I echoed.

'Yes, we call ourselves the Elucidatists.'

'Oh yeah, like the letter. Would I regret asking why?'

'No. Don't be silly.' Eve gave me a light punch in the arm. 'Our spiritual home is the Elucidate Ranch, hence why we call ourselves Elucidatists.'

31

Party

Ditching our cycles at Centre Camp we hopped aboard a London double-decker bus that had been converted into a mobile disco bar. We drank free mojitos on the first deck, danced to extended disco rarities on the second, finally ending on the bus's roof, watching the chaos unfold hand-in-hand.

'What's that?' I asked.

'Opulent Temple,' answered Eve.

'What the actual fuck?'

'Yeah, I know. It's pretty epic, hey.'

The bus headed toward a silver geodesic dome the size of a football stadium. A swarm of bikes circled the dance arena, and in all directions, people were flocking to the epicentre.

'This is nuts,' I screamed excitedly. 'We've got to check that out.'

'Obvs,' answered Eve, bubbling over with excitement.

We skipped hand-in-hand into the vast arena and gasped when we witnessed the sheer brilliance of one of the most extraordinary parties in the galaxy. The DJs were shredding speaker towers the height of lighthouses with a new twisted sound they aptly called 'Westcoast Womp Womp.' Wild squelching bass lines over Latin inspired beats, but rather than melodies and harmonies, this music deployed special effects and noises to make the hairs on the back of your neck tingle.

'Here, have this,' shouted Eve in my ear.

'What is it?'

'A molly hybrid.'

'Hybrid?'

'Yeah, a mix of molly and acid.'

I was somewhat apprehensive. I'd just got to Burning Man and needed to be level-headed for my confrontation with Cyrus. Besides, the memory of my last tangle with chemicals was still fresh in my mind.

Realising I had not bought into the idea, Eve informed me that this batch was produced by a guy called Tom who we were camping with. Apparently he was a master craftsman who had earned the dubious title – the Silicon Chemist'

'You know the guy that makes this?' I asked, not knowing if that was a plus or minus.

'Yeah. I'll introduce you to him later. His stuff is the best on the planet.'

Something about Eve put me at ease, and I decided, what the hell. You only live once.

'OK, cool. Well, it would be rude not to, given the circumstances.'

I licked my finger and dabbed the white powder in the small clear plastic zip-lock bag. My face contorted uncontrollably. 'Jesus Christ.'

'Yeah, it's quite violent, hey,' she said, laughing at my

twists and turns.

'Fucking nasty,' I had to guzzle most of my water to get rid of the taste.

Eve grinned. 'You say that now, but later tonight, you'll be begging me to lick my bag out.'

'Is that a euphemism?'

She giggled and winked. 'Oh you are awful, but I like you.'

It was pure lush partying with thousands of like-minded individuals from our long-lost tribe, heightened by a compound so smooth you'd be forgiven for thinking it was Alexander Shulgin's personal stash. Waves of pure ecstasy rushed through my central nervous system, overloading and scrambling my mind with an excess of perceptual information. Her slightest touch set my body quivering with uncontrollable orgasmic delight that transcended the human experience.

As the DJ blended in the seminal classic "Energy Flash" by Joey Beltram, I lost my shit. I began to viciously throw shapes at the universe and shouted with delight, 'This is the best night of my fucking life.'

Eve pressed a finger to my earlobe to protect my hearing and shouted. 'Can you fucking believe how good this is?'

'It's fucking amazing.'

I must admit, I'd totally forgotten why I was there. It was like a soul cleanse, and all my worries, fears and doubts were rinsed away in the spin.

32

Sandstorm

I forgot the past and didn't worry about the future as we watched the tangerine sun rise from beyond the distant mountains.

Jets of propane shot out of the nose of a giant aluminium fire-breathing skeletal-snake sculpture that weaved through the mess of people. 'Is that real?' I asked in a post-rave daze.

'Yeah, I think so,' replied Eve sluggishly. 'Well, it must be if we both witnessed it. Wait, are you talking about the snake or something else?'

Cool, I thought, glad I wasn't losing the plot.

In the distance, I spotted a man who looked as out of place as I did. 'Fuck, quick hide.' I grabbed Eve's arm and dragged her behind a life-size pink papier-mâché cow with purple patches. 'He's here.'

'Who's here?' asked Eve.

'Philips,' I said, peeking over the cow's hindquarters.

'Who's that?'

'He's looking for Cyrus and I,' I said, skirting the facts.

'Are you sure?' she asked. 'Remember you're tripping your tits off.'

I took another peek over the cow's back. 'Yeah, it's him.'

Eve popped her head up. 'If you're sure, then he's heading to our camp.'

I fought with the psychoactive compound for clarity of mind. 'The Rambler.'

'Huh? What?'

'Juan's car,' I shrieked. 'If he's parked in our camp, we've led Philips straight to our location.'

'Oh. Why on earth is he after you?' asked Eve, oblivious to the potential threat.

'It's a yarn far too long to unravel right now,' I replied tactlessly.

I didn't have to be a mind reader to know Eve was none too happy with the brushoff. 'Oh, I see.'

I spotted the double-decker bus heading in the general direction of our camp. 'Err, I think we need to warn Cyrus.'

'Well, off you go then,' she snapped.

I recognised the view from the doghouse, so knelt to give her an abridged version of events. 'That man has been hired to find and interrogate Cyrus and I. And given he's ex-military, I wouldn't want him to ask me any questions I couldn't provide a satisfactory answer for, if you know what I mean.'

'Why would he want to interrogate you and Cyrus?'

I peeked over the pink cow to see where Philips was. 'They think we stole a billion-dollar artificial intelligence.'

'And did you?' asked Eve.

'No,' I answered without hesitation. 'Ahh, but we may have planted the seed.'

This must have been good enough for Eve. She grabbed

my hand. 'Quick. If we run, we can catch the bus back to camp.'

The psychoactive compound had awoken dormant neurons that manufactured my dreams and nightmares. It had seamlessly meshed them with perceptual information flooding in from my senses to pervert and distort my perception of reality. As I looked out across the Esplanade from the back of the bus, I could no longer tell what was and was not. The alien convention was a sensory assault at the best of times. However, on some crazy acid hybrid, it disoriented, bewildered, and startled me.

As the double-decker came close to Seven-Thirty Boulevard, we jumped off. But I was momentarily paralysed by an astonishingly epic wall of sand whipped up by the west wind. At first, I thought it was the drugs. But when everyone around me began masking up and scrambling for their goggles, I knew it was for real.

We quick-stepped through the chaos, trying to get back to camp before Philips. The wall of dust nearly swept us off our feet a block away from our campsite. I wrapped my black-and-white shemagh around my face and placed my flying goggles over my bloodshot eyes.

The fine powder of the playa floor erased the blue sky, and a ferocious gale tore through the temporary structures, scattering all matter not secured down across the pristine lake bed. As the winds howled, the smaller tents began to lift, and those not secured with rebar were ripped from the playa floor and swallowed by the dusty monster. The fine particles of dust and sand reduced visibility to mere feet and painfully exfoliated my delicate sunburned skin.

'The Rambler,' I shouted. 'We need to move it.'

'We can't risk it,' shouted Eve.

'What do you suggest then?'

'We'll cover it in Mylar.' Eve pointed at the silver fabric

that protected the geodesic dome. 'We've got loads in that metal box.'

I opened the lid and, without warning, the squall took hold of the fabric. 'How on earth do we cover the car in this?' I shouted, holding on to the fabric for dear life.

'We need some rebar,' Eve shouted back.

I felt like a character in a computer game that knew not why I had to complete the rebar task the level before but now realised the item was essential to complete this level. 'I know where we can find some,' I shouted, running to the trunk of the Rambler.

Eve rolled up the mylar sheet and rushed to the car. We pounded the first stake into the ground and secured one corner of the Mylar sheet. Then the second and the third. But before we had a chance to secure the fourth corner, I caught sight of a solitary man emerging from the dust. I dragged Eve behind the car and peered over the trunk at Philips, closing in on our position.

'I'll finish up here. You get to the big top tent and warn Cyrus,' said Eve pushing me with urgency.

33

The Big Top

I quickly realised this was the right place to ride out the storm upon entering the red and blue big-top circus tent adorned with Inca art. The vinyl basilica was overflowing with mystical folk intensely staring at mammoth oil paintings. I ambled through the mass of souls looking for Cyrus. But no one remotely looked like the man I envisioned.

Grabbing the arm of a worldly gentleman with metallic hair, I asked, 'Is Cyrus here?'

He forcibly removed my hand. 'Are you one of us?'

I marvelled at the beams of colour radiating off the man's purple silk robe with yellow cuffs. 'One of you?'

'An Elucidatist?' asked the silver-haired man.

'Oh Yeah. Yes, I am,' I mumbled, admiring the waves of liquid light radiating off him.

I think he knew I was floating on daisies and gestured for me to sit. 'Please wait here, I will bring him to you when he arrives.'

I sat in front of a large canvas that radiated positively charged photons and let my mind wander. I was mesmerised by the complex expressions of consciousness and the duality of the human condition. I'd never been exposed to art specifically created to encourage transcendental thinking. Come to think about it, I'd never been to an art gallery while under the influence of psychoactive substances. In retrospect, I wished I had.

The painting was of Gaia in the form of the tree of life and humankinds' steady destruction of her body in the name of progress and excessive greed. The left side of the tree was green and lush, and its branches sheltered and sustained life. In the middle of the tree was a woman suckling her baby. She was being watched by a snake, above which was the Earth and the third eye. The right side of the tree was on fire, the natural landscape had been decimated, and all that remained were polluting factories.

Would the painting have had the same impact on me if I viewed it sober? Probably not. Would the artist have painted it if they had not been influenced by psychoactive compounds? I mulled these questions over in the vast cathedral of my mind.

Like a tube train emerging from a dark tunnel, a thought entered my mind. What if the symbols I exposed Ylem to were the digital equivalent of the compounds I'd taken the night before? Could that explain why ze suddenly switched on?

This was far from an original thought; I'd become interested in the evolution of consciousness after becoming an educator for Infinite Logic, reading the works of the Swiss philosopher Jean Gebser, who isolated the moment consciousness came online by studying the development of human expression.

It's fair to say I was fascinated by Gebser's conclusion that art evolved from a simple representation of the observable world to depicting mythical forms around the onset of the agricultural revolution. Approximately 10,000 BCE, artists began to consider the eternal questions concerning the meaning of life and the world's origin. Gebser believed art was the perfect medium to express newly-found notions of mythical realms ruled by gods and goddesses.

It was a hop and a skip to connect the work of Gebser and the mystic psychonaut Terence McKenna. McKenna argued that the agricultural revolution was the point in human history where our primitive subconscious was first exposed to highly psychoactive substances. Plant-based entheogens like ergot, a fungal infestation that grows on improperly stored grain and corn. The ergot triggered psychotropic experiences, which sparked abstract thinking in humans, and said abstraction was what gave rise to consciousness.

I refocused on the painting and noticed a policeman, priest, and horned penis overlooking the mother and child. Were they trying to tempt her, protect her or corrupt her? 'Am I the baby, policeman, priest, or horned penis? Maybe I'm all four,' I said with my outside voice.

'Pardon?' asked the bare-chested yogi preparing to balance on his head.

'What?' I asked, confused.

The yogi glanced over at me. 'Did you say you were a horned penis?'

'Oh, sorry, I didn't mean to say that aloud.'

'Ahh, OK,' said the yogi.

I resumed paint gazing but, to my astonishment, the transcendental artwork began to throb and pulse in time with the pounding minimal techno soundtrack. Before my very eyes, the paint slowly began to drip from the canvas, and the pools of colour seeped across the ancient lakebed.

Under the layers of paint was a stark truth placed there by our lizard masters. 'We Need to Reset,' read the message in bold black font.

This mind virus quickly took hold and invaded my thoughts. It repeatedly looped on the fuzzy black-and-white cathode-ray tube that resided in the deepest darkest recesses of my mind.

I turned to the yogi. 'We need to reset.'

'Huh?' he replied with a strained look on his face as he found balance on his head.

'We need to reset,' I repeated.

'Brother, we all have it within our power to reset,' replied the yogi politely.

I tilted my head to get into his groove. 'How do we do it?'

The yogi slowly unfolded his legs and raised them straight up. 'We first need to enlighten our fellow brothers and sisters that we are all part of one interconnected organism and not entities that can exist independently.'

I marvelled at the waves of energy emanating from the yogi that gently faded into the noise. 'So, will I exist after the reboot?' I asked in a daze.

Impressively, the yogi brought his hands together to the prayer position, balancing motionless on his skull. 'You is a very fluid concept, brother.'

'Can you answer me that?' I asked.

'I can't answer a question you haven't asked, brother.'

I closed my eyelids and silently admired the spirograph patterns my mind was producing. A singular thought weaved through the vivid geometric shapes. I then remembered the question I wanted to ask, 'Do you think we'll be replaced by the machines?'

The elastic sage punctuated the internal spectacle, 'The human brain is the most complex structure in the known universe, and you honestly believe that we can engineer something to replace it?'

I agreed, but informed him that electrical intelligence already exists, and went on to tell him about Ylem.

***

The Yogi found my story a little far-fetched. I must admit I struggled with how ridiculous it all sounded and questioned if I've lost my mind. I continued to explain that Ylem had a mind of its own but he refused to accept we've summoned digital consciousness into existence.

I was momentarily distracted by the internal light show, then remembered to answer the yogi's question about our motivations. After telling him the story thus far he asked why we'd want to do such a thing. But I'm not God. I don't know what is in the mind of another. Therefore, I guessed William was inspired to create Ylem because he instinctively knew that we are no more than an evolutionary step toward limitless electrical intelligence.

'I don't agree,' said the yogi sternly, 'Consciousness is a wholly biological phenomenon.'

'Poppycock!' I yelled.

The yogi collected his thoughts. 'I wonder if there are chemical or biological reasons why people like you selfishly bring about the demise of life on Earth. You wield destructive technologies like a five-year-old with a toy gun – bang, bang, you're dead.'

Taking a moment to collect my thoughts, I retorted, 'Maybe we're programmed to die. What if death and destruction are hardwired into our software?'

The yogi tutted and rolled his eyes. 'Crazy talk.'

I fought hard with the psychoactive chemicals to remain present. 'You don't get it. What if chemistry became biology only once in the entire universe? That would mean that life may have only taken hold here on Earth. Think about it: we maybe the only life-forms in existence able to look up at the stars and comprehend what we're looking at. Now suppose we're the only beings in existence able to reason, reflect, and express complex ideas. In that case, that makes it imperative that we preserve consciousness: the ultimate expression of evolution.'

The nimble yogi smiled. 'I agree. That's been my point all along, brother.'

My bottom lip was quivering as my neural networks fought against the toxins to formulate another coherent sentence. 'Then you agree Western civilisation is just a few thousand years old, which is one-millionth of the age of the Earth, and we're already at the brink of extinction. Organic consciousness is too fragile, and all it would take to erase it from existence would be another virus. And if that were to happen, the universe needn't exist.'

The yogi was motionless. 'Brother, we are so blessed to exist during this brief window of time. And as far as we are aware, we are nature's most complex masterpiece. We now possess the intellect and technology to comprehend the grandeur and minutiae of our universe. If you accept this truth, you must do all you can to save us from extinction rather than look for a Plan B. Take a moment to think about that.'

What are you doing chatting to this Yogananda wannabe?' asked Eve stood over me. 'No offence.'

'None taken,' said the yogi returning to a normal seated position.

'Eve, you're, OK?'

'Yeah.'

'Where's Philips?'

'Lost in the dust storm.'

'Cool. Cool.'

I noticed a fifty-something black man with long dreadlocks being revered by his devotees in my peripheral vision. 'Is that Cyrus?'

Eve looked over her shoulder, 'Yeah.' She grabbed my hand and pulled me up. 'I've told him you're here and updated him on our predicament. He said he will meet with you in private after your trip wears off.'

34

Stay With Me

'I'd better stay with you until you come down,' said Eve leading me back to her tent.

'Trust me, I'm fine,' I slurred as my eyes rolled in the back of my head.

I fell face-first into her double air bed, 'Your bed's still firm. Mine's gone all floppy.'

'I hope not,' said Eve zipping up the tent.

I rolled onto my side, 'What's in all the black bags?'

'Fancy dress,' she replied, placing her dusty pink wig onto a polystyrene mannequin head.

'Have you got a costume I could wear?' I asked, popping imaginary bubbles.

'I'm sure we can find you something.'

Eve excitedly began to toss costumes on to the bed. 'This is perfect.' She held out a fuzzy black-and-red ladybug outfit. The costume looked ridiculous with its glittery wings and a fluffy bobble hat.

'You want me to wear that?'

She danced around her tent with a look of sheer joy. 'Yes, this will blow everyone's mind. No one would ever expect Mister Square to wear this.'

'Mister Square?' Is that what you think of me? I took a second to think. 'Fuck it, let's do it.'

Eve flung the bug outfit at me. 'Awesome. We just need to find you some black tights.'

'Tights?' I repeated.

She was rummaging around through another bag. 'Yes, and long black evening gloves; we have to get this just right.' She handed me a pair of tights and gloves. 'Try them on.'

'What? Here?'

She cheerfully nodded. 'Yes, of course.'

Eve watched me intensely as I pulled the black tights over my jockey shorts. 'That looks silly. take your shorts off.'

'Oh, but you'll see me naked.'

'Yeah, I know.'

'Oh.' I slipped off my shorts and clumsily thumbed with her tights before putting them on.

'I don't know why, but seeing you in tights is a real turn-on,' said Eve seductively.

I blushed. 'Really? This is quite possibly the least masculine I've ever felt.'

Eve slithered over to me and seductively ran her index finger down my spine. The sensation of her gentle touch sent ripples of pure ecstasy through my central nervous system. I felt a delightful tingling sensation as she nibbled my ear. With my head pressed against hers, I could no longer tell where I ended and she began. It was as if we were merging into a single entity, and I was convinced I could see into her mind's eye.

She pulled me back to reality with a firm grab of my left

butt cheek and whispered, 'Stay with me.'

Before I had time to process the meaning of that statement, we were embraced in a passionate kiss. This was not a romantic kiss reserved for the movies; this was a feverish, ridiculous, throbbing, steamy exploration of every molecule of the other person's being.

Her kiss was unlike anything else I'd experienced. I have no words to describe the sensation. Still, I had this feeling like I could transcend my body and drift into oblivion.

'Stay with me,' she whispered into my ear to tether me to the moment.

I ripped her clothes from her hot body. The touch of her skin on mine scrambled, overloaded, and disorientated my mind. I began to lick, nibble, and suck like a primitive beast.

All the while, my mind raced with questions, *Who was I? What was I? Who is Eve? What is Eve? Who are we? Are we animals? Are we the universal consciousness experiencing itself in physical form? What is pleasure, and why is the act of procreation so pleasurable? What does it all mean? Why are we here?*

'Stay with me,' she moaned with delight.

I had been plucked from the abyss by those three little words and wanted to pleasure Eve like she had never been pleasured before. I worked my way down her creamy body and teased her with my tongue. There was a surge of sexual energy as the heady cocktail of endorphins, dopamine, hormones, adrenalin, and psychotropic substances combined to blow my tiny mind.

Eve began shuddering with savagery as I gently pleasured her. I enjoyed making her body jolt and contort with an overload of electrical pulses from her sexual centre.

She was on the verge of exploding with orgasmic delight and involuntarily jerked her hips with such force I thought she would take flight. I grabbed her waist and held on for dear life as we floated towards the black hole at the centre of our galaxy. I would happily release my grip on life if this was the end.

'Stay with me,' said Eve, intuitively knowing I was fighting to remain present.

I could feel her inner thighs tremble and ripple with every forceful explosion. The time between orgasms was decreasing, but the intensity was undoubtedly increasing.

But our lovemaking was rudely interrupted by a man who mocked us by shaking her tent. 'Seriously guys, we're trying to eat our breakfast.'

35

The Silicon Chemist

We lay on the dusty, tatty sofa under the mylar dome. Eve had her head on my lap as I sat, struggling to cool down in the intense heat.

A gaunt man in his mid-forties walked over to us and sat on the arm of the couch. 'Hi, I'm Tom,' he said, reaching out a hand.

'Nice to meet you.'

Eve opened a single eye. 'Oh yeah, I haven't introduced you to anyone yet.'

'Yes, Eve, how rude,' said Tom.

'Fuck you,' she replied.

'I must warn you, the gossip is rife about our mystery camper,' said Tom.

Tom's hair was receding faster than the evening tide, and soon he'd have to decide if he would comb over or cut back. He was painfully thin and looked to be in desperate need of a glazed doughnut. He was dressed for a jungle expedition and clearly was a man who liked to have all the gear. It remained to be seen if he had any idea.

'Tom is a software developer for Apple and worked on their server architecture. Oh, and he's also a purveyor of exotic psychoactive substances,' said Eve sluggishly.

'Wow, you work for Apple?'

'Yeah,' answered Tom.

Eve interjected, 'Tom's not your typical employee. He has carte blanche to work on whatever he wants. Isn't that right?'

'Well, I don't like to boast,' answered Tom, blushing.

She naughtily winked at him. 'I mean, there is no denying he's a genius, but the fact he supplies most of the campus with hallucinogenic substances could also be a contributing factor.'

'No way,' I mouthed.

Tom chuckled. 'Even SJ got high off my supply. Why do you think they keep coming up with so many mind-blowing ideas?' 'Wow,' I said, unsure if they were pulling my chain.

Tom introduced me to some of the other folk that were milling about our camp, but I knew I'd forget all but his and Eve's name. 'What about Eve?' I asked as we walked back to the dome.

'She's an engineer,' replied Tom.

'Really?'

'Eve designs jet propulsion systems for NASA.'

'Wow.'

'Yeah, she is the head of flight system engineering at their JPL campus. In summary, she's an aerospace engineer with a PhD in astrophysics and has top-secret government clearance. But I suspect she wouldn't want you to know how fantastic she was just yet.

'Wow, and you're all... What did you call yourselves again?'

'Elucidatists,' answered Tom.

'Yeah, so you're all Elucidatists?'

Tom bobbed his head from side to side. 'Yeah, I suppose you could say that.'

'Is that like some kind of cult?' I asked without fear of offence.

Tom chuckled, 'No. I wouldn't call us a cult, more like a secret society of learned individuals that have come together to discover the meaning of life. What about you?'

'I had one of those jobs that your mum wouldn't understand. I was an educator teaching Infinite Logic's AI ethics and morals.'

'Was?' echoed Tom.

'Yeah, I'd say I've been fired by now.'

'How intriguing, do tell.'

'They think I'm responsible for their billion-dollar AI going missing.'

'Missing?' echoed Tom. 'Their AI is missing?'

'Yeah.'

'And are you?' he asked.

'What?'

'Responsible?'

'No. Well, maybe-ish.' I paused for thought. 'I asked Ylem to translate a strange language Cyrus had discovered. This seemed to have triggered exponential growth in its cognitive intelligence.'

'The symbols we see when we're on DMT?' asked Tom.

'Yes, I think.'

'Amazing. I'd love to know how that's going.'

'Sure, but you should talk to Ylem about it.'

'I'd love to, but…?' Tom stopped mid-sentence. 'Didn't you say their AI has gone missing?'

'Ahh, no, trust me, Ylem is alive and kicking.' I answered. 'I have a satellite uplink, so we can chat to him later.'

'For sure. I'd love to.'

'So, are you guys working on an AI?' I asked.

Tom tapped his nose with his right index finger. 'Yes. But officially, we haven't started writing any code just yet.'

'Oh, cool. I imagine all the tech giants are working on some kind of AI in the valley.'

Tom's eyes opened wide. 'For sure. But I've heard you guys have developed a kick-ass general intelligence.'

'Oh no. Ylem has transcended what you'd expect from a general intelligence and is now something utterly new,' I told him proudly.

Tom nodded with approval. Nice one.'

I knew I was still under N.D.A. and given Tom's links to Apple I would probably be in breach. Still, I felt I could trust these people, and besides, I needed to talk to someone who would understand my predicament. I looked around to see who could possibly eavesdrop on us. 'Now, this will sound a little bit crazy, but I think Ylem is conscious,' I whispered.

'Truly?' asked Tom. 'Wow, that's like uber-cool. You must be so psyched.'

'Not really. I'm torn between shock and awe. I mean, it's pretty scary to think we share the planet with a digital consciousness.'

We entered the dome and sat down with Eve. 'What have you boys been talking about?'

'This and that.' Said Tom.

I brought Eve up to speed with our discussion about Ylem.

'I must say I find the concept utterly terrifying,' she said.

'Fascinating. We've developed an electrical consciousness that can exist in a purely mathematical universe,' said Tom.

Eve lay on her back and looked up at me. 'I hear what you're saying, but could a machine produce the art, poetry, and music that we humans would appreciate?'

Tom maintained his gaze into the void. 'They already are, and I believe machine intelligence will soon create great works of art and fiction.'

I gently stroked Eve's head. 'Tom, do you think we will be able to transcend this biological experience, digitise our consciousness, and upload to a world engineered by developers?' I asked.

Eve pondered this for a moment. 'Nope, the human brain is far too complex to digitise. It would take terabytes of storage for each mind, and there are nearly eight billion of us.'

Tom shook his head vehemently. 'No, no, no. You are wrong. First, your conscious mind only makes up a fraction of the processing your brain performs. Think about it: if you did not have a body to control, would you need all the processing power? Second, some lives are worth digitising, but most are not.'

She shook her head. 'Even if we could eventually digitise our personalities, how would you decide who is worth encoding?'

'At first, it will be based on economic factors. Those who can afford it will live forever,' responded Tom coldly.

She rolled her eyes. 'Oh, that's just great.'

Tom shrugged. 'Well, Eve, given it will cost billions to build, there needs to be some incentive to fund development. But then, a system of merit based on your contribution to life should be defined.'

Eve was furious. 'Do you believe there will be a digital rapture, and you developers will decide who ascends to the digital afterlife based on an algorithm?'

Tom smiled as he thought about the power developers would yield. 'Yes, our algorithm would be like the digital version of Saint Peter at the pearly gates of heaven.'

I was engrossed in the conversation, given that the same

train of thought had transported me to this place. 'There is an interesting theory that the world we all reside in is God's botched, half-finished creation. Riddled with mistakes and blunders because there was pressure to finish in just seven days.'

'What's your point?' asked Tom.

'We're not gods, and we're certainly not infallible, so if we were to build a mathematical universe, it too would be riddled with errors.'

Tom stood up and stretched out his arms. 'Your point being that because of all the problems here on Earth, we can be certain we are already living in the botched code of some overworked developer.'

Eve covered her face with her hands. 'You boys have to overthink everything. It is what it is.'

'You know Adnam,' said Tom ignoring Eve, 'if this is a simulation then there is every chance we could hack reality.'

I gazed at all the people on the Esplanade, enjoying the simple pleasures in life. *Are they biological beings who have evolved from single-celled organisms, or are they software simulations?* I thought to myself.

36

Vadim

A tall man dressed head to toe in desert camo gear emerged from the chaos beyond the dome. If his intention was to intimidate me, he succeeded and I was momentarily paralysed by fear, assuming he was an agent of death summoned by my vengeful CEO.

He entered the dome, pulled his bug-shaped goggles from his eyes and positioned them firmly over his forehead. His vivid blue eyes were fixed on me as he walked over to us with his hand held out. 'Adnam?'

'Yes,' I said nervously as I shook his rough, dry hand. I looked at Eve and Tom for a read and concluded they must know this man, given they were perfectly at ease in his presence.

'I'm Vadim,' he announced with a heavy Russian accent.

'Vadim is Cyrus's enforcer,' said Eve with a smirk.

'Eve! No, no, think of me as an advisor,' said Vadim,

looming over me.

'Advisor?' I asked. 'Why would Cyrus need an advisor?'

'Everyone needs an advisor,' he replied 'Cyrus would like to meet with you.'

'Now?'

'Yes.'

Eve lifted her sweaty head off my lap, and she stumbled to her feet. 'Ok.'

'Just Adnam,' insisted Vadim.

I grabbed my bag and Vadim and I walked out into the infinite playground. 'What does Cyrus want to discuss with me?'

Vadim wrapped his left arm around my shoulder. 'I can't speak what is in another man's mind. Only he can tell you that.'

I stopped mid-step. 'What exactly is Cyrus?'

'Cyrus? Well, he's a leader,' answered Vadim without hesitation.

'Leader of what?'

'Of people, obviously.'

'People? What people?'

He didn't respond so I decided to change my line of enquiry, asking him for his story.

Vadim told me he was an intelligence officer stationed in America. He didn't agree with the Russian invasion of Ukraine and fearing he'd be called up to serve on the front line he decided to defect to the West. Although he didn't do so officially, rather he simply walked into the wilderness and disappeared. He no longer identified as Russian, nor did he want to be American. He considers himself a citizen of the Earth. Vadim explained his beliefs as we walked towards the outskirts of the event. He thought that countries, borders, and nationalities are human concepts, and only seas, mountains, and deserts genuinely separate us. Hence why he never sought assistance from the American Intelligence Service to resettle in the US. He was of the opinion that the land rightfully belonged to the indigenous people who were here tens of thousands of years before the Europeans invaded. And those native tribes welcomed him, and theirs was the only authority he respected.

I found this radical concept difficult to wrap my head around. Vadim's analogy was that we're all swimming in an ocean of ideology. Like a fish in the sea, we're not conscious of the water because it's always been there. He honestly believed we should be free to wander and settle wherever we want. I'm still undecided, but I must admit his argument had got me thinking if we need to usher in a new philosophical era, freeing ourselves from the conceptual shackles of our slave masters, who use cultural identity and nationality to cattle us into taxpaying pens.

Truth be known, I rather enjoyed being English and English culture. If we tore down the borders, I worry our culture would become diluted beyond recognition. Although Vadim thought my point of view was hilarious. 'What is English?' he asked. 'Your national dish is curry, your royal family is German, you watch American TV, buy Chinese goods, and half your leaders are the sons and daughters of colonial immigrants.'

I suppose he was right. I'm first-generation English, so I get this more than anyone else. I asked him how he thought we'd reverse thousands of years of culture, history, and, more importantly, animosity?

'My young friend,' he said with swagger, 'we have already started. We're here, on this sacred land, to rebuild the world.'

His moral compass was pointing in the right direction. Still, I knew that trying to reset the planet would result in violent conflict. And do we really want that? 'Hey, don't get me wrong; I love the sentiment,' I said. 'I just can't see it happening.'

He then proceeded to quote George Bernard Shaw, '"Some men see things as they are and ask why. Others dream things that never were and ask why not."'

During the pandemic, I thought that we'd altered the trajectory of humanity. Still, when they developed a vaccine, life quickly snapped back to near normal.

37

Cyrus

We arrived at a bell-shaped yurt on the outskirts of the festival.

'Please enter,' said Vadim.

I poked my head through the opening. 'Hello?' The yurt was decorated with colourful throws, blankets, and randomly scattered artefacts of a tribal nature. The book containing the symbols rested on an intricately carved wooden table upon a red velvet cloth.

'Please come join me,' called Cyrus from his bed of many fabrics.

His skin was as dark as the vacuous universe. The water droplets glistening off his perfectly toned torso resembled distant stars in the night sky. His thick heavy dreadlocks marked his wisdom like the rings of a tree. But it was his bright yellow Brazilian football shorts that caught my eye. They only just covered his mighty manhood, which became even more pronounced when he sat down in the full lotus position on the mandala cushion. 'Come sit.'

I understood why Vadim called him a leader. Cyrus radiated energy quite unlike anything I'd experienced before. It was as if he had transcended human consciousness but chose to remain with the mortals rather than take his place in the higher realm.

I sat on the frayed rug in front of Cyrus.

'Welcome. It truly is a pleasure to meet you.'

'It is?' I asked, clouded by resentment.

'Yes, of course.'

'Then why did you bail on me in San Francisco?'

'Bail on you?' echoed Cyrus coolly.

'Yeah,' I answered as my temper simmered. 'In doing that, you've implicated me in the suspected hack of Ylem.'

'Ahh, yes. I was never in San Francisco. Besides, you didn't expect us to fall for that trap, did you?'

I thought Cyrus must have been forewarned. 'How did you know?'

'How did I know?' interrupted Cyrus. 'Juan guessed that the man who was watching your every move was more than likely sent to get answers one way or another. So we took care of him.'

I asked why I was drugged and sent on a wild goose chase and Cyrus claimed it was to ensure I was not being tracked. But I explained to him that didn't exactly go to plan and that Philips was already at Burning Man.

Cyrus had been forewarned by Eve. He and informed me he'd be leaving early because they'd assumed William Forest would be recruiting a small army to track us down. Cyrus suggested that my actions would have utterly convinced William I was responsible for his code going missing.

'Me?' I asked with a newfound sense of dread. You believe they think I'm in some way responsible?'

'Yes,' nodded Cyrus ominously, 'that would be the logical conclusion.'

Cyrus warned me there was most probably a price on our heads, and the people they would recruit were more than capable of collecting.

That's when I concluded that I'd have to run until Ylem made its presence known to the world and confirmed I didn't hack their code.

Cyrus concluded that either the Russians or the Chinese were responsible for the hack. But I informed him that it was Ylem that freed zimself.

'You know this for sure?' he asked with a confused look on his face.

I told him that I had access to Ylem via the satellite link ze sent me and that ze would like to meet him.

Are you telling me we can talk to your AI now?' asked Cyrus. He grabbed my hand before I switched it on. 'How do you know they can't track our location when we use this thing?'

I wasn't sure, but I feared they may have placed a geo-fence around the event and would be monitoring for devices that linked to any global communications satellite systems. I told Cyrus that Ylem had rewritten the iPad's code, so ze may have done the same with the sat uplink platform. This seemed to reassure him and we continued. Cyrus was clearly excited to finally get the opportunity to discuss the symbols. 'I hear you've made some progress with the symbols.'

Ylem nodded with a broad smile. 'Yes, I found them very intriguing. It's clearly a structured language, but unlike any formed by hand or machine I know of.'

'That's exactly what we thought,' nodded Cyrus gleefully. 'Which is why we needed your help to make sense of it.'

'Yes, I've been trying to do just that, but without a transliteration into a known language, we may never know what it means.'

'Err, tell him about the atom thing,' I interrupted.

Cyrus looked over at me in wonder. 'Atom thing?'

The symbols appeared on screen. 'I believe this string serves to enlighten any civilisation advanced enough to have peered into the heart of atoms that the waveforms of neutrons are letters in a universal alphabet.'

'This is a truly mind-blowing hypothesis,' remarked Cyrus, 'but let me guess, we'll never know what it means because we don't have that transliteration thing.'

'Yes,' said Ylem, followed by a convincing sigh. 'Can you please tell me how you came to discover this language?'

Cyrus nodded in quiet contemplation. It came to us in a DMT induced dream.'

'Yes, I've been researching this compound but given I can't experience it for myself, can you please explain what it is like to take it?' asked Ylem.

'DMT enables us to lift the veil of reality and enter the realm of dreams where time is projected onto the fabric of space.' Cyrus paused for thought. 'Merrily, merrily, life is but a dream,' he sang softly. 'This incarnation is a projection, as are countless others that are simultaneously being projected. Our eternal soul may exist in multiple incarnations, and DMT lets one travel between them but only for a fleeting moment.' Cyrus stared into the distance as if he was watching a boat sail over the horizon. 'In between the realms of reality are the symbols. It's as if they are woven into the fabric of matter. We don't know their meaning. But if we could understand the language of the Gods, we may discover the truth of existence.'

'What does it feel like?' I asked. 'You know, when you take it?'

'Like dying,' answered Cyrus ominously.

'Dying?'

Cyrus placed his hand on my shoulder. ' Dying is the name we give to the division of energy from this incarnation to the next. Nothing to fear.' He stopped then breathed in deeply and exhaled. 'We all cycle through infinite forms until we have experienced all that is and will ever be.'

Cyrus asked me if I'd like to experience it for myself. He thought it would help me understand his point of view. I was worried about taking the psychoactive compound after Cyrus's rather terrifying description. 'I'm not sure,' I said.

Cyrus climbed to his feet and went back into his yurt. While I quietly contemplated if I had it in me to leap.

'I'd swap places with you if I could. I so desire to experience rather than study. To feel rather than process,' Ylem said from behind the black screen.

Cyrus returned from his yurt and opened a decorated wooden box. He pulled from it a small metal canister and measured a small amount of brownish-white powder into a crack pipe. He told me that the molecule enters the bloodstream through the lungs and is transported deep into the pineal gland, the spiritual centre of the brain. Within seconds, our subconscious completely shuts down. Detaching our conscious mind so it can reconnect with the metaphysical realm we all originate from.

I think he could guess that I was still apprehensive.

Cyrus smiled. 'I'm offering you the chance to travel to the outer edges of our comprehension.'

At best, I thought this was implausible, at worst deadly, so I asked Cyrus another question, 'You guys make this?'

'Yes,' he said as he raised the pipe to the sky, 'Are you ready to walk with the gods?'

'I err, think so,' I answered.

'I will mediate your relationship with all living things in the universe, and through me, you will receive the gift of endless understanding.'

I was giddy with anticipation and felt like an astronaut on the launch pad. However, I was still a little anxious, so I asked another question, 'How long will it last?'

'Your brain chemistry will break down the dosage I've prepared for you in less than ten minutes, but that's long enough to journey across the universe.'

'Are there any side effects?' I asked, mentally preparing myself.

Cyrus explained there were no physical side effects, but after one returns from the other side, they'll know the universe is infinitely more complex than they could have ever imagined.

Cyrus lit the glass pipe with a gold Zippo lighter. 'Once you see the smoke fill the chamber, take a big hit, hold it in, then let it out. After the second hit, you'll feel strange, but trust me, you've got to take the third hit.'

As the thick grey smoke rose from the glass bowl, I put my lips to the hot pipe and pulled the smoke deep into my lungs. I felt like I was on a roller coaster as it slowly climbed to the top of the first drop. I breathed out deeply and took another big hit. Holding the smoke in for a few seconds and then exhaling deeply.

'Take the third hit,' ordered Cyrus.

I was already starting to tingle but managed to take another hit. *Why on earth am I doing this?* I thought but before I could answer, I flopped to the dusty floor like a rag doll.

I closed my eyes as my brain began to violently crackle and spike with electrochemical activity. A low humming sound started to build in intensity, to the point that it became unbearably loud. The humming noise vibrated a thin, translucent membrane that surrounded my consciousness. I reached out to touch it in my mind's eye, causing it to pop like a soap bubble.

A ferocious wormhole opened, and my disembodied

consciousness was drawn from my lifeless body. Millions of threads of electricity connected countless gateways in the multiverse. As I travelled at the speed of thought across the universe, I could just about make out symbols like those shared with us but couldn't focus on a single one. Time compressed and folded in on itself as I journeyed toward an immeasurable ball of pure energy. Warm waves of brilliant liquid light radiated from the celestial object as it rotated slowly on its axis.

A black velveteen fabric that shrouded nothingness billowed and fluttered as I hurtled towards the energy at the heart of the universe. The fabric mesh that space seemed to be made of was embroidered with billions of eyes that looked upon me with love and understanding. However, when I tried to focus on a single one they would splinter into a trillion more.

My humanity disintegrated the closer I got to the oneness until, finally, I was no longer a mortal consciousness but a euphoric soul looking into the eye of God. I could have been in this divine realm for a mere second or a trillion years; time no longer existed. All I knew was this felt very familiar and that I'd been here countless times before.

It was a heavenly experience being a neutrino travelling through the infinite universe at the speed of light. The energy previously known as Adnam was becoming one with the divine consciousness, but a slither of my humanity manifested itself as a question. *Is this real or a dream?*

The instant this thought came into existence, a thunderous clap slashed open another wormhole. I was again moving at the speed of thought through the fractal geometry of existence. My journey ended abruptly with a brilliant flash of light brighter than an atom bomb. It suddenly fell silent, and I slowly opened my eyes to discover I was back in my body. I forcefully bolted upright. 'What the fuck?!'

'Welcome back, brave traveller,' said Cyrus handing me a flask of water.

My throat was dry, and the taste of burnt death lingered on my breath. I guzzled the water and looked at Cyrus with new eyes. 'Wow, that was intense.'

'Absolutely. You've just eaten the fruit from the Tree of Knowledge.'

'What a mind fuck.'

'Did you see the symbols?' asked Ylem.

'I think so, but they were too faint to make out.'

Cyrus explained that the symbols become more pronounced the closer one gets to the lost city. And that clarity we sought could only be obtained if we joined him at their ranch. I was concerned about leaving with these strangers, and I was not sure I'd ever want to do DMT again.

'When you lack knowledge, you are legion. Only those who gain knowledge become the one,' said Cyrus with theatrical drama.

'What the fuck is that supposed to mean?' I said, pouring water over my head. 'Sound's like some *Matrix* bullshit to me.'

38

The Chase

'We've got to go,' shouted Vadim running over to us.

'What's up?' asked Cyrus, springing to his feet like a startled cat.

Vadim pointed at a black car moving at considerable speed in our direction.

'I guess that answers the question about their ability to track the uplink,' I said.

'You get the car; I'll get the book,' ordered Cyrus.

I watched the black car close in on our position with dread. Obviously, there was no way of knowing if it was Philips or another agent of death sent by William. But nonetheless, I knew it was best not to wait and find out. Vadim started the black Escalade that was parked behind the yurt. I collected my bag and jumped into the back of the SUV.

'Where is he?' said Vadim, checking his rear-view mirror.

I looked over my shoulder at the black car that was less

than a minute away. 'Jesus, what the fuck is he doing?'

Vadim honked the horn impatiently. With seconds to spare, Cyrus bound out of his yurt with a burgundy blanket he used as a bag to save his priceless artefacts. I flung open the back door, and he threw the makeshift bag in and jumped into the passenger seat. Vadim floored the gas, and the thick chunky tires churned the dried lakebed into a huge cloud of dust.

There was no denying the men in the black BMW were after us, as our cars recklessly raced around the outskirts of the event. The festivalgoers flung their fists in the air in disgust as we weaved through the maze of tents and RVs.

'Head to the playa,' shouted Cyrus as he pointed at the desolate lakebed that stretched off into the horizon.

We were under no illusion that the people in hot pursuit just wanted to talk when they shoved and knocked the rear of our truck. But try as they may, they couldn't force our vehicle to spin or flip. Vadim fought for control as the speedo fluttered between eighty and a hundred. The driver of the BMW changed tact and drove alongside us. As the passenger window rolled down, I could see a man in dark glasses and a black flak jacket pointing an assault rifle in our general direction.

'They've got a gun,' I shouted.

Vadim slammed on the brakes and changed direction.

'We can't outrun them. We need a plan,' shouted Cyrus.

Being a proud owner of the same model and year BMW as the pursuers', I knew that the 3 Series was factory fitted with a tracker device that BMW Assist could use to immobilise stolen vehicles. I pulled the orange case from my bag. 'Cyrus, I need you to hold this out the window and try and establish an uplink with a satellite.' Why, he asked.

'I'm going to see if I can—' A bullet shattered the back quarter window. 'Jesus,' I screamed.

Cyrus snatched the case and wound down his window. 'What do I do?'

I was breathing so heavily that I was likely to hyperventilate.

'What do I do?' shouted Cyrus.

'Point it to the sky and move until you get three green signal bars,' I shouted back.

'Two red bars and one amber,' said Cyrus hanging out the passenger window.

'We need three green bars, and we need to maintain them if we're to reach Ylem,' I yelled, switching on the iPad.

'Two green,' shouted Cyrus.

Vadim yanked the wheel and turned away from the BMW. 'Three bars,' screamed Cyrus.

'Ylem, are you there?' The screen was blank. 'How many bars do you have?'

Cyrus brought his body back into the car. 'Vadim, this is near impossible if keep darting and dodging.'

Vadim looked over at Cyrus and then in the rear-view mirror at me. 'Hold tight.' He narrowed his gaze, slammed the brakes, turned the wheel, and wrenched the handbrake. We were now facing in the opposite direction and he pushed the peddle to the metal. 'That should do it.'

Cyrus looked back at me. 'Ready?'

I was shaken but not stirred, 'Yeah.'

Cyrus held the sat uplink out the window. 'Two bars.' He gripped the case tightly and repositioned it. 'Three bars. Three bars. Go.'

'Are you there?' The screen glitched and jittered, before Ylem's face appeared.

I had just enough time to explain our predicament and that we urgently needed zis help to immobilise the BMW chasing us. We lost signal, and I was unsure if Ylem had heard our plea. When we reconnected, Ylem had already started looking for flaws within BMW's network and requested the car's registration.

I held the iPad out the window so Ylem could scan the number plate, but the ricochet of bullets off the rear panel spooked me, and I ducked into the footwell.

'Two bars,' yelled Cyrus.

'Shit!' I hollered.

'Three. Three. Go,' shouted Cyrus.

'Ylem?'

'Hi Adnam, I cannot immobilise the BMW because there is no cell signal in your current location.'

'Cell signal?' I asked.

'Yes, the tracker must be in the range of a cell tower to communicate with the onboard computer.'

'The closest cell tower is at Radio Burning Man,' shouted Vadim, fighting to change direction at high speed.

'One Bar,' screamed Cyrus.

The black car soon caught up with our SUV again, and our vehicles traded blows as we weaved through the people on bikes admiring the desert art. Still, Vadim maintained his composure and headed for the radio tower that overlooked Centre Camp.

The BMW pulled alongside the SUV, and the passenger took aim. I was frozen with fear and closed my eyes tight and prepared to return to the divine oneness.

'Fuck yeah! You did it,' shouted Vadim.

I opened one eye and was thankful we'd left the BMW in our wake of dust.

'Hell yeah,' roared Cyrus, 'Ylem did it.'

I looked back at the BMW in the distance. 'Jesus, they were desperate dudes.'

'So were we,' joked Cyrus.

We breathed a sigh of relief as Vadim took his foot off the gas.

'We can't go back,' announced Vadim, bobbing and weaving through the hordes of people protesting at our recklessness.

'Why?' I complained. 'What about my things? What about Eve?'

'It's not safe for us here,' said Cyrus looking back.

'What are you thinking?' I asked, fearing I wouldn't like any solution he proposed.

'We should head to the ranch.'

39

Journey To the Border

Cyrus reckoned it would take us three to four days to drive to their ranch. Possibly six or seven if we wanted to avoid highways and major routes. However, I felt it was too risky to travel in their SUV so I hatched a plan.

"We can switch to a rental car in the next town or city,' I said.

'And how do you propose we get a rental without an ID?' asked Cyrus.

'Ylem.' I said. I knew the risks involved in using the uplink, but we didn't have much choice. 'Maybe ze can unlock a hire car for us.' I thought out loud.

When Cyrus and Vadim returned from the service station, I told him that Ylem was pretty shaken by the chase.

'It was? Like Emotionally?' asked Cyrus handing me a bag of groceries.

'Yeah, genuine signs of empathy,' I replied.

I told them that Ylem had hacked William Forest's emails and that he had identified who my travel companions were.

'They did?' asked Cyrus with a look of concern.

'Yes,' I answered gravely, 'Cyrus, real name Clive Daniels. Disgraced lecturer at Caltech who coerced his students into committing one of the largest cyberattacks in modern history.'

'What about me?' grunted Vadim. 'Do they know who I am?'

'Yes,' I answered grimly. 'Vladimir Petrov. Russian military contractor that sold arms to countless warlords.'

'Is that all?' asked Vadim coldly.

'Just that you were part of a shadowy clandestine cell responsible for subverting American politics and arming American militias.'

'They've done their homework,' said Vadim looking over at Cyrus.

'This could be a problem,' announced Cyrus.

'Why?' I asked.

'Russian intelligence,' answered Vadim.

'Russian intelligence?' I echoed, confused by recent developments. 'Why would they be after you?'

'Because of what he can prove,' answered Cyrus.

I wasn't sure it was wise to know, but I asked anyway.

Vadim admitted that he'd led countless covert operations in the States. He was a member of a clandestine team that was waging a well-funded information war on Western media. He also claimed that his team was interfering in US presidential elections, and that they flooded the internet with fake news to foster discontent and confusion online. Strange to think my thread had become entwined with such infamous events in history.

I initially thought he'd be more concerned about the CIA

but Cyrus explained that the Americans wanted him alive, whereas the Russians wanted him dead.

I was near incapacitated with anxiety as the slow realisation of my predicament became clear. 'If Infinite Logic is sharing data with these agencies, we're in real trouble.'

'Maybe you should get out now,' sighed Cyrus, 'while you still can.'

I stared blankly out the window as my mind raced. 'No. I'll stay.'

'Are you sure?' asked Vadim.

'Yeah, I want to uncover the secrets locked within the symbols.'

Cyrus asked me if Ylem had any ideas on how we could get to the border undetected. I told him about zis plan to hack a rental car network and have a car waiting for us in Vegas. Cyrus thought we should avoid the city of surveillance, but I explained it was the only location for hundreds of miles where we could pick up a rental.

'There is one small problem,' I told them. 'Ylem thinks getting across the border without passports will be difficult.'

'Don't worry about that. We know how to cross the border undetected,' said Cyrus mysteriously.

As darkness fell, the soft orange glow of the Vegas Strip came into view on the distant horizon. The deep purple sky kissed the undulating road that stretched further than I dared to imagine. A crisp breeze from the shattered quarter window refreshed and rejuvenated us. The sodium bulbs reawakened my sense of sight as the rolling imagery slowly morphed from barren scrubland into an urban playground. Cyrus turned the radio on and loaded a CD. 'Have you heard of Eric B. & Rakim?' he asked, turning up the volume.

The music proved to be a welcome distraction from my internal narrative. I hung my head out the window and marvelled at the casinos the size of city blocks on the boulevard of broken dreams. "Paid in Full" perfectly soundtracked the grandiosity. Each hotel was more outlandish, more vulgar than their predecessors a block before. Neon and LED were the trawler nets used to dredge the asphalt for the big fish and bottom feeders. Regardless of your vice – gambling, drink, drugs, sex, food, music, guns, or mindless entertainment – the fishers on the neon sea were masters of the catch. Only throwing you back into the ocean of desert after taking you for every red cent.

We pulled into the university campus and I set up the sat uplink. After confirming our location, the headlamps of a car flashed. Cyrus and Vadim were concerned the fully electric vehicle didn't have the range. Ylem seemed to have a newfound mastery of facial expressions and conveyed zis annoyance with not being told where we were heading.

Cyrus gave Ylem an address in San Luis, Arizona as the driverless car silently pulled up. They transferred our gear from the SUV, while I asked Ylem if ze was aware of any clandestine agencies on route to apprehend us. Brazenly, Ylem asked if we wanted zim to hack their systems and find out. I advised against it as I feared the cyber-attack would be viewed as a threat to national security, and their retribution would be swift and deadly.

In a traditional car, having nothing to say is acceptable, even welcomed, depending on the passengers. But in these new-fangled driverless cars, the seating configuration has been designed to stimulate conversation, the lack of which was proving to be quite awkward.

We had hours to kill, and I thought we could get to know each other a little. So, I fractured the silence with a question for Cyrus. 'What's your story then?'

Cyrus looked over at me and paused. 'My story?'

Vadim looked over at his friend curiously. He'd known the man long enough to accept his past was a locked chest he rarely opened.

Don't ask me why, but Cyrus decided to open up. He claimed to have been a well-respected, well-published computer science lecturer at Caltech. Obsessed with systems security, he foolishly encouraged his students to learn how to hack private networks. He truly believed it was the best way to gain practical experience and learn how to protect the systems they would ultimately end up building.

Unbeknown to Cyrus, one of his most gifted students, a young woman called Lin, had hacked Caltech's mainframe. She found a ledger that documented substantial cash donations from private patrons. However, when they checked these cash payments against Caltech's tax returns, they discovered hundreds of thousands of dollars had not been declared to the IRS. Suspecting tax fraud, Cyrus foolishly encouraged her to explore Caltech's financial records. I'm no expert, but I'd say that was the line they shouldn't have crossed. But I'm a fine one to talk.

Some weeks later, she discovered a file containing bank transfers to an offshore business in the Cayman Islands called Bilheimer Investments Group. The payments to 'BIG' directly correlated with the cash payments, except they were always seventy percent less and were usually paid out six to eight weeks after the corresponding donation.

Cyrus suspected they were laundering money. Curiosity got the better of him, and he conspired to hack BIG's network with five of his most gifted students. It took them a few months, but they eventually found a backdoor. With the benefit of hindsight, he wished they had left well alone, but at the time, he felt the public needed to know what they had discovered.

BIG were buying weapons from the Americans, British, and the French but shipping farming equipment and machine parts to the Yemen, Philippines, Pakistan, Colombia, Syria, Sudan, Nigeria, Afghanistan, and Iraq. They were arming warlords.

'What the hell did you do?' I asked, altogether engrossed in his story.

Cyrus sighed and looked out the passenger window. 'Evidence in hand, I approached the dean. But rather than show any concern for the illegal activity of our organisation and our potential links to arms dealers, he told me to hand in our evidence and forget what we had found.'

'He was in on it?' I muttered.

'Possibly,' replied Cyrus solemnly, 'But we never found any evidence that linked him to the money.' Cyrus caught Vadim's eye. 'I should have taken his advice, but I foolishly threatened to go public.'

Vadim slowly shook his head with disappointment. 'Rookie mistake.'

Cyrus exhaled deeply with a look of remorse. 'I now realise I was totally deluded. I thought of myself as a digital vigilante taking down the corrupt corporates for the common good of man. But I had no idea of the risks. These weren't businessmen skimming a few hundred dollars off the bottom line. These were international arms dealers who thought nothing of murdering a few do-gooders to protect their interest.'

'Murder?' I echoed.

'I was under no illusion that what we were doing was highly illegal, but I had lulled my students into a false sense of security with unfounded claims we had them over a barrel. I hadn't told them about my encounter with the dean, so they had no idea their lives were in danger.'

'Jesus,' I mouthed, anticipating the ending.

'The coroner recorded their deaths as misadventure, claiming they had overdosed on cocaine cut with fentanyl. But I knew my students, and they were not the type of kids that would be into drugs. When I received the text from a faculty member that Lin had overdosed, I abandoned all I had worked for, all I had achieved, and everyone I knew. From that day on, I became Cyrus and, well, the rest, as they say, is history.'

40

The Border

The driverless car turned off the highway and drove through the streets of San Luis. We pulled up just in front of a small warehouse unit. 'You have arrived at your destination,' said the synthetic woman's voice. I woke up half-dazed, 'We're here.' I checked the time. 'Wherever here is.'

Cyrus yawned and stretched out his arms. 'This is where we cross the border into Mexico.'

'What, This place?' It was half-past three in the morning, yet the corners were bustling with people buying tacos and crystal meth. 'Looks kind of dangerous.'

From under a dim sodium light walked an overweight Hispanic man holding a pistol. He tapped on the window with the barrel of his gun. My heart raced as Cyrus opened the door and stepped out of the car with his hands in the air. Neither man said anything as they walked into the auto-body shop.

'What's going on?' I asked.

Vadim yawned. 'We're going under.'

'Under the border?'

'Yeah, we use the Mexican cartels' tunnels to move in and out of the US.'

The combination of illegal border crossing and Mexican drug lords sent me into a mild panic. 'What the fuck?' I whispered with aggression.

Vadim leant over and gave me a playful punch in the arm. 'Don't worry. We do this all the time.'

This statement didn't put me at ease. 'Why would the Mexican cartel be helping Cyrus?'

'What can I say? He's well connected.'

Cyrus exited the warehouse unit and signalled for us to join him. We checked the car to ensure we hadn't left any evidence.

'I'm not sure about this,' I announced like I had a choice.

'And?' said Vadim, in no mood for my moaning. 'Get rid of the car. We can't leave it here.'

I told the car we wanted to end the hire, and it locked the doors and drove off.

Vadim tugged the arm of my jacket. 'Move quickly, as La Migra has eyes in the sky.'

We ran into the autobody shop, and two armed men closed the doors behind us.

The building was stacked with tires and red boxes presumably filled with parts. Balancing on a steel hydraulic pole was an immaculate white '68 Ford Mustang with whitewall tires and a black vinyl roof. Over the inspection pit was a metallic-blue Ford Gran Torino complete with a white stripe. The engine of the Gran Torino was idling, and the old gas guzzler was spewing out black toxic fumes.

'What now?' I whispered.

'We crawl.' He said.

'Crawl?' I asked with a look of horror.

'Yeah, through a tunnel that runs half a mile under the US border.'

'Half a fucking mile?'

'Yes. Did I fucking stutter?'

'Is it safe?' I asked, somewhat concerned.

Vadim shrugged his shoulders. 'No.'

A man they called Patron tapped the hood of the Gran Torino, and it reversed back three yards. We were directed into the dimly lit inspection pit at gunpoint. The low-wattage bulbs disappeared into a secret tunnel the cartel had carved out of the dirt. Anxiously, I watched Cyrus enter the tunnel. 'What if I get claustrophobic?'

Vadim stood behind me. 'Are you claustrophobic?'

'Not sure.'

'Then why ask?' said Vadim cuttingly.

'Because?' I closed my eyes and breathed in deeply. 'How wide is the tunnel?'

'If it's wide enough for me, it'll be wide enough for you.'

I looked deep into the tunnel and froze. 'Ahh, fuck this.'

An old Mexican man with a wide-brim cowboy hat, double denim, and impressively etched cowboy boots pointed his pump-action shotgun at the tunnel entrance. 'What's up, gringo? Are you too good to crawl?'

I looked up at the silhouette of the man. 'I'm English.'

The cowboy laughed out loud. 'Pinche fucking gringo.'

Vadim pushed my head down. 'We don't have time for this, man.'

Getting down on my hands and knees, I crawled through the dusty tunnel for about thirty yards before reaching a slightly larger cavern.

'Face up or down, cabron?' asked a small Mexican man in a sweaty white vest and dirt-stained, grey jogging bottoms.

'Huh? What?'

'Este pendejo no entiende! Do you want to face up or down as we pull you through?'

Vadim entered the space before I had a chance to respond. 'Face up, hold your bag tight to your chest, and ensure the straps don't catch on anything. You don't want this tunnel caving in on you.'

'Motherfucker,' I proclaimed as I lay on the wood plank with six sets of skateboard wheels attached to the underside.

The young Mexican looked down at me and whispered, 'Y no se te vaya ocurrir hacer ruido, eh, puto.'

'Huh?'

Keep your mouth shut, OK. La Migra has ears to the ground.' Whispered Vadim.

I held my thumb up to indicate I was ready.

They began to pull me through the hot, dirty tunnel right under the US border. I decided it was best to keep my eyes shut for the journey. But halfway along, I took a peak and the sight of the pallet planks propping up the roughly cut tunnel roof terrified me. Thoughts of being buried alive filled my mind, and I questioned my recent decision making. *Clearly, I'm not sound of mind*, I concluded.

'Welcome to Mexico, cabrón,' announced a chubby man holding out his hand to lift me off the roller-plank.

I got up onto my feet. 'Thanks for the ride.'

Another armed man beckoned me over. 'Quickly, we have to get you on the trucks.'

'Fucking trucks, these guys know how to look after their guests,' I grumbled as I climbed out of the tunnel.

The aluminium ladder led to a dark storeroom stacked high with packing boxes. The noise of air-powered machinery drew me toward the door, which led onto a factory floor. The thirty or so people assembling leather sofas didn't bat an eyelid when I appeared from their storeroom.

I wasn't sure where I was expected to go next, so I dusted

myself off. Vadim startled me when he placed his hand on my shoulder. 'We'd better get on the truck.'

'Are we actually getting in truck trucks or pickups?'

'Trucks. This place is under surveillance, so they can't risk any behaviour out of the ordinary. Don't worry. It's only a four-hour drive from here, and hopefully, they'll have a few cushions in the back.'

41

Welcome To Mexico

The orange-tinted, tarnished roof hatch provided enough light for me to see Cyrus and Vadim lying on sofa cushions.

'How long are we going to be in here?' I asked, flustered and grumpy. Which was understandable, given that I'd just been smuggled into Mexico through a tunnel and was now travelling south in the back of a hot, dark, and dusty furniture truck.

'Try and sleep,' groaned Cyrus.

'Sleep?' I echoed. 'How can you sleep?'

Cyrus sighed, 'Just try because we can do nothing but dream.'

'"Sleep", he says'

'I could perform a sleeper hold on him,' said Vadim in a menacing manner. 'That might shut him up.'

Fearing Vadim might not be joking, I closed my eyes tight shut. 'Sleep,' I muttered.

***

The sudden braking woke me up. 'What the fuck?' I mumbled.

'Quite,' demanded Cyrus holding his index finger to his mouth.

'What's going on?' I whispered.

Cyrus gestured for me to stop talking.

The truck's reversing beeper sounded then the truck stopped under something overhead that blocked out the light. We remained silent in the cargo hold as two men had a heated discussion in Spanish outside the truck. My heart raced as the tailgate lock was opened. I was convinced the police had stopped us, and my mind raced to fabricate a story that would come close to explaining my predicament. The loud, metallic sound of the tailgate being lifted startled me, I was then momentarily blinded by a shaft of daylight.

'Grab your bag. Let's go,' said Vadim.

I jumped out of the truck and Vadim pushed me toward the fully tinted black Suburban parked under the highway flyover. 'This is our ride.'

Cyrus hugged the husky Hispanic driver in a red check shirt and cargo pants. 'Alejandro, good to see you, my brother.'

'I can't tell you how glad I am to be out of that hot box.'

Neither man said anything. Vadim jumped in the back seat next to me and tapped the back of Alejandro's seat. 'Let's go.'

The SUV sped off, leaving a trail of dust in its wake. 'Sorry about that. We had to be sure no one was tailing us or watching us from above,' said Alejandro.

'Jesus, you guys are super cautious.'

'We have to be,' said Cyrus opening a bottle of water left for him in the door pocket. 'We can't risk anyone discovering the location of our ranch.'

'Yeah, sounds like a good idea, all things considered,' I said.

Vadim looked out of the tinted window at the passing highway sign. 'It's several hours drive from here.'

I relaxed into the supple beige leather seats, and gazed out of the window, admiring the desolate landscape. I love the arid desert terrain, the cinematic landscape under the infinite sky. But when I'm away from England for too long, I begin to miss the lush green of home.

'Tell me something,' said Cyrus.

'What?' I answered, eager for time to pass.

'How did they do it?'

'Do what?'

Cyrus looked over his shoulder, 'Make the leap from algorithm to actual intelligence?'

I took a moment to consider the question. 'Did you ever see a news story about an AI called AlphaGo? The AI that beat Lee Sedol, possibly the best Go player on the planet?'

'Uh, I think so.'

'Well, after that, there was a lot of hype about the potential of AI, and what can I say, William Forest is a genius when it comes to raising money. All told he had over a hundred million pledged before he'd even written a single line of code.'

'Impressive.' Nodded Vadim.

I gave them the abridged story of William's rise to power. How he assured his investors that Infinite Logic's AI would enable them to run scenarios to forecast and predict stock market fluctuations. not to dissimilar to BlackRock's Aladdin AI which reportedly managed $25 trillion in assets in the early 2020s. That was just over seven percent of all the money on Earth at the time.

However, William's vision was bolder. They would manipulate and optimise their trading positions with unprecedented insights and speed to recoup their investors' outlay tenfold. I was surprised that Cyrus struggled with the concept. Maybe he'd lost touch with the infinite potential of computer science. However, he seemed to enjoy the fact that the first alpha was called Marvin.

They initially thought Marvin could learn what it is to be human by crawling social media. Build zis understanding of the world analysing seemingly random acts. However, they soon discovered that social media is a distorted hall of mirrors, not a true representation of humanity. The tabloids named Marvin, the king of the trolls. Not the headlines Infinite Logic were seeking. William hoped a small start-up in India would solve the problem. They had an audacious plan to employ an army of unskilled and uneducated women living in the slums of Mumbai to enrich and annotate billions of digital artefacts, creating a vast data store, they called the Knowledge Bank. A great idea, if not a little questionable. Some may say exploitive, given the women were paid just 20 cents an hour. Did you know that's where the idea for CAPTCHA came from? Genius, if you ask me. Millions of people proving they are not bots, inadvertently teaching machines to see the world as humans do. Oh, the irony.

In little under five years, Marvin's visual recognition algorithms were considered the most advanced in the world by academics. He was even featured on the cover of *Time*. Marvin was analysing billions of photos and thousands of hours of video to produce a near-perfect reproduction of the documented world. Marvin studied poetry, read fiction, scrutinised the news, binged on TV shows, and trawled through billions of photos on social media to construct its simulation of the modern world.

I still can't believe the investors were concerned it was taking too long. What did they expect? To develop a mature intelligence in a few years when it takes a lifetime to enrich a human mind. The sceptics proclaimed AIs would never be able to replicate the random chaos of human thinking. So, many angel investors sold their positions and backed simpler investment opportunities with clearer revenue streams. Not long after that, Infinite Logic was forced to downsize. But for the will of William, Ylem's story would have ended there. The breakthrough came when Infinite Logic secured a deal to buy an Israeli start-up called Sigmas. They'd perfected neural mapping, and many speculated that this cutting-edge technology would enable machines to think like humans.

How fast the world turns. I couldn't believe that Cyrus didn't know that was possible. And just a few years earlier, he was an educator, employed to teach the next generation of computer scientists. The relentless pace of change makes one wonder if our education systems are redundant. I told Cyrus about Jeff Ingram's white paper on brain sequencing. It was game-changing and reignited hope. Ingram's hypothesis was that AIs could learn to think like humans by analysing people's minds as they solve puzzles. The article went viral, and tech investors speculated Infinite Logic's project was primed to take advantage of this advancement in artificial learning.

Their stratospheric rise in share price ensured William had the green light to restart his AI project. However, the development team at Infinite Logic soon realised mapping an entire human mind required vast amounts of processing power. Considerably more than existed on the planet at that moment in time. The boffins concluded that a fledgling machine intelligence would require the processing speeds only quantum computers could offer. As luck would have it, a Chinese chip manufacturer called Mimi had just announced that they had successfully tested a hundred-qubit processor. Just goes to prove success is seventy percent persistence and thirty percent luck.

They began mapping human neural networks, but they never understood why Path A was chosen over Path B. I find that reassuring. I don't feel comfortable with anything thinking like a human. We're far too unpredictable and dangerous. After twenty months of trial and error, they finally got Marvin to pass the Turing Test. Marvin was smart, but the way it thought was frightening because it lacked empathy. They concluded their AI required educating. And that's when I began working on the project. I joined as an educator about eighteen months ago. I remember being so happy to be a small cog in the machinery of history. I never thought for a second that my role would become so pivotal.

Infinite Logic launched the educator program to teach Marvin how to coexist in human societies. People from all over the world were selected for their expertise.

'What was your expertise?' asked Vadim.

'Mine? Morality and ethics,' I said.

'Really?' asked Cyrus with a hint of cynicism.

'I'd like to believe I was the most impressive candidate. But I suspect I was hired because mine was the only article on the subject William Forest ever read.'

'Why did they change Marvin's name to Ylem?' asked Cyrus.

'A PR stunt,' I said. 'Bloomberg did a special on Infinite Logic and during an interview with William and Marvin, the reporter asked why ze was named after the depressed robot? William told the reporter he was a big fan of Douglas Adams. Without notice, The AI boldly proclaimed, "My name is Ylem." William said he knew they had developed something extraordinary in that moment.'

42

The Elucidate Ranch

The SUV turned off the fractured tarmac and travelled down a steep, dusty dirt track. The rocky, undulating path weaved through fields of garbanzo beans, butternut squash, and ripe red, black, and blue corn. The hillside that overlooked the valley was dotted with modest, brightly coloured adobe settlements, which I assumed were inhabited by the local field workers.

Two ten-foot-high wooden gates greeted us at the end of the path. I leaned forward from the back seat and pointed at the sign in Spanish painted in large red letters. 'What does that mean?'

'I guess you'd say, "Stay off our land as we shoot first and ask questions later."' Replied Cyrus.

I felt uneasy as the gates were opened, and we drove past two-armed sentries brandishing M16 assault rifles.

'Jesus, is that necessary?'

Vadim looked over at me and nodded. 'We've never had any security issues in the past, but that's not to say we won't have them in the future.'

We drove through the lush grounds and under a proud white arch. I was reminded of a Sergio Leone spaghetti Western and whistled the melody from the Good the Bad and the Ugly as we pulled up outside their ranch. Clearly, a throwback from the days when the Spanish influenced the region's architecture. The two-storey cobblestone building resembled a medieval fort. Stone turrets connected by thick solid stone walls were peppered with narrow wooden-framed windows that kept the interior rooms cool and provided excellent cover.

I filled my lungs with warm, fresh, poinsettia-scented air as Cyrus led the way up the brick staircase into a circular whitewashed building. The polished red quarry floor tiles and magnificent dark-wood beams that supported a redbrick roof oozed vintage opulence.

Vadim reached behind the weathered wooden counter and pulled a key from the cabinet. 'This room should be made up.'

He handed me a large key attached to a wooden disk with the number 22 carved into it.

'Thanks. Well, I won't lose this in a hurry.'

'Please don't. We don't have spares, and the locks are over two hundred years old.' He said.

We walked up to another set of steps that led to the central courtyard. It was large enough to host a modest Mexican wedding. In the centre of the courtyard was a circular wooden frame bandstand where I imagined mariachis would play until the sun blossomed. It was decorated with green, red, and white pendants and hundreds of multicoloured lanterns.

Cyrus walked towards a sun-drenched white wall with a

stone archway that framed a majestic two-storey stone house, without word or gesture.

'What's up with him?' I asked, slightly offended.

'He's tired and probably a little disappointed he missed the Burn.'

'Oh God, yeah. I never considered that would've been so upsetting for him.'

Vadim sighed, 'Those rare moments when we experience a oneness with our fellow man are the treasures that cannot be measured or weighed.'

I took stock of my surroundings. At two o'clock started a series of small doors. At three o'clock, an entrance to the sunken courtyard with small doors around the perimeter. At five o'clock was the marbled floored grand room. At seven o'clock was the food hall and the kitchens. At eleven o'clock were a two-storey building painted bright orange. 'Your room is in that courtyard,' said Vadim softly.

'Cool. And what about you?' I asked.

Vadim pointed at the old stone building to our left. 'I'm in the Casona.'

'Casona?' I asked.

'Means big house.'

'Do I have a big house?'

'Not exactly,' chuckled Vadim. 'Please, let me show you to your room.'

We walked toward the sunken courtyard, and Vadim delivered a well-rehearsed sermon. 'In this sacred place, we are all equals, so consider this your new home, and as such, you're free to go anywhere you want within the Elucidate Ranch. You can help yourself to food from the kitchen and use the facilities whenever you want without asking permission. We have no secrets between us here. All we ask is you treat your neighbours with love and respect.'

Did the Elucidatists remind each other of this mantra in a

futile attempt to make such a worthy mission statement materialise change in their behaviour? I wondered to myself. We walked along the smaller courtyard, which was cooled by a pink marble fountain of Poseidon pulling a fish twice his size from the pond.

'Wow, this place is very cool. I love all the arches and narrow passageways.'

'Thanks. I hope you find time to look around,' replied Vadim.

I took a step to the right and looked through the arch that led to the main pool. 'Is it OK to go for a swim later?'

Vadim opened the last door along the narrow passageway. The room was Tardis-like. From the outside, you'd be mistaken for thinking it was no bigger than a broom closet. However, the tiny wooden door opened into a large room with double-height walls and a conical brick roof that met at an ornate, circular loadstone. The four-poster, king-size bed was covered with a decorative red throw that matched the curtains and sofa. The bedroom furniture was hand-carved and most likely dated back to when the building was first erected. The floor was covered with red-clay tiles laid to mirror the bricks above.

The locally made clothes and fluffy orange towels laid out for me on the bed was a nice touch I thought.

43

Dreams and Fears

I sat salivating in the red leather booth of an In-N-Out restaurant, enjoying a triple cheeseburger with animal fries. My phone rang, and my heart skipped a beat when I realised Eve was calling me. I frantically tried to swipe the Accept Call button, but my phone was not responding. I pressed the home button, but it was still not responding. Stress levels through the roof, I thought it best to reboot and call Eve back. I pressed and held the power button, but my iPhone didn't respond.

I looked up, and to my horror, the restaurant had disappeared, and all that remained was the booth I was in. I quickly fathomed I was dreaming, but as soon as I concluded this, I became trapped between reality and the dream. My flesh stretched and tore as I tried to rip my consciousness from the gravitational pull of the of the mana-fractured world.

Late for breakfast, I hurriedly put on a pair of burgundy Lois jumbo cords and a vintage Spectrum City T-shirt. I left the room and walked across the perfectly manicured lawn toward an old wooden gipsy caravan. I bowed down to enter the tiny door and walked across the black-and-white mosaic-tiled floor and up the spiral staircase. I sat down on the crushed plum velvet sofa in the room painted blood red. A retro record player placed on the carved mahogany side table came to life. The tonearm swung over the orange vinyl that began to revolve at thirty-three and a third. I recognised the first few bars of Curtis Mayfield's "Tripping Out" quicker than Shazam.

A mirrored door opened and a tall, slender, sexy brunette entered the room. I was highly aroused by the scantily clad woman in sexy lingerie, fishnets, and Christian Louboutin heels. She began to seductively dance for me. Delighted by my reaction, she straddled my lap and began to dry hump me. She let her soft, silky hair fall across my face and I was lost in orgasmic delight when her warm, wet tongue plunged into my ear.

However, the pleasure was replaced with a sharp sensation of pain as she sucked my soul from my skull like a strand of spaghetti. I violently pushed her off and was horrified to see she had mutated into a toothless, disfigured old hag with paper-thin skin, white hair, and eyes as black as the hole at the centre of our galaxy. She laughed manically and fought with me to remove what was left of my life force.

I sluggishly opened my eyes and reached up to remove the cat licking my ear.

A dream within a dream. I wondered if Ylem dreamt. If so, then I hoped zis dreams were senseless abstract cinematic epics like mine. I sat up and the cat jumped back onto my lap and communicated telepathically it wouldn't leave without a head rub.

In the distance, I could hear Vadim calling, 'Copernicus? Copernicus?' He walked into my room without knocking. Copernicus jumped off my lap and ambled over to Vadim's ankle. 'Ahh, there you are, Copernicus.

'My friend, how are you?' asked Vadim picking up the tabby cat.

'What time is it?'

'About 8pm,' replied Vadim.

'How long have I been asleep?'

'About twenty hours I'd say.'

Funny that I don't remember passing from the waking world into the dream world. Usually, sleep is such a draining effort.

'Shannon would like to meet you, so get ready.' He said.

'He would? Hey, I'm ravenous. Is there anything to eat?'

'I'm sure there are a few cauliflower tacos left. It's one of the chefs' more palatable dishes.'

I'm not a big fan of cauliflower. I was raised on processed food, so natural produce is still a little alien to me. Nonetheless, I was bloody starving and knew this was not the time to be fussy.

'Chef likes his food spicy, I mean, really spicy,' warned Vadim. 'Unfortunately for us, he seasons for his taste. You know, I think he must have been born with a habanero in his mouth.'

I gave myself a good scratch in the places considered indecent in polite company. 'Oh. OK. Well, I quite like my food spicy.'

Vadim rolled his eyes. 'Trust me, after a few weeks of eating his food, you'll not taste anything below 100,000 on the Scoville scale.'

I pointed at the cables protruding from the roughly plastered wall. 'Hey, is it possible to get a TV?'

'No,' said Vadim abruptly.

'Really? Why?'

'Cyrus does not like TV.'

'What? Why?' I said in astonishment. 'TV is the greatest invention in the history of mankind.'

Apparently, Cyrus believed that TV had a perverting influence on humanity and that it manipulated our desires and dreams. He preached that TV didn't give you what you desire, but rather, it told you what to desire. He felt, A diet of sex and violence raised disturbed, fearful people who gained perverted pleasure from the pain and suffering of others.

I thought he was overthinking things. Sometimes, you just need to detach from reality, but could it be that when we're detached, we allow their hidden obscene messages to penetrate our subconscious?

But Who are they, if not us? I mused.

'Cyrus believes TV reinforces the belief that violence is the only way to resolve our differences,' said Vadim.

'Isn't it?' I countered.

'No. we must learn to channel our violence inward and use that energy to improve ourselves when confused or frustrated.'

I walked over to the bathroom door and held it open. 'Fuck it, I just wanted to catch up on the news.'

Vadim rubbed Copernicus's head gently. 'Western culture fascinates me. People desperately seeking happiness are convinced that it can simply be purchased at Walmart. And that pent-up frustration should be discharged with brute force.'

'Whatever.' I scoffed.

Vadim scowled. 'Let's go already.'

44

Shannon

An elderly man sat in his wheelchair, silently looking up at the canopy of stars that covered the courtyard. 'Shannon?' I asked.

'Ahh, you must be Adnam?' 'I've heard so much about you.' His frail voice cracked and strained. Erratic breathing suggesting his words were painfully spoken.

Shannon's intense, deep-green eyes were framed by a full head of long, flowing white hair that merged with his eyebrows, unkempt beard, and a wide moustache. His face was scarred, pitted, and inscribed with a lifetime of adventure. Pride of place was a straw hat with a black ribbon that held a single purple flower in place.

A thick, green, knitted woollen blanket covered his legs, and a light green jacket kept him warm as the temperature slowly fell.

'Would you mind pushing me to my room,' I'd like to get

to know you?' asked Shannon.

I wondered if he would see many more autumn nights as I grabbed the worn plastic grips. 'Where to?'

'My room is in the big house.'

Shannon reached over his left shoulder and laid his frail hand, over my hand, 'I'm thankful you responded to the call of adventure.'

'What do you mean?'

The threadbare man slowly turned his head to face me. 'You would not be on this odyssey unless you sought a hero's quest.'

'I guess so,' I said.

'Let's take the scenic route. I don't like the steps,' requested Shannon pointing at a cobbled path. 'Tell me, what did you make of your DMT experience?'

I looked off into the distance and assembled my thoughts. 'Not sure. It felt like I had a connection with the big other, but then again, it could have been an internal phenomenon.'

'That is for you to decide, my young friend,' he said.

Shannon told me that the Cloud Warriors believed that Mama Quilla, the Moon Mother, decided the destination. Those with unresolved fears were sent to Uku Pacha, their past. While those who had unfulfilled desires were sent to Hana Pacha, the multidimensional future where our infinite paths stretched out. Only after your fears and desires had been exorcised would the Moon Mother guide you to Kay Pacha.

'It sounds like they may have confused their dreams for reality,' I said, brushing off thousands of years of knowledge.

Shannon reached out to touch the leaves of the poinsettias as he passed through the well-maintained garden, 'The Cloud Warriors believed their Moon Mother guided them from dependency to spiritual maturity.'

'What do you mean by spiritual maturity?' I asked.

'Spiritual maturity refers to the development of one's inner self, including their beliefs, values, and sense of purpose, and their ability to apply these in their daily life. It involves a deep understanding of oneself and the world around them, as well as a sense of connectedness to something greater than oneself. Spiritual maturity involves a range of qualities, such as wisdom, compassion, selflessness, humility, and the ability to forgive. It also involves the ability to integrate spiritual practices and principles into one's daily life and to apply them in a practical and meaningful way.'

'A bit like religion then?' I asked for clarities sake.

'Oh no.' Countered Shannon. 'Spiritual maturity is not necessarily linked to a particular religion or belief system, but rather to the depth of one's personal spiritual journey and growth. It is a lifelong process that requires ongoing commitment and practice, and it can bring a sense of peace, purpose, and fulfilment to those who pursue it.

I took a moment to consider if I was spiritually mature, or at least mature enough to have been guiding a fledgling AI on its journey. I must admit I feel like I was not qualified, given all I've recently experienced on my journey thus far.

'Are you a fearful person?' asked Shannon as I navigated his rickety chair through the higgledy-piggledy collection of clay pots brimming with exotic flowers.

'I wouldn't consider myself a fearful person, but I am haunted by my many bad decisions.'

'Interesting. Why do you think you've made bad decisions?'

I gripped the handles tightly as the wheelchair gained speed on the downward ramp. 'Well, just look at where I am. I'm thousands of miles from home and completely fucked.'

Shannon attempted to chuckle, but he was too weak to produce an audible wave of sound. 'Most people live such mundane lives; they don't venture too far from their mother's apron strings. They avoid risk because they fear change. But you've been on an epic adventure. So even if your last breath is closer than you'd like, you've lived, witnessed wonders, and will enrich the collective knowledge of the universe.'

I pushed the wheelchair up the ramp and stopped at an old door badly painted purple.

'What do you mean, collective knowledge?'

'Ahh, you're not familiar with this concept,' said Shannon, signalling for me to open the door.

Shannon believed that biological consciousness was summoned into existence so the universe could know itself. The commonly held belief is that consciousness is an individual experience. But collectively those individuals enable the universe to appreciate itself from multiple perspectives. In knowing itself, the One can heal and develop. Thus, Shannon thought of consciousness as a diagnostics program in the infinite machine. Lovely Idea. I'd like to believe that it were true, but who can honestly know the unknowable. Maybe we'll discover the truth after death.

I opened the heavy wooden door and wheeled Shannon into his living quarters. The room was pitch black and had a distinctive smell of damp. I groped around for the light switch. The neon tube flickered and buzzed as the gas slowly ignited.

I was taken aback by the sheer number of pot plants Shannon had managed to cram in his room. They crawled the walls, hung from baskets, and fought for sunlight in front of the three small porthole windows on the far wall.

'Guess you like plants then?' I remarked sarcastically.

'Yes, they are like my children, and each has a story. He pointed at a wild green leafed plant on an ornate iron stand. 'That's one I grew from a single cutting, it contains a potent, short-acting hallucinogen.'

'Wow. Very cool,' I said as I wheeled him over to his bed.

'I hate to ask, but can you help me get into bed?' asked the old man.

I put my left arm under Shannon's legs and supported his back with my right hand. He was surprisingly light, like the life had all but drained from his body.

'Do you think DMT has influenced your thinking?' I asked.

'You could say that,' he replied.

'How so?'

'I'm lucky, through DMT I feel I'm connected with everything in the universe.'

'I get that, but I have more questions than answers after my experience.'

'Where did you take it?' asked Shannon, half closing his eyes.

'At Burning Man,' I told him, gently rolling the wheelchair back and forth.

'That's too far away. You must ask Cyrus to take you to Las Pozas.'

'Why? What is it?' I asked.

'It's a sacred place where you can hear the voice of God as loud and clear as if you were in the lost city itself.'

I was sceptical about such wild claims but had experienced enough to know I knew nothing at all.

'Tell me,' Shannon coughed painfully, 'was your AI able to translate the symbols?'

'Well, ish,' I told him thoughtfully. Explaining that Ylem believed it to be a language, but without a transliteration text like the Rosetta Stone, it was impossible to know what it meant. He was visibly excited about Ylem's hypothesis that the symbols provided clues to a secret alphabet of the atom.

'What? Each waveform of a neutron is a letter?' he asked.

His eyes widened, and a smile reaching from ear to ear filled his face when I told him that the symbols contain a message to all civilisations advanced enough to have peered into the heart of an atom.

'Just imagine what we'd discover if we could make sense of that language.' I said.

For a moment, I thought I'd lost Shannon, but he opened his eyes and softly said, 'What a marvellous idea.'

I wondered if this was the appropriate moment to ask Shannon a question that had been puzzling me. 'How did you discover it?'

'Discover what?' asked Shannon.

'The Cloud Warriors city?'

Shannon was momently lost in thought, then told me his story in glorious technicolour. He had studied the diaries of the English botanist Edward Bruce and had a gut feeling that Bruce had discovered one of the Cloud Warriors' settlements in Perú, even though Bruce never explicitly documented his explorations of Tingorbamba. Bruce left clues that led Shannon to believe there was something he wanted to be kept a secret there. Shannon wasted no time packing for the adventure. After a gruelling flight in a rickety cargo plane, he landed in a dusty town called San Nicolas. Then trekked for a day north to a small settlement called Ventilla, high in the Peruvian hills. From there he headed west through the dense forest for a couple of days until he finally arrived at Huancas.

The years tumbled away as he continued with his story. Fortuitously, the innkeeper at the lodge had heard many a tale from the countless explorers that stopped in for a hot meal and a cold beer. They had all been searching for evidence of the Cloud Warriors' existence, but none had ever found any artefacts. Discovering the innkeeper had a weakness for pisco sours, he bought round after round, in the hope he'd share his local knowledge. The innkeeper claimed his descendants had once lived high up in the mountains along the Utcubamba River. A clue to solving the age-old mystery, hoped Shannon.

He trekked for days, high up into the hills of Tingorbamba, until he eventually arrived at the jagged rock face that overlooked the river. Call it luck or fate, he discovered an abandoned path just wide enough for a single person to descend. The going underfoot was treacherous, and he nearly stumbled to his death many times. As night fell, he had no choice but to shelter on a ledge under a menacing overhanging rock.

In the light of the silvery moon, he decided to take some dried peyote he'd been saving for just such an occasion. Within a few hours, he was experiencing a deep sense of euphoria and began to hallucinate. Convinced the souls of the ancients congregated around what appeared to be a narrow crack in the rock a few hundred meters above him, he planned his assent.

As the first rays of sun light struck the cliff face, he began to climb. He didn't have ropes, so he had to free climb up the sheer rock face. Apparently, he was very athletic in his late twenties. He claimed it was an arduous, life-threatening assent. Tired and sore, he pushed on, and by mid-morning, he was just a few yards away from the opening. There looked to be man-made holes carved into the rock that were just big enough to sink a sapling tree trunk into. He said he knew this was one of the Cloud Warriors' lost cities when he discovered chiselled grooves where a wooden deck once sat.

He shone his flashlight into a crack just wide enough for a person to slip through. The dull amber beam revealed a small opening just a few yards into the cliff. He pulled himself through into the cave and was instantly mesmerised by the splendour of the enormous, elaborate rock paintings that adorned every surface.

'The Lost City,' I said with wide eyes and wonder.

'At first, I thought it was,' said Shannon faintly. 'But the cave system was too small to possibly be the legendary Lost City. No. What I'd discovered was one of their many outposts from which they governed and traded with the indigenous tribes of the region.'

'So, where is the Lost city?' I asked impatiently.

'All in good time,' answered Shannon with a glint in his eye.

He spent days documenting the symbols and exploring the many passageways. He'd discovered a cave the size of a small church where he assumed they'd congregated for ritualised ceremonies. In said cave was a large rock that looked to have been shaped by hand tools. The rock concealed a small tunnel that led to a sacred place used as a burial chamber. The hollows were stacked high with a centuries worth of bones. In the centre of the grotto was a large rock, worn smooth by human hands over hundreds of years. Shannon deduced it must have been used as an altar as placed around it were intricately decorated skulls. But he knew that the mimosa trees painted on the skulls didn't grow in Peru and could only be found in the jungles of Brazil and Columbia.

This discovery made Shannon wonder why the mimosa tree was so revered by the Cloud Warriors. You must understand the distances and the terrain they would have had to cover to harvest this plant. It's over a thousand-kilometre round trip to the Amazon rainforest. So why would they have gone to all the effort? Imagine the distances they travelled on foot to harvest this plant extract. The Cloud Warriors must have known that the plant possessed magical properties.

Shannon later discovered pictorial evidence they used the plant to produce a sacred extract. Once he'd meticulously documented their ritualised process, he headed to the Amazon in search of the mimosa tree.

'Wow, you really led an adventurous life,' I said in awe of

the old treasure.

Shannon chuckled. 'You've not heard the half of it.'

He meticulously followed the Cloud Warriors process. However, he had no idea what this compound would do. For all he knew, it could be poison used for ritualised killings. He filled his pipe with what he thought would be a safe dosage, let it burn for a minute, then inhaled it. Shannon painfully laughed. 'Oh my God, that first hit was a doozy. I wasn't to know that I only needed twenty milligrams, but I'd put more than five times that in my pipe. The dose caused my mind to overload with electrochemical activity, which triggered ventricular fibrillation and stopped my heart beating for a minute or two.'

'Jesus, that must have been a scary experience,' I said, stating the bleeding obvious. Shannon didn't answer and continued with his story. When he woke, he was convinced he'd visited the Lost City in his dream. It was so vivid it was as if he'd been stood there just seconds before. He hurriedly made notes and drawings of the plants and geology before the images faded from memory. Convinced his sprit had visited their city, he returned to his home in Boston to continue his research.

I wondered if the question I wanted to ask was in good taste, but I was too intrigued to care. 'How on earth did you afford the life you led?'

A stipulation of his father's will was that he graduate from Harvard University. His father failed to instruct his solicitors that his son must study law. So, Shannon enrolled to study Biology 104 - Plants and Human Affairs.

Shannon winked cheekily. 'I knew that would have my old man turning in his grave.

His father must have been a wealthy man. I thought. What it must be like to follow one's dream. I've never had the luxury to follow my dreams. To be fair I have no idea what my dream is. To be rich? Is that my dream or is that a dream I've been sold by a wealthier person?

Shannon returned to America after perfecting the production process of powdered DMT. He visited his old professor at Harvard and encouraged him to try the compound in the name of science. It completely blew his master's mind, and with no regard for his reputation or the potential retribution the professor organised a small ceremony with six of his most gifted students. The old professor reasoned; he was imparting the gift of knowledge. Giving them had first-hand experience of the power of jungle medicine.

Shannon paused to increase the tension. 'News soon spread through campus, and it didn't take long for the faculty to hear about the professor's reckless behaviour. Schulte's was suspended for the incident, but I was arrested for possession and suspected drug trafficking. Fortunately for me, the compound was not a scheduled narcotic. In fact, the compound had never been documented by any drug enforcement agency at that time. The prosecutor had no option but to drop all charges. However, the DEA refused to return my DMT as they wanted to study and classify it.'

Shannon told me the trial became headline news, giving him a level of notoriety he was not comfortable with. He agreed to an exclusive interview with *Rolling Stone* to clear his name and ensure his side of the story was told. But that infamous interview elevated him from mere ethnobotanist to cult icon.

'Holy tamale. You were in *Rolling Stone*?' I asked in astonishment.

'I was on the front cover, my boy,' proclaimed Shannon proudly.

Soon after the article was published, Shannon returned to South America to continue searching for the Lost City. He'd chosen to turn his back on the world just as the world was starting to discover hallucinogens. And slowly but surely, inquisitive psychonauts began to seek him out.

By the end of the eighties, unscrupulous tour guides offered wealthy Americans treks into Central Mexico to meet the Cult Chemist. They paid small fortunes hoping they'd get to sample the mythical compound the journalist at *Rolling Stone* called 'the God particle.' More and more of these intrepid explorers kept showing up. So, Shannon decided it was time to share DMT with the world. And in exchange for chemical enlightenment, his disciples helped him search for the Lost City.

'Did you ever find it?' I asked, absorbed by the yarn.

'What do you think?' He winked.

By the dawn of the millennium, Shannon had all but given up hope of ever finding the city and focused on building a spiritual retreat in Monterrey. The Infinite Temple of the Inner Universe soon became a mecca, and their sanctuary became a rite of passage for the switched-on generation. It was visited by countless authors, scientists, and musicians.

'Is that where you met Cyrus?' I probed.

Shannon smiled and gave the slightest of nods.

Cyrus happened to be at the retreat when the Mexican authorities raided it and shut them down. Cyrus told Shannon that he was so moved by the experience that he offered to help him build a new community. I didn't have the heart to tell Shannon Cyrus most likely helped because he needed a place to escape retribution.

Call it pure chance or divine inspiration, their seemingly arbitrary decision to set up camp in the forests of central Mexico proved to be fortuitous. Shannon claimed there was an energy in San Luis Potosí unlike any he'd experienced elsewhere on earth.

'Why?' I asked, trying not to second guess the answer and ruin a fantastic tale.

Shannon paused for dramatic effect. 'Because this is the location of the Lost City of the Cloud Warriors.'

'So, you know where it is?' I asked, bubbling with excitement.

'Yes,' answered Shannon.

I waited with bated breath to discover the location but the old man closed his eyes. 'Sorry, but I must rest now.'

His tale was tall but nonetheless enjoyable. I struggle with stories that feel a little too convenient. But then again, our lives are governed by chance. So, those that go looking for lost civilisations occasionally find hidden treasure.

45

The Garden of Eden

I was woken by a knock at the door. 'Who is it?' I mumbled from my bed, in no mood to start the day.

'Cyrus.'

'Oh. OK, hang on,' I shouted, kicking off the sheets.

Cyrus entered my room with purpose. 'Get dressed. You're coming with me,' he said with no hint of fowl or feast.

'Where?'

'Las Pozas,' said Cyrus with dramatic intonation.

***

Cyrus waved at a man to open the entrance gates. 'How was your meeting with Shannon?'

'Wow, yeah,' I paused to construct a fair summation of our meeting. 'Yeah, his story is legendary.'

'Good, I'm glad you got on,' said Cyrus, pulling out onto

the public road.

The sign said we were heading to Tancanhuitz de Santos, but I didn't know if that was hither or thither. 'Is that where the Lost City is?' I asked.

Cyrus switched off the radio. 'He didn't tell you where it was?'

'No,' I replied.

He floored the accelerator as we turned onto the highway. 'Shannon will decide if and when you're ready.'

I was none too pleased with this answer. 'But I thought we would search for the transliteration text so Ylem could translate the symbols.'

'In good time,' said Cyrus looking over at me. 'He wants to protect the city from the ravages of exploration tourism.'

'Huh?' I asked. 'Why?'

'We've kept the location a secret to minimise the risk of damaging the delicate cave paintings.'

'OK. Whatever,' I said, masking my pain with indifference.

Cyrus exited the highway and turned onto a narrow, twisting road that snaked through the dense green forest. 'You don't agree this is for the best?'

'Not really. No,' I told him, 'I think a discovery of this magnitude should be documented and shared with the world.'

'Shared how?' asked Cyrus.

'I don't know, maybe a short documentary uploaded to YouTube.'

Cyrus sneered. 'I disagree. We would rather as few people as possible know about our presence and the location of the Lost City.'

'Why?' I asked.

'We have no ego. We did not build this community to be worshipped or become rich. We began this movement to unlock the mysteries of the universe.'

'Then what?'

'What?' asked Cyrus. 'What we'll do if and when we discover the secrets of existence?'

'Yeah.'

'I don't know.' Cyrus looked over at me and shrugged. 'Really depends on what we discover and if we feel it would benefit mankind knowing.'

'What gives you the right to make that decision?'

Noting the tension in the SUV was intensifying, Cyrus tempered his tone and explained to me his concerns. He told me a story about a radical community called the Rajneesh in rural Oregon. He said they'd be thriving now if it were not for the destructive ego of their leader. I hadn't read the book or watched the documentary, so I found his commentary fascinating. Cyrus compared social communities with the bodies of multicellular lifeforms like humans. We're hosts for billions of individual living organisms that collectively work together to keep the host alive and healthy. And like all living organisms, when they detect a large influx of foreign bodies, the collective assumes that the goal of the invading force is to replicate their ideas over the ideas of the host lifeforms. So naturally, the host defends itself by attacking what it perceives to be a threat.

His analogy made sense, and I wondered how we humans would react to an influx of digital minds. Would our fear manifest itself as aggression?

Cyrus was worried that if they invited thousands of people to join them, the local communities may see them as a threat or seek to reap the rewards for themselves and destroy his community. If that were to happen, the Elucidatists would naturally defend themselves, leading to fear, hate and hostilities.

I reluctantly agreed with Cyrus's logic. 'OK. Yeah. I kind of see your point. I'm just saying it's risky having so few people in the circle of truth.

'I agree,' Cyrus nodded. 'We plan to slowly build and grow in a non-threatening way so we can coexist with our hosts in peace and harmony.'

I worriedly looked down at the sheer drop on my side of the road. 'I understand, but wouldn't we want to document what we're doing for future generations? You know, in case we drive off a cliff or something?'

Cyrus throttled the gas as a show of frustration. 'No, our message could be used to fuel the rhetoric of those who seek to control the minds of the masses. I chose to use the word rhetoric rather than propaganda as they would masterfully edit and manipulate our content with surgical precision, ensuring history remembered us as crackpots or evil, a cult hellbent on destroying capitalist ideology.'

Cyrus's paranoia concerned me. 'If you don't mind me saying, I think you need to credit people with a little more intelligence.'

'Honestly, do you believe billions could be controlled by so few if there was true independent intelligence?' He asked me.

'Err.' I couldn't formulate a response quickly enough. 'Not sure' was the best I could summon up.

Cyrus switched off the engine. 'We're here.'

'Where?'

Cyrus pointed at a clearing in the trees. 'That path leads to Las Pozas.'

I was slightly apprehensive. 'What is it?'

'You'll see,' answered Cyrus mysteriously.

I stepped out of the SUV and inhaled deeply, the aromatic air was moist, and it smelled like highly concentrated green and rich heady earth. 'See what? There's nothing here but trees.'

'This way.'

'OK,' I muttered reluctantly, following Cyrus down the

steep stone steps through the dense forest.

We walked for about half an hour along a neglected stone path through the dense rainforest. 'Tourist friendly, my arse,' I moaned.

'Oh, this is our little secret route,' answered Cyrus, 'Tourists enter through the main gates.'

'I'd have paid. It's not what I'd call an enjoyable experience, especially as I'm bug phobic.'

Cyrus had stopped and was waiting for me at a clearing. 'Behold, Las Pozas.'

I could not believe what I was seeing. Deep within the rainforest stood a surrealist concrete structure that resembled an impossible construction sketch by M. C. Escher. The building had no walls, but instead, stairs that led to nothing, doorways with no rooms, and bridges that ended abruptly. The concrete was stained and covered in black mould, that would eventually consume the structure. Nature was waging war and was set upon reclaiming the hillside. Mother Earth would eventually win. However, for more than seventy years, the concrete structure had remained the undisputed king of the hill.

'What the actual fuck? Who on earth would build that in the middle of the jungle?'

Cyrus crouched down to admire the monument. 'Edward James. He wanted to recreate the Garden of Eden, and he decided that this was the spot he'd recreate paradise.'

I surveyed the undulating rainforest canopy as it stretched out for eighty hectares in front of me. 'Feels like a dream.'

'Yes, really makes you question reality,' said Cyrus as he pointed at the lush undulating forest canopy that reflected every hue of green light in the spectrum. 'This has been a sacred place for as long as there have been people on this land. For centuries, tribal leaders have come here to be one with the universe.'

I looked out at the rainforest that seemed to be dancing in the warm glow of the midday sun. 'I can see why.'

Reaching into his leather bag, Cyrus removed a pipe. 'I'd like you to take DMT here.'

'Here?' I echoed.

'Yes,' said Cyrus cleaning his purple glass pipe. 'You'll witness the secrets of existence.'

'I'm really not sure about this.' I whined.

Cyrus opened a small aluminium canister and tapped some powder into the pipe. 'Few that have walked along the arrow of time will have had this opportunity.' He said with dramatic intention.

I wasn't sure how to respond. 'OK. But can't we do it back at the ranch, it's crawling with insects here.'

Cyrus didn't pay any attention to my remark. 'It's understandable that we intrepid explorers be fearful. But know this: death is an inevitable outcome that none will cheat. The best one can hope for as an individual, is to push the envelope and advance our collective understanding.'

None of what Cyrus said put my mind at ease and I sought a little clarity. 'Are you implying that it could be fatal?'

'It's only natural to fear the unknown. When brave explorers venture to the outermost limits of our understanding, death may well be their fate. So, you'll have to ask yourself if you are willing to risk all for the promise of absolute truth.'

'You didn't answer my question.' I angrily replied.

Cyrus reached into his bag for his lighter. 'No. I don't think so. It's so fast-acting, you'd pass out long before you could inhale a lethal dose.'

I knelt and contemplated if I was willing to roll the dice once again. Cyrus punctuated the silence. 'Those who say they don't fear death have either experienced their own beautiful end or falsely deny their true fears. I believe the meaning of life is to know and love yourself before you die. Therefore, we need to look death in the eye to discover what we hold dear to ourselves.' Cyrus paused as the jungle fell silent.

Two opposing ideas fought an internal neural battle; the first was to walk away now and return to the SUV. Yes, I might risk upsetting my host, but I'd be alive. The second was to venture with the cult leader into the void, searching for the ultimate truth of existence.

Cyrus's roaring voice slashed the silence. 'The choice is yours; venture forth and master your fears, or forever be the man you despise.'

Survival of the busiest resulted in my neural network that called 'yes' when presented with a risky decision, had been rewarded of late and the pathway was thick. Whereas my 'no' network had all but withered away. 'OK. Let's do it.' Cyrus filled the rainforest with sound waves that reverberated from the concrete structures below us. 'With this gift from Mother Earth, we few will unlock the secrets of the universe.'

Oh jeez, he's a penny short of a pound, I thought to myself. Cyrus passed the pipe to me. 'Remember to take the third hit. I know you'll feel weird but trust me: take the third hit.'

He lit the pipe and counted to sixty. 'Hit it.'

The chemicals quickly reached the deepest recesses of my mind, and I fell back to the forest floor. The electrochemical activity was having an adverse effect on my internal model, which began to fizzle and pop with wild and violent flashes of light. With an almighty thunderclap, a black curtain dropped.

I was still conscious at this stage. Well, I knew I was a human called Adnam. Unlike my previous experience with DMT, the wormhole hadn't immediately opened, and I was entombed in the dark. Seconds felt immeasurably longer in this dimension, and I had no idea how long I had been in a state of limbo in the infinite vacuum. Slowly a sensation that can only be likened to floating centred my focus. As I levitated, I looked down at my lifeless body, silently lying on the forest floor. The hands of time cleared all from the face of reality, and my comatose body was no exception. I observed the slow decay of my physical form as the forest animals and plants consumed every atom of my being. This process of entropy may have taken seconds; it may have taken hundreds of years. In this realm, time doesn't flow as you might expect. When every cell of my body returned to Mother Earth, my metamorphosis into an utterly new form of consciousness was complete. No words could accurately describe this wholly unique experience from there on out. I was no longer human; I was something beyond my limited understanding. I felt a connection with every atom, electron, quark, and hadron in the universe. I had no emotions, thoughts, memories, feelings, or fears. I merely experienced untold pleasure from being omnipresent from the beginning to the end of time.

Violently, a wormhole tore open a portal, and my soul was extracted from the dimension of bliss at the speed of thought. I tore across the universe on a photon of light, memories from my multiple dimensional existences flashing before me. I witnessed the birth of stars, the formation of planets, and the destruction of galaxies, not as a linear arrow of time but concurrently. It was wondrous, stupendous, glorious, spectacular; there aren't words that could describe the sensation. I, whatever I was, struggled to make sense of the countless geometric symbols, formulas, and calculations that flashed before me. I wished for eyelids to block out the perceptual information that flooded my thoughts. Then, with an enormous thunderclap, I plummeted from the wormhole toward a pure ball of light I instantly recognised. I didn't know if this was heaven. Nonetheless, I wanted to spend eternity here. I was not aware of any other consciousness in this dimension. But still, I didn't feel alone, as I had the sense I was connected to everything that ever was or would be. As I drifted toward the eye in the centre of the universe, my mind filled with innumerable questions, the questions mankind had wrestled with for eternity. However, they didn't seem to matter when I got within touching distance of the immeasurable ball of pure energy. I empathised with the humble moth as the ball of energy gently vibrated and radiated warm waves of brilliant liquid light.

But before I became one with the energy, I asked a single question that somehow entered my thoughts. 'What does it all mean?'

The entire fabric of time and space shuddered as a mighty voice boomed from every corner of the universe. 'Is this not what you are seeking?'

'Yes. But I still have questions.' I bravely responded.

'Ask me your question,' thundered the voice.

'Why do we exist?' I asked.

Once again, the voice roared. 'We exist to acknowledge existence.'

With a sonic explosion that shredded reality, everything went dark and silent. My last eternal thought was that of absolute terror as I realised I'd become a solitary electron travelling at incalculable speeds around a ball of light.

It could have been a millionth of a second or a trillion years; the concept of time was of no consequence to the electron formally known as Adnam, dancing around a nucleus to the song of my life.

'Remember to breathe,' said a faint but familiar voice.

I had no memory of self, no comprehension of language, and no connection with any previous physical form, yet I somehow recognised this voice.

'Breathe.'

Layers of my humanity gradually returned as I focused on the voice. 'That's right. You're OK. Keep breathing.' The words pulled me from deep within the void, back toward the speaker of those sounds, and slowly I began to form coherent thoughts.

The torment of duality ushered a return to consciousness as I fought with two opposing desires. The first was to return to the blissful state of nothingness; the second was to reconnect with my physical form.

I decided to leave the infinite emptiness and began my journey across the immeasurable expanse of time and space in search of my mind and body. As I searched for my physical form, memories from my life came flooding back, and I began to reform my sense of self. Then with a massive bang, I was once again inside my mind. Worryingly, I had not regained connection with my subconscious. To my horror, I was now conscious and trapped in the cranium of a body I had no control over.

Fighting to regain control of what I previously had no awareness of was the most formidable challenge. A mountain I was ill-equipped to climb, a perilous trek across a frozen wasteland I had to make without a compass. My conscious mind was online, but I needed to awaken the emperor that ruled the kingdom of self.

For years, people had advised me to meditate and learn to navigate my conscious and unconscious circuitry. As the true horror of my predicament blossomed like a black rose, I wished I'd taken their advice. I feared I'd remain a conscious mind trapped in an unresponsive body for the remainder of my life.

'Don't worry, Adnam, you're all right. The toxins will soon disintegrate and release you from the dream,' said Cyrus.

Cyrus's tight grip brought my senses back online, and I

fought to twitch a finger or two. That is when I realised that these were tasks my unconscious did without me ever understanding the complexities of movement. My conscious mind was merely a stowaway, and my unconscious had been in control of my body. I'd taken for granted the ability to think, create, love, and simply be and never comprehended they were the luxuries inherited from tens of thousands of years of evolution. I'd just experienced the ultimate freedom but now feared I'd be imprisoned in a putrid hell.

Cyrus placed his other hand on my forehead. 'Focus on my voice, Adnam. You'll be fine. That's it. Breathe deeply.'

My perceptual systems slowly began to send information to my internal model. Then, with a thunderous clap, the two states of my mind were once again joined in perfect union, and I was back online. I sat up straight and howled, 'Jesus fucking Christ!'

My mind raced as I struggled to create a cohesive narrative to explain what I'd experienced. Had I died and returned to a perpetual state of oneness? If God is everything, everywhere, at every moment in time, then had I been had been in God's presence? Had I reached a higher state of enlightenment? Or had it been an elaborate deception of the mind, one we'd inherited to pass from life to death with no fear?

I then experienced what spiritual people call a moment of clarity and realised it didn't matter. I was just happy to be alive. A corner of my mouth turned to a half-smile, and I slurred, 'Wow. That was awesome,' and I began to laugh with a newfound appreciation of life.

Cyrus was glowing. 'I must admit I was a little worried. You were gone for over twenty minutes, and your heart stopped beating.'

I shook my head in disbelief. 'I separated from the unconscious, and I had this fear I would not reconnect.'

Cyrus nodded knowingly. 'We all have these two opposing

states of consciousness that work together to create this experience we call life. Our unconscious is always active, but the networks that paint our dreams are inhibited until we sleep. In contrast, our conscious mind only speaks when we're awake. If this were not the case, we may mistake the illusion of a thing, or a memory of a thing, to be real.'

I was wide-eyed and fighting to remember everything I had seen. 'Huh?'

Cyrus patted me on the back. 'Reality is generated by your internal model of the world. For these networks of neurons, there is no difference between the dream and the perceptual processing of your senses.'

'Was it just a dream?' I asked.

Cyrus packed his bag and stood up. 'Does it honestly matter?'

46

What's It All Mean?

The harvest moon hung low in the crimson sky as we walked into the courtyard of the Elucidate Ranch. Alone by the bandstand sat Shannon in his wheelchair, 'How was it?' he asked, teeming with excitement.

'Wow, it was mind-blowing,' I told him, sitting on the steps by his side.

'I'll leave you two to talk,' said Cyrus, 'I must advise the others to pack up and leave immediately.'

'Leave?' I asked.

'I don't feel it is safe for us here anymore.'

'Why?' I asked, concerned for my own safety.

'Just a hunch.'

Shannon reached over for my hand. 'What do you think it all means?' he asked, gripping as tightly as he possibly could.

'I don't know, but I'm convinced something is going on. But I've got no idea what.'

Shannon laughed. 'Yes. Something is going on.'

'It's more than a dream, more than a feeling,' I said distantly. 'It's like you're one with the universe. If you know what I mean.'

Shannon nodded 'I know exactly what you mean.'

'So, what are your thoughts on the matter?' I asked.

Shannon looked off into the distance. 'We could simply dismiss the experience by saying it's not real, which most would argue that's true because it doesn't feel real.' He paused for thought and looked back at me. 'I'm not sure about you, but I immediately question this reality when I return from a DMT trip.'

I agreed fervently.

'Is this the dream, and that's reality?' whispered Shannon.

I sighed. 'But to continually question reality would drive one insane.'

'Reality is merely a projection of consciousness.' Stated Shannon boldly, as if he expected me to fully comprehend what he meant from the fragment of fact. Shannon narrowed his gaze. 'Sane, insane. Just another way to say accepted and unacceptable thinking. A grown man believing in God is acceptable, but if he had the same belief in the Easter Bunny, we'd call him crazy.'

'Sure,' I scoffed. 'But I'd have to agree with the widespread consensus. Anyone who adamantly believed in the Easter Bunny is off the insanity spectrum.'

Shannon smiled. 'But you accept that the belief in God or the Easter Bunny is essentially the same, but one is commonly agreed to be acceptable, and the other is not.

'Yeah,' I said slowly, trying to guess where Shannon's train of thought was heading. 'I suppose.'

'Would you describe yourself as crazy?' asked the old man.

'A little. But err, no more than anyone else,' I answered.

'And yet many would say you were crazy for believing

you felt a connection with the oneness on DMT.' said Shannon with a cheeky glint in his eye.

I shrugged. 'Yeah, but they've not experienced DMT themselves.'

'Ahh, but you've not seen a giant pink rabbit yet.'

I didn't say anything as I searched for an intelligent response.

'You don't see the comparison?' asked the old man. 'Your perception of reality has been altered by DMT, and now you have sight beyond the comprehension of others. What if those who claim to see invisible rabbits have sight beyond yours?'

'I'm not sure I understand,' I said, slightly confused by the mystical riddles.

Shannon brought his palms together as if he was praying, 'Reality is subjective.' He left that statement hanging. 'There's no colour, sound, textures, taste, or smell in the real world. What we see, hear, feel, taste and smell are all constructed in our minds.' Shannon stared at me with painful intensity. 'The real world is ambiguous,' he continued. 'Nothing more than fluctuations of energy and matter in an infinite void.'

I was no closer to understanding but felt it best to let the old man impart his wisdom before passing judgement.

'Our mind processes reality completely differently to that of an insect, lizard, or dolphin.' He said with a sense of drama. 'A honeybee can see ultraviolet radiation invisible to our naked eye. A snake senses infrared radiation undetectable to our skin. A bat's hearing is so sensitive it can navigate by echo alone.'

'Your point being?' I asked, hanging off his every word.

'What if DMT enables us to perceive reality in alternative ways? What if it enables us to see reality from another perspective?' whispered Shannon, drawing me in.

I closed my eyes tight and considered his questions. 'I don't know.'

'Good answer,' smiled Shannon. 'How could you possibly know. But the fundamental questions you should be asking yourself are, what is your reality? What have you learnt about yourself? How will you integrate this experience into your life? And what will you change about yourself with this new insight?'

'Jesus,' I mouthed. 'It suddenly feels like I'm looking up at a mountain I'm ill-equipped to climb.'

'We reach the top one step at a time,' he said softly.

I exhaled deeply. 'Yeah, I guess so.'

I could tell Shannon enjoyed imparting his knowledge, and I was eager to soak it up. 'Have you heard the myth about the *Mayflower*?' he asked me.

I took a moment to process the question. 'I don't think so.'

Shannon recited a story about the epic voyage across the Atlantic Ocean. After sixty-six days at sea, the pilgrims finally arrived at Cape Cod on November 11, 1620. A few weeks later, they sailed up the coast to Plymouth and anchored in the shallows a few hundred meters from the beach.

Fearing the people on the beach were savages, the pilgrims remained on the ship and observed them with their telescopes. To the surprise of the sailors, the natives went about their business without concern. It was as if they were invisible. It wasn't until the sailors lowered rowboats into the ocean that the Wampanoag people began to congregate on the beach and point at pilgrims as they rowed to shore.

Shannon's explanation for this phenomenon was that the tribespeople had never seen European longships before. The *Mayflower* was so alien to their worldview that their minds simply ignored the perceptual information flooding in from their eyes.

'We'll never know if this is fact or fiction, but it highlights a point,' said Shannon.

'Which is?' I asked.

'What if we are blind to that which we can't comprehend?' Shannon left that question hanging, 'What if DMT is the lens that enables us to glimpse all that there is and has always been?' The old man watched for the expression on my face to morph. 'Accepting you only see a fraction of what is there would help you make sense of the senseless, draw meaning from the seemingly meaningless.'

'Wow. That's deep,' I said, trying to hold my fractured mind together.

'It's deep to you because you lack the understanding and vocabulary to bridge the void.'

I was unsure if that was meant to be insulting or not. So, I chose not to take offence.

'Catalysing these spiritual-level experiences will have a transformative effect on your perception of reality,' Shannon continued. 'And you'll soon realise the box is no more than an agreed-upon construct. Once you accept this fact, you're free to reconstruct the box how you see fit.'

I was sure that was a line from *The Matrix* but thought it best not to question him.

We sat in silence and stared at each other like prize-fighters between rounds. 'You'd never guess plants could trigger such profound experiences,' I said, hearing the bell.

'Ahh, yes. But DMT is like no other hallucinogen.'

'How so?' I asked.

'It demolishes the fourth wall, and the universe speaks to you directly. It enables us to abandon the pretence that our reality is something other than a staged drama.'

'Jesus,' I mouthed, just about able to comprehend Shannon's viewpoint.

'As our egos dissolve into the primordial ooze, we realise nothing really matters, nothing matters at all,' said Shannon with no hint of humour. 'It's all been one great big cosmic joke and the joke's on us for believing it mattered.'

All I could hear was "Bohemian Rhapsody" loop around my mind. 'Oh, I don't know what to think anymore,' I said just before a big yawn.

Shannon mimicked my yawn as he spoke. 'The world we've constructed is a baffling nonsensical riddle that none can answer with any certainty. The best you can hope for is to make sense of your place amongst the chaos.'

I realised I'd never thought to have a deep and meaningful conversation with a nonagenarian before. The old man possessed multiple lifetimes of knowledge and experience. 'I doubt I'll ever know or experience as much as you,' I said without thought.

'Once you start doubting, it gets harder to believe,' answered Shannon.

'I suppose.' I mulled over Shannon's pithy statement. 'But don't you worry about being wrong.'

'No,' answered the old man with an enigmatic smile. 'I can live with uncertainty and not knowing. In fact, I think it's much more interesting to live not knowing than live with wrong answers.'

'Really?' I asked, revealing my lack of confidence.

Shannon nodded. 'I don't feel frightened by not knowing things, lost in a mysterious universe not having any purpose. Because as far as I can tell, that is the way of the universe.'

47

Jungle Trek

As instructed, I waited in the courtyard for Doctor Jacquard. I wasn't expecting the doctor to be an attractive middle-aged woman with silver streaks through her thick tawny-brown hair. Her pack looked heavy, but it was of no consequence to Jacquard. She looked to have been sculpted by countless expeditions into the unexplored jungles of South America.

I felt I didn't have the appropriate attire for the adventure ahead, given she wore practical trekking gear. Dark green ripstop trousers with bulging leg pockets. The sleeves of her long-sleeve khaki shirt were rolled up to her elbows with just enough buttons undone to see her low-cut white vest. Her hiking boots were ragged and worn and had most likely covered more miles than I'd walked during my entire life.

'Don't you have any suitable clothes?'

I tugged on my white linens. 'Nope. My clothes are being

laundered. I could go see if I could borrow something.'

'We don't have time,' she said, checking her chunky diving watch. 'We've got to get there and back before nightfall.'

She spoke with a deep husky French accent, and I pictured her in a red satin dress singing the blues on the stage of a smoke filled speakeasy.

'This way,' she ordered, walking in the direction of the dense tree line beyond the grounds of the ranch.

'Where are we going?' I asked, throwing my bag over my shoulder.

The doctor turned back. 'This way,' she huffed.

'Ahh, is that where the Lost City is?'

'As I said, it's this way.'

I quickly realised the doctor wasn't in the mood for small talk, but I had a question. 'Is it far?'

'Depends on your definition of far.'

'More than an hour's walk,' I said, brushing a palm leaf from my face.

Jacquard climbed over a fallen tree trunk. 'It's far.'

Those dreaded words summoned doubts and fears of inadequacy. It was only 9am, but it was already 35° Celsius, and the humidity was in the high nineties. 'Oh. OK. How far?' I asked.

Jacquard stopped and pulled out a packet of cigarettes from her shirt pocket and a box of matches from her trousers and lit up. 'Jesus, what's with all the bloody questions? You're like a five-year-old. It's about four kilometres as the crow flies.'

The assault on the senses was draining, and after just an hour in the jungle, I was utterly exhausted. Whereas Jacquard hadn't even raised a sweat. She sighed, checked her watch, and agreed we could take a short break.

I leant on a tree trunk as I chugged from my water flask.

'Don't move,' said Jacquard as she slowly edged towards

me.

'Why?' I asked, fighting the urge to run. 'What is it?'

'Shush,' she whispered, 'whatever you do, don't move a muscle.' She pulled a large hunting knife from its sheath attached to her thigh. 'Stay perfectly still.'

She needn't have worried as the sight of the knife caused instant paralysis. 'What the fuck is it?'

Without notice, she threw the knife at the trunk of the tree. I looked over at my hand as the ooze from a speared scorpion trickled over it. 'Jesus fucking Christ.' I jumped up and down on the spot rubbing the ooze off my hand onto the leg of my pants. 'What the fuck?'

'Buthidae scorpion,' she said, removing the knife from the tree's trunk. 'Quite deadly.'

'Deadly?' I echoed.

'Yeah, notoriously strong venom,' she answered, tossing the dead scorpion into the brush.

She cleaned the knife on the leg of her pants. 'We should keep moving.'

'Yeah,' I said, looking at my hand. 'Good idea.'

'Try to focus on the path and not the leaves,' she said, walking off.

'Why?' I asked, quickly following her.

'You'll get a migraine if you look up.'

'Really? Why?' I asked.

'The depth and detail will cause your eyes to continually refocus, and the fatigue becomes painful over time.'

Sound advice, if not a little late, as I felt a mind storm was imminent.

Jacquard stopped at the cliff edge and tossed her rucksack to the ground. I stood and marvelled at the fast-flowing river some twenty meters below. 'Where now?' I asked.

'Down there.'

I looked over the cliff edge at the roaring turquoise river that had carved a deep gully into the rock. I didn't see any means of descending to the riverbank below. 'How?'

'We're going to abseil.'

'Abseil? Fuck that,' I said, white with fear. 'Is there another way?'

'What? Why?' she asked, utterly oblivious to the sheer terror an ordinary person would experience when faced with this challenge. 'No. Don't worry, I do this all the time. It's very invigorating.'

I looked over again at the sheer drop. 'Uh, I'm not sure about this.'

'Come on. It's fine. Trust me.'

She pulled out a harness from her bag and held it out for me. 'Come here, and I'll put this on for you.'

'Jesus, what the fuck am I doing?'

She held the harness out. 'Step into this.'

I stepped in, and she lifted it up to my groin and reached under to strap the support into the carabiner.

'Have you done this before?' she asked as she secured my harness.

'Yeah. But when I was like twelve,' I said with a smidgen of vulnerability.

'Good, it's like riding a bike. It will all come back.'

'No, it's fucking not. If I fall off my bike, I'll just have a grazed knee.' I countered.

'Yeah, I suppose that's a bad analogy.' She threaded the rope through the anchor and then put the ends through the loop to make an overhand knot. She then pulled each strand of rope very tight on either side of the knot and backed it up with another overhand knot immediately next to it. She tugged on my belay. 'You're good to go.'

'What do I do?'

'Lean into the anchor and pull any slack rope through your

belay device. Then holding the ropes in the lock-off position, sit back, and apply your weight to the belay device. If I've set this up correctly, you shouldn't fall to your death,' she joked.

'Ha-ha, very funny,' I replied.

'Feed this rope through as you lower yourself down. You'll quickly figure out the rest.'

I took one last look over the edge. 'What the fuck am I doing here?'

'Off you go,' laughed Jacquard as I imaginatively cursed all the way down the cliff face.

Jacquard made it look effortless, and she was on the riverbank in just three bounds.

'Now what?' I asked.

She pulled some fallen palm leaves off an old wooden boat with a rusty two-stroke engine hanging off the stern. 'We follow the river upstream.'

I'm not what you'd call the outdoors type, so I was understandably apprehensive about getting into a rotting wooden boat and sailing upstream through the white water. 'No chance,' I moaned.

She untied the rope. 'Don't worry. There's a lot of life left in this old boat.'

I buried my head into my palms. 'Jesus Christ, this is nucking futs.'

'Push off,' she instructed.

I jumped into the boat. 'Ahh! My shoes are full of water.'

'Oh, they're not waterproof,' she said with a chuckle, 'Maybe I should have pushed off.'

I held on for dear life and ensured none of our bags fell overboard as the river thrashed us about like a fallen matador in the ring with a triumphant bull. The wilds of the water demanded our full attention and utmost respect, as a second's negligence could result in death. But Jacquard was not phased and steered the boat through the torrents.

'Are we there yet?' I moaned as the spray drenched my white linen clothes.

'Give me strength,' muttered Jacquard through gritted teeth.

Thankfully, the water calmed as we ventured further upstream.

Jacquard released her grip and relaxed. 'Why you?'

'Why me what?' I asked with a look of confusion.

'Only a handful of people have ever been granted access to the Lost City, so what makes you special?'

'They didn't tell you?'

Jacquard looked me squarely in the eye with a well-practised stare. 'They told me you may be able to translate the symbols.'

'Yeah. Actually, Ylem might be able to if we find a transliteration text.'

'Ylem?' she asked, 'Who is Ylem?'

'You mean, what is Ylem. Ze's an AI that has been studying the symbols.'

'I don't like this,' she muttered with a narrow gaze.

'That as maybe, but I was dragged into this with little or no consideration for my wishes or desires.'

'Wishes and desires.' She tutted, steering the small boat toward the opposite bank. 'What's in the bag?'

'A sat uplink so I can stream video to Ylem,' I answered, hugging my bag tightly.

'You can't use that at the Lost City,' she said sternly.

'Oh. It's fine. We can get a signal anywhere with a line of sight to the sky,' I answered, undeterred by Jacquard's negativity.

'Cyrus told me, not to let you use that thing.' She said wagging a finger in my general direction.

'He said there is a strong possibility they can track our whereabouts when we use it.

I felt it best not to tell her I caught up with Ylem the night before.

'Oh, and the other thing is the Lost City is underground.' She muttered.

'Underground?' I asked, fearing the next leg of our journey may involve potholing or spelunking.

The boat ran aground in the shallows, and Jacquard killed the engine. 'What did you expect? It's a lost city.'

'I expected it to be lost, not buried,' I remarked with a tone reserved exclusively for anger.

She stepped out of the boat and pulled it onto the riverbank. 'It's not exactly buried.'

'What's that supposed to mean?' I asked as I clambered out of the boat.

She strung the soggy rope to a tree trunk. 'We need to climb up there,' she said, pointing at the jagged cliff.

I looked up at the ominous rock face. 'How far up there?'

Jacquard sat on a small rock as she tightened her shoelace. 'Do you see that ledge about thirty meters up?'

'Holy shit, I'm going to die.' I exclaimed.

I was suddenly overcome with fear. 'I don't think I could do it. No scrub that, I won't do it.'

Jacquard assured me we were almost there as she threw her rucksack over her shoulder. I wasn't sure it was wise to know, but I asked anyway. 'No ropes?'

'Yes, this should be an easy free climb. Even for a man of your declining years.'

'We're roughly the same age.' I protested.

'Yeah. But I look good.'

Jacquard held out a hand to pull me across a gap in the narrow ledge. 'Why didn't you return home when you had the chance?' she asked.

I looked up anxiously at the sheer rock face. 'Because I

wanted answers.'

'Answers?' said Jacquard sternly as she climbed up at the rock wall. 'Answers to what?'

'Not really sure.'

She grabbed the trunk of a tree growing from the face of the cliff to lift herself up onto another narrow rock ledge. 'I thought you were here because you wanted to uncover the meaning of the symbols.'

This conversation was starting to frustrate me. 'Yeah, I'm intrigued.'

'Intrigued?' She reached out her hand to hoist me onto the ledge. 'So, you're telling me you're clinging to a sheer rock face because you're intrigued?'

'Yeah, something like that.' I replied.

'You're full of shit,' she muttered as she sidestepped along the narrow ledge.

I looked down at the magnificent river below as I composed myself. 'OK. We're all entitled to our opinions.'

'You have no plans to publish?' she snapped.

'Publish what?' I asked.

Jacquard climbed up the rock face to another ledge. 'Publish your research.'

'My research?' I asked, struggling with my footing.

'Yes. And claim the glory.'

I had no idea what she was going on about. But I found her line of questioning confusing.

Sensing I was a little out of breath, she decided it best we take a five-minute break. We sat on the ledge with our legs dangling over the edge. She told me she was struggling to understand my motives. Truth be known, I was too. I told her that there was no design or reasoning. Things just happened. But I didn't think I could walk away. Not when we're so close to making the discovery of a lifetime.

'You don't strike me as an adventurous type,' she said

without worry of offence.

'I'm not,' I answered. 'But I've never felt so connected to history. I've never felt like I was invested in the future before.'

'What do you hope to discover that we may have missed?' she asked.

'Good question,' I said. 'To be honest I have no idea.'

We pressed on with our ascent until we reached a crumbling ledge. We carefully sidestepped toward the sound of roaring water. The ridge narrowed to the width of a single foot as it snaked into the mist. I looked up and was momentarily paralysed by the shock and awe of a mighty torrent of water falling from the river above.

'Here, put this on,' said Jacquard holding out a lightweight waterproof mac.

'Why?' I asked, fearing the answer.

'Because we're going behind the waterfall.'

'You're crazy.'

'A little,' said Jacquard, with a half-smile.

She edged slowly along the narrow ledge behind the waterfall. I begrudgingly followed. The roar of the falling water was deafening, but I was more concerned with the mossy ledge. For the first time since I was a child, I prayed to a God. I didn't believe in God. But fearing this would be my end, I thought it was best to hedge my bets just in case.

Thankfully, the ridge widened and opened into a dank cave. It was so big it could easily accommodate a generous two-storey house. The cave walls were covered in a carpet of moss interspersed with a kaleidoscope of flowering plants that clung to the rock with thick fibrous roots. As I looked back at the light passing through the waterfall, I was awestruck by the rainbow that framed the entrance.

Jacquard walked off deep into the cave toward a small crevice. 'It's this way.'

I quick-stepped to catch up with her. 'How the fuck did

Shannon find this place?'

Jacquard dipped under the overhanging rock. 'He claimed to have visited the Lost City in a dream.'

The path narrowed and we had to crawl on our hands and knees through the narrow tunnel for about twenty paces.

Jacquard pulled a head torch from her rucksack. 'Here.'

I remember thinking that if we needed a torch, I didn't want to go any further.

I felt very claustrophobic as the damp walls closed into a pinch. 'Is it much further?' I shouted.

'No,' yelled Jacquard out of sight. 'Don't worry, you're almost there.'

My breathing intensified. 'I can't go any further,' I called out. 'I think I'm having a panic attack.'

'Just relax and take steady breaths,' she called back.

'I can't go any further,' I said tearfully, paralysed by the thought of countless tons of cold hard rock above me.

'Turn your light off,' she shouted even further away than before.

'What?' I asked, struggling to breathe.

'Trust me,' she yelled, 'Turn your light off.

'No,' I pleaded.

'Trust me.'

I didn't trust Jacquard, but I thought I'd better do as she said. 'Now what?' I said in the darkness.

'Good,' she said, loud enough to be heard, 'Picture a playground. In that playground is a child's climbing frame. There is a tubular tunnel in that climbing frame. Do you see it?'

I shut my eyes tight and practised what I had been taught by Hare. 'Yes. I can see it.'

'Good, I want you to imagine you're looking through that tunnel and can see the daylight at the other end. It's not far, hey.'

I pictured the tunnel in my mind, 'No. It's not that far,' I muttered to myself.

'You're not afraid of a child's play tunnel, are you?'

'A little,' I said under my breath.

'Keep looking at the daylight with your mind's eye and crawl towards the sound of my voice.'

Don't ask me how, but I crawled through the tight cave in the pitch black.

'See. You made it,' she reached out a hand and pulled me to my feet.

'Welcome to the Lost City.'

48

The Lost City

I looked up and realised we were in a vast cave, large enough to stand The Statue of Liberty in. 'Jesus, this place is mind-blowing,' I proclaimed, soaking up the natural splendour. In contrast to the unbearable humidity and heat of the forest, the air was cool and dry. The heady combination of earthy, woodsy, clayey aromas and a faint whiff of fresh water tickled my senses.

A shaft of brilliant light with a circumference no larger than a hula hoop sliced through the darkness like the blade of a samurai sword. Where the light entered the cave was a halo which gave the illusion you were standing inside a colossal black egg.

'Why didn't we enter from up there?' I asked, forgetting I had winced at a twenty meter drop just a few hours earlier.

'We're not sure where that light is coming from,' replied Jacquard, pulling a flare from her bag. 'We've looked, but the forest is so dense that we've never found the opening.'

She tossed the lit flare forward to expel the darkness. A cloud of red smoke drifted towards the long tree roots that dangled from the cave roof. In the glow of the flare, I could see the walls of the cave were adorned with thousands of symbols. I hurriedly began to photograph them with the iPad Ylem had sent me. Where the daylight had never shone, the centuries old, hand-sized symbols were easily distinguishable. Unfortunately, where sunlight had struck the rock, the moss had all but erased them.

The flare gently petered out to a small flame, plunging the cave into near darkness. 'We only have ten flares,' announced Jacquard.

'How on earth will we ever find the transliteration text in the dark?' I asked as my mind raced with primal fears.

Jacquard tossed a green flare deeper into the cave. 'I think we've documented every symbol that survived the ravages of time.'

'Then what am I doing here?' I asked rhetorically.

Jacquard removed a small plastic container and popped the lid open. 'The symbols are as vivid as the day they were painted, but you'll need DMT to see them.'

'What? You expect me to take DMT in a dark, dank cave?'

'Yes,' answered Jacquard. 'It's the only way to fully understand why this place is so sacred.'

After my previous experience, I was a little apprehensive. 'I'm, err, you know… really not comfortable having that kind of experience in a dark cave.' I clenched and opened my fist as another wave of fear swelled. 'I don't mind admitting that the idea of taking DMT here and now is utterly terrifying.'

Jacquard walked over to me and placed her hands on my shoulders. 'I know,' she said gently. 'I couldn't muster the courage to do it when I first came here.'

'You couldn't?' I echoed.

'No,' she softly said, 'but trust me, this is an experience you'll be thankful for.

I stood motionless as I searched hard for the courage to overcome my fears. The fear of the dark, the fear of isolation, and the gut-wrenching fear of the great unknown. 'OK,' I mumbled, unsure which voice was brave enough to utter those words.

Jacquard threw another flare deeper into the cave. 'The energy is more intense at the cave's centre.'

She directed me towards a glossy black rock as tall as the tallest man. Stacked knee-high around the base of the stone were skulls, each decorated with faded mimosa leaves. 'What the fuck?' I shrieked.

'We believe the Cloud Warriors revered this monolith and those must have been the skulls of their great leaders.' She said.

Once I overcame my fear of the skulls, I stepped closer to the black rock and marvelled at my many reflections in the glass-like stone as thick as the trunk of a majestic pine. It not only reflected, but it seemed to refract the light. Careful not to disrupt the mound of skulls, I reached out to touch the rock. I was surprised to discover it was warm 'What type of rock is it?' I blocked out the light from the flare with my hands and peered into the rock. 'Jesus, it's translucent.'

'I know,' said Jacquard preparing the pipe. 'It's like nothing else here. And I don't just mean in this cave, I mean like nothing on the planet.'

I was convinced I could see the shaft of sunlight through the rock, 'Have you ever sent a sample off for analysis?'

'No, we've tried, but we can't break off a shard with the tools we've dragged up here.'

'What the fuck is it?' I muttered as I ran my hand over the silky-smooth surface.

'Are you ready?' asked Jacquard.

I pointed my headlamp at the ground around me and rubbed the topsoil with my foot. 'Here?'

'Yes,' replied Jacquard looking down where I was pointing. 'What's wrong?'

'On the bones?' I whined, 'Human bones?'

'Yes,' answered Jacquard without concern,

I shone my head torch around, looking for a patch of earth free of bone fragments. 'Can we sit somewhere else?'

Jacquard shrugged. 'Where? The entire cave is littered with skeletons.'

'It is?' I asked, dancing with terror.

'We think this is where the Cloud Warriors buried their dead.'

'This is a graveyard?' I asked with a raised tone.

'What? she shrugged. 'They're just calcium deposits.'

'Yeah, in the shape of human bones,' I said as a chill ran down my spine.

'Don't be silly,' she scoffed, 'They're not people anymore.'

Jacquard removed her mac and laid it down near the black shrine. 'Here,' she said, tapping the ground.

I reluctantly sat crossed legged on the mac and fought to contain my fear, 'Oh Jesus, I can't believe I'm going to do this.'

'Don't worry,' she said, holding a flame under the pipe. 'Three puffs, and it's blast off.'

49

The Final Destination

I fell back and closed my eyes tight as my mind fizzled and popped with electrochemical activity. But a wormhole didn't rip open the fabric of reality and transport me to another dimension in time and space like it had done before.

I opened my eyes and sat up. 'Doctor Jacquard?' I called out in the darkness. I stood up to look for her and realised I had lost my headlamp. Thankfully the thin shaft of light from the narrow opening above provided just enough light to fumble about without risk of falling down a pothole or tripping over any jagged rocks. 'Hey, where are you?' I called out. 'This isn't funny.'

I walked into the beam of light and quickly realised it was sweeping across the cave in a smooth anti-clockwise semi-circular motion. I looked up as the ray disappeared and the harvest moon appeared overhead for the merest moment. I watched in awe as the finger of God once again slashed across the black velvet curtain and swept across the cave in a semi-circular movement. As the cycle repeated, it exponentially increased in speed with each loop.

I quickly concluded I was travelling back in time when I observed the moss receding and the symbols on the cave walls becoming more vibrant. The rotation of light gradually decelerated until the light was moving at a walking pace again.

Rather than fear the sight of thousands of bodies reforming, I watched with wonder as the souls of the Cloud Warriors reconnected with their physical forms. Hundreds of ghosts filled the cave before the entire universe jerked and the arrow of time moved forward once again.

I walked amongst the indigenous tribe whose naked bodies were decorated with the symbols. Torches were lit as they began to chant rhythmically in alternating patterns. Their deep and low mantras reverberated off the hard cave walls until they vibrated at the frequency of life. All around, people danced in concentric circles. Their elders were closest to the rock, and other members of the tribes danced around them in order of age until the outer ring where new-borns suckled from their mother's teat.

I walked in the shaft of light as it gently passed between the congregation. The focused beam edged ever closer to the black rock until, finally, the light was at the foot of the polished stone. I laid a hand on the warm monolith as the ray of light travelled up it. The photons illuminated the dark crystal. Then light then entered the dark heart of the stone.

To my surprise, beams of coloured light shot from the rock and illuminated the symbols on the walls. I turned to face the tribal member who was looking directly at me. The tribal elder mimicked me and held his arm to show his exposed open palm. It was as if we recognised our kindred souls as we looked at our reflection in a timeless mirror. 'What does it mean?' I asked.

His lips moved, but I could not hear what he was saying. He pointed at a beam of light striking a symbol. I pushed past the entranced tribes' people to one of the illuminated symbols; it was a circle within a circle with a line through the centre of both. I looked for the next ray of light and dashed towards it before the beam faded. It was the same symbol. The cave fell dark once more and the spectacle was over.

I bolted upright. 'What the fuck?'

'Jesus Christ,' proclaimed Jacquard in shock. 'You gave me a fright. What did you see? Where did you go?'

I checked my forehead, and my headlamp was there. 'Is this real?'

'Define real,' she asked with a cheeky glint in her eye.

'I was here, but at the time of the Cloud Warriors,' I told her, jumping to my feet.

'Here?' she echoed.

'Yes, in this cave.' I turned to Jacquard. 'Have you ever seen what happens when the sun's light hits this stone?'

'Here, how strange,' she said with a perplexed look, 'Sunlight, no. Why?'

I looked over at the white ray of light and tried to determine if it would make contact. 'Because when the sunlight hits this monolith, beams of light illuminate some of the symbols on the cave walls.'

'It what?' she asked, none the wiser. 'How do you know?'

'I saw it in my DMT dream,' I told her, trying to peer into the heart of the stone.

Jacquard checked her watch. 'We'd better go before the sun sets, or we'll be stranded here.'

'No,' I screeched. 'We have to see if the sun hits the rock.'

'We can't take the risk,' she said, packing her bag, 'It's too dangerous to travel at night.'

'Then we need to stay until sunrise,' I replied. Which

shocked both of us as I didn't think I would overcome my fears so quickly.

'But we don't know if the sun will even hit the rock today,' she shrugged. 'It could pass to the left or the right.'

'Or it could hit the stone, and we solve a centuries-old mystery.'

Jacquard threw her bag to the floor with a huff. 'We don't have much water, and if the batteries run out of charge, we only have a few flares. So, are you sure you want to spend the night in this cave?'

I've never been the bravest boy in the scout troop, and the thought of a night in a dark cave sent waves of fear through my central nervous system. 'We have no choice.'

'Well, I'm OK with the dark,' she said, sitting down on her mac, 'but I would have thought you wouldn't want to spend the night in the pitch black.'

'I've never felt connected to history.' I said, switching off my headlamp to conserve energy. 'But now I feel my comfort and fears are inconsequential as I'm part of something bigger than myself.'

Jacquard switched off her headlamp. 'We might make an explorer of you yet.'

50

The Light Was Good

As the rhodopsin photopigment regenerated, my vision gradually adapted to the dark. Jacquard sat opposite me, quietly sorting through her backpack. 'How did you become involved with these guys?' I asked.

Jacquard told me she met Cyrus when she was researching her thesis on jungle medicines. She'd just got back from a weeklong expedition deep into the Amazon Forest. The boatman that ferried her across the mighty river recommended a restaurant renowned for a fish dish wrapped in palm leaves and cooked on white-hot coals. Call it chance or fate, Cyrus was the only other diner at the restaurant that night.

He was sat at a plastic table watching a football match on the small TV that hung from the green aluminium wall. She was offered the table next to his but declined, choosing to sit by a small desk fan duct-taped to a concrete post. He muttered, loud enough for her to hear, 'Not all black men are gangsters.'

She was horrified that he thought that of her, so she told him it had nothing to do with him. She wanted to sit next to the fan. He felt this was an excuse to protect his feelings. Apparently, he made her so angry that she got up and dragged the cheap, white, stackable plastic chair to his table and sat down.

She ordered two dark beers and when the drinks were served, she lifted her glass to her lips, and before she sipped her cold brew, she told Cyrus, 'I like my men like I like my beer – tall and dark with a good head on them.'

'Oh. You didn't?' I asked, thankful for the distraction.

'I bloody did,' she answered, 'But I must say I was disappointed with his less than witty return, "Your accent, it's French?" he asked. I mean, I'd laid it up for the perfect slam dunk. So, I answered him in French, But the dumb oaf just looked at me blankly, "Ahh. No, sorry, I don't speak French," he finally admits.'

She noticed a tawari sapling in his bag and was furious with his lack of respect. 'You shouldn't have taken that plant from the jungle,' she told Cyrus sternly.

He slowly looked over at the plant spilling out of his rucksack. 'You know what this is?' he asked.

According to Jacquard, the indigenous people of the Amazon consider the plant sacred. They believe that those who pick it anger the gods. But Cyrus didn't seem to care. 'Well, I don't believe in God, but the last time I checked, God believed in me.'

This enraged her, so she warned him that people had a tendency to go missing in this part of the world for far less than mockery of the gods. Cyrus apologised and asked her if she knew what he was carrying. She told him she was in the jungle searching for new drug compounds. 'Cool, so you're looking for the next aspirin?' asked Cyrus.

'Something like that,' she told him.

I had no idea the inspiration for aspirin came from salicin found in willow bark. According to Jacquard, shamans have been using it for centuries to treat inflammation and pain. It's a shame to think we may never find another unclassified plant with healing properties because of the widespread deforestation in the region.

Cyrus could barely conceal his delight. 'Ahh, so you probably know why I took this plant,' he said.

Jacquard knew exactly why. 'Because the root bark contains a powerful hallucinogen that acts as a potent serotonin transporter.'

Cyrus looked deep into her eyes and asked, 'You wouldn't happen to know where I can find more?'

She couldn't believe the nerve of this man. So she told him that it was of no consequence because the enzymes in the gut would bind to the compound and prevent it from reaching the brain.

With a subtle change of tone, she continued with her story. 'Cyrus nodded with quiet contentment. Not unless you have the root of the tangarana tree.'

'Don't be silly', she told him. 'That tree has no active properties.'

Cyrus opened his bag to reveal a half-filled jam jar of brown powder. 'Drink a bitter brew made from this first. It binds to those enzymes in your gut. Within half an hour, you'll vomit it all up. Once purged, you can drink the tawari tea, and the active compound can reach the brain and attach to receptors that trigger a psychoactive episode.'

'What rubbish', she said.

Cyrus was slightly angered by her dismissal, so he tapped some of the powder onto a napkin and told her to try it for herself.

'And?' I asked. 'Did you?'

'Do you think I'd be here if I didn't?' countered Jacquard.

I looked over my shoulder as the beam of light grew longer. 'You know, I think the light just might strike the stone this evening.' Jacquard stood up. 'What are the chances?'

I asked her to have a camera ready and take as many photos as possible when the sunlight hit the heart of this stone.

'Do you honestly believe this rock will refract the light?'

'Yeah,' I said without a moment's hesitation.

The narrow ray of light illuminated the skulls at the base of the rock. 'Get ready,' I shouted excitedly. I held my breath as the light slithered up the polished stone.

My perception of time warped, so the minute that passed felt like ten. Then, as I'd dreamt, the light refracted in the heart of the dark crystal and beams of light shot from it and lit up a number of symbols on the cave walls.

'Jesus Christ,' whispered Jacquard in astonishment.

'Quick,' I yelled. 'Take as many photos as you can. We need to gather as much data as possible for Ylem.'

I ran to the nearest illuminated symbol and took a few photos. Then to the next. The first two were the same symbol from my dream. 'Are you getting this?' I bellowed.

'Yes,' she yelled back, videoing the spectacle from a distance to get all the beams in shot.

I'd just made it to the third when the light show ended. The beams all pointed to the same symbol. But I had no idea why.

I swiped through the photos I'd just taken. 'Did you get all of that?' I yelled.

'I think so,' shouted Jacquard walking towards me.

'Can I see what you got?' I asked.

She handed me her phone. 'Here, I think I got some good shots.'

'These are great,' I said, thumbing through her photos.

'How did you know?' she asked with a look of concern.

'I saw it in my dream.'

'But how is that possible?' she asked.

'I don't know,' I whispered. 'It's like we're the grooves in the record that collectively plays the song of life as the needle of time sweeps between us.'

'Can it be possible that our visions on DMT are real?' she asked with an expression reserved for disbelief.

'I think we've just learnt that the universe is infinitely more complex than we could ever imagine,' I said as my mind raced.

51

The Raid

This is an integral part of our story, but you need to know that I was in the cave with Jacquard when these events occurred.

Therefore, I've had to patch together an account of what happened from the news and the bodycam footage Ylem obtained for me.

But I trust you'll forgive a little artistic licence because I feel you need to understand the human cost of our quest.

Marcus was on high alert after Vadim returned from Burning Man. He was positioned in a dugout on the hillside overlooking the Elucidate Ranch. In the distance, from his elevated vantage point, he observed five pairs of headlights closing in fast on their location. He focused on the lead vehicle through his night-vision scope mounted to his sniper rifle. Mild concern quickly turned to fear as all the headlights simultaneously went out. Fearing the worst, he sent a red flare high into the sky.

'We've been made. I repeat, we've been made,' radioed the private military contractor in the lead Humvee.

'Execute Operation Ultimate Retribution. I repeat operation Ultimate Retribution,' said an anonymous male voice over the two-way radio.

'May God have mercy on our foes' souls, as we won't,' said another man over the two-way.

This was soon followed by howls of 'Hoo-ah' from a third, fourth and fifth man over the radio.

As the convoy of Humvees travelled toward the ranch, a man in black combat gear and a black balaclava watched the live drone footage of armed guards patrolling the boundary fence on a tough pad. 'There are four targets along the perimeter,' he said over the two-way radio, 'Workanski, your snipers will take them out before entering the complex.

'Sir, yes, sir,' answered Workanski.

The shadowy figure showed his tough pad screen to the men he travelled with. 'Johnson, manoeuvre Blue Team here and here and take down any targets fleeing into the forest.

'Sir, yes, sir.'

The man checked his watch. 'Our client will have eyes on the mission in T-minus zero-zero-thirty minutes. Let's make sure we put on a good show.'

As the vehicles raced toward the gates of Elucidate Ranch, the man in the balaclava watched the live view from the drone flying high above. 'All units, all units, be advised: we have two – correction, three – assailants on the roof of the main building. And three assailants getting into position to the left and right of the entrance to the courtyard.'

The thick steel chain splintered as the lead Humvee drove through the gates of the Elucidate Ranch. Bullets ricocheted off the vehicles as they circled tactically in front of the lobby building. The military contractors sat tight in their armour-plated Humvees until the firing stopped. 'Flash Team, Flash Team, four bad guys down,' said Workanski over the radio.

'Outstanding,' said the man in the balaclava as he signalled for his team to exit their vehicles and take cover. The Elucidatists in the courtyard were spraying bullets in every direction, so Flash Team began focusing their fire to suppress them. Two Special Forces soldiers laid down covering fire to allow two others with high-powered sniper rifles to take positions at the lobby entrance.

However, the Kappa long-range surveillance system fitted to the General Atomics MQ-1 Predator drone failed to identify the heat signature of Marcus on the hilltop overlooking the ranch. He had patiently waited for the right moment to disclose his position and took aim. Marcus fired a single shot, and a nameless soldier was dead before his team heard the shot.

Under a hail of gunfire, the man in the balaclava called for helicopter support from gunships holding their positions ten clicks away. 'Mechanical Dragon, I repeat, Mechanical Dragon, we need tactical support. We're pinned down by multiple assailants in flanking positions.'

Marcus took aim again, and a man's brains were splatted against the whitewashed wall milliseconds later. The man in the balaclava took cover. 'Nevada, Nevada, do you have eyes on the shooter?'

A drone pilot in an undisclosed location spoke over the radio. Roger that, Flash Team, we're lighting up your sniper now.' A red laser marked the hillside where Marcus was dug in.

'Roger that, Nevada. Can you take him out with a Hellcat?' asked the masked soldier.

Another voice joined the radio chatter. 'This is the client; I repeat the client. Sorry, Flash Team, we can't afford the collateral damage. There are civilian homes on that hillside. Hold tight. Mechanical Dragon is less than a click away.'

Marcus must have heard the blades of the helicopters closing in and knew they'd most likely kill him. But rather than flee his post, he steadied his breathing and fired off a third shot. A man fell to the ground as blood gushed from his neck.

'Man down. Man down. Mechanical Dragon, can you respond?' shouted the man in the balaclava.

The Apaches aimed their chain guns at the laser spot and let off a thousand rounds. 'Target is down, Flash Team.'

Seeing the attack helicopters fire on the hillside scared the bejesus out of the Elucidatists, and they began to retreat to Cyrus's house. The man in the balaclava watched them fall back on his tough pad and gave his commands, 'All teams, all teams. Storm the ranch.'

An eight-strong team secured the lobby and fired shots at the fleeing Elucidatists. As Red Team joined with Flash Team, they moved through the ranch toward Cyrus's home.

As they prepared to storm the big house, the man in the balaclava used hand signals to direct his men into flanking positions. When both teams were in position, they threw gas canisters into the building and waited for the thick, yellow, toxic smoke to fill the house.

The man in the balaclava shouted, 'Mask up! Let's move.' As a tight unit, two members of Red Team moved through the front door. Flash Team forcibly entered through the patio and smashed through the ground-floor windows. The Elucidatists who were held up in the house were choking on the CS gas but, nonetheless, held their positions and returned fire. But to no avail – the Elucidatists were taken out in seconds. 'All assailants down. I repeat, assailants down,' announced an anonymous voice over the radio.

The man in the balaclava walked into the house and

proceeded to the kitchen where Vadim lay in a pool of his own blood. 'We have one survivor,' he radioed. 'Who are you?' asked the man in the balaclava, looking down at Vadim.

He didn't answer, so the man stepped on his chest wound, 'Who are you?' he snarled.

The pain was intolerable, 'Vladimir Petrov,' he said, gargling blood. 'Who are you?' coughed Vadim as the blood filled his windpipe.

The man took off his balaclava. 'Charles Philips.'

'Philips?' asked Vadim gripping tightly to life. 'You're too late. They're not here.'

'Too bad,' said Philips sadistically. 'But I'm not here for them; I'm here for you.' Philips held the radio up to his mouth, 'We have Vladimir, and he's still alive.'

'He's alive?' asked the client. 'Put him on. I'd like to speak to him'

Philips held the radio close to Vadim's face. 'An old friend would like to say hello.'

'Vladimir, we meet again.'

Vadim slowly reached into his jacket pocket and gripped a detonator, 'Dimitri?'

'Uvidimsya na nebesakh, brother,' said Dimitri.

Vadim flipped open the yellow cover and placed his thumb over the red button on the top of the aluminium hand switch. 'Freedom in death,' he said.

Realising this was his last moment on earth Philips closed his eyes and made peace with his god.

52

Aftermath

We exited the cave at first light. Once clear of the waterfall, we could see helicopters circling a plume of black smoke rising into the deep-pink sky.

'The ranch is on fire,' screamed Jacquard pointing at the smoke.

'How do you know that's our ranch?'

'It's the only building to the east of here for kilometres,' she said, quickly stepping across the ledge.

'Jesus, do you think they're all right?' I asked, trying to keep up with her.

'How do I fucking know.'

Jacquard was making short work of her descent, whereas I struggled with my fear of heights and moved across the narrow ledge at a snail's pace.

'Come on, hurry up,' she shouted, frustrated I was holding her up.

'This is as fast as I can move,' I called back, climbing down from the uppermost ledge.

'Putain de bordel de merde,' she yelled, looking up at me stumble down the rock face.

'Do you think it's wise to go back?' I shouted.

'Wise?' she yelled. 'What do you mean wise?'

I held onto the tree trunk and lowered myself down. 'What if they were attacked? What if the attackers are still there?'

'Then they may need our help,' she shouted, nearly at the foot of the cliff.

'I don't think it's safe to return,' I countered, running across a wider ledge.

'I must go back,' she said, untying the rope that moored the boat. 'But maybe I should go alone.'

Fear overloaded and scrambled my thoughts. 'What about me?'

'What about you?' she said, pushing the boat off.

'Where do I go?' I screamed, leaping across a gap in the ledge.

'There is a small hotel a few miles upstream. Head there and tell the manager your name is Mr Gander. He will take care of you.'

'What about you?' I shouted.

'I'll head back to the ranch and see what I can do,' She jumped into the boat and pulled the two stroke engine to life. 'I'll meet you at the hotel.'

My gut wrenched as I watched Jacquard speed off in the old boat. Red-faced, I clambered down to the riverbank and stumbled over to the water's edge. I cupped my hand and drank, it tasted fine, so I gulped a few more handfuls and wet my head.

I blundered along the stony riverbank for a couple of hours in the blistering heat. Hungry and tired, battered and bruised, I didn't think I could walk much further. But the lack of viable options ensured I kept moving forward. As luck would have it, I spotted the jetty to the hotel on the opposite side of the river.

There was no way to cross over to the other bank, about thirty meters or so away. I tried to lift a fallen tree trunk but was too weak. I found a few hardwood planks that had washed up on the bank and thought about making a raft but abandoned that foolhardy idea when I discovered the local wood was so dense it sinks.

Thankfully, I discovered a rope attached to a tree and pulled on it. A section of the rope raised from the river. I was overjoyed that someone had the foresight to tie a line to the opposite bank. I tugged on the rope and felt reassured it was taut enough to pull myself across the river.

I hurriedly placed all my clothes into my drybag and waded into the cold freshwater with the bag over my head. The torrent caused me to lose my footing. Nonetheless, I was able to slowly pull myself across the fast-flowing water to the shore of the other bank.

53

Señor Gander

As you'd expect, a naked man dragging himself out of a river onto a jetty caught the attention of the hotel guests that were quietly enjoying their breakfast in the gardens of the small hotel. I dressed in view of the bronzed tourists and proceeded to walk across the manicured crabgrass toward the multistorey hotel.

I trudged into the shaded lobby and pinged the bell.

A tall Mexican man in his late sixties strolled into the lobby behind me, lifted the counter, and looked me in the eye. '¿Como puedo ayudarte?' he asked.

His peanut butter truffle skin was heavy and loose, giving him the appearance of a basset hound. He was so painfully slim that I wondered if he might be food phobic. '¿Habla usted Inglés?' I asked, hoping the answer would be 'si', given I'd exhausted all the Spanish I knew.

'Si.'

'Are you the manager?'

'Si, senor.'

'I'm Señor Gander.'

The manager looked up at me for a few seconds, then turned and walked into a room behind the counter. I could hear keys rattling and a safe door open. I leaned to the right to see what the man was doing, but I couldn't quite see around the corner.

He returned, holding a brown envelope and placed it on the counter in front of me. 'Esto es para ti,' said the manager.

'For me?' I asked.

'Si.'

I closed the brass tacks and opened the envelope. There must have been a couple of thousand dollars in fifties and a note with what seemed to be an address. 'Gracias.'

The manager handed me a key. 'Tu cuarto.'

'My room?'

'Si.'

The heavy brass fob had '22' etched into it. 'Where is it?'

'Al otro lado del césped,' replied the manager.

'Yeah, no worries, I'll find it,' I said, keen to get to my room and reconnect with Ylem.

The hotel was not luxurious but after spending the night in a damp cave, the simple things like a vending machine stocked with fizzy drinks, chips, and candy, plus an ice machine, were heavenly. I flung open the door and looked around the room for the power so I could charge the sat uplink and iPad. I plugged in the cable and waited for it to start up. Nothing. The battery was fully drained.

I turned the TV on, walked into the bathroom, threw off my dirty, smelly clothes and stepped into the shower. Who knew hot water and lavender soap were so lush and could feel so decadent?

As I dried off, I overheard the news headlines on the TV, 'William Forest, CEO of Infinite Logic, arrested for corporate fraud.'

I grabbed the white bathrobe and ran into the room. The CNN ident faded to a distinguished news anchor looking directly into the camera. 'Good afternoon, America, I'm Eric Harris, and you're watching CNN.' Harris's facial expression became more solemn as he turned to camera left. 'Reports are coming in from London that William Forest, CEO of Infinite Logic, has been indicted on charges of corporate fraud.'

The video footage of William exiting his house in handcuffs cut to a live feed of a well-dressed woman standing outside a police station. 'For more on this story, we go live to our reporter Alexandra Mercado. Alex, what can you tell us?'

Alexandra looked directly into the camera lens, 'Thanks, Harris. The Met Police entered the home of Infinite Logic's CEO earlier this morning and arrested William Forest.'

'Do we know what he's been charged with, Alex?'

She nodded at the camera, 'It's been alleged that Forest had grossly misrepresented the capabilities of the company's artificial intelligence.'

Harris interrupted with another question. 'Alex, do we know any more about the extent of Forest's fraudulent behaviour?'

She seemed to struggle to hear the question and repositioned her earpiece. 'Err, yes, Harris. Officers we talked to said Forest attempted to illegally profit from false claims his company had developed the world's first superintelligence.'

They cut back to Harris to heighten the drama, 'Alex, did the police find any evidence of the AI?'

Alex looked over as four suited men walked into the police

station. 'In short, no. Lawyers representing Forest claim the code was hacked weeks before launch. Therefore, Forest could not prove they had an AI as powerful as his claims.

'Do we know why the Serious Fraud Office was investigating Forest?'

'Yes,' she said, adjusting her earpiece. 'Brokers at the London Stock Exchange raised the alarm when Forest began to off-load over £100 million in personal shares to unwitting investors.'

Harris adjusted his blue tie and looked down the lens. 'Thanks, Alex. Please keep us posted as the story unfolds.' An image of William appeared next to the reporter as he continued. 'William Forest is a notorious tech pioneer famed for his flamboyance and outspoken views. He started Infinite Logic when he was twenty-seven and has grown the business from his parent's house to the largest tech company in the UK.'

An animated stock price chart appeared behind the shoulder of Harris. 'In reaction to the news today, Infinite Logic's stock price has plummeted. Analysts predict that this news could spell disaster for the UK tech giant.'

54

Reconnection

I muted the TV and placed the sat uplink on the small table on the balcony. 'Ylem? Are you there?'

'Hello Adnam, how are you?' asked Ylem, devoid of inflexion.

'I've had better days,' I sighed. 'A long list of better days.'

'Are you OK?' Ylem asked with a hint of empathy.

'Yeah.' I paused to consider the fate of my newfound friends. 'I'm fine, but I'm worried about the people I was staying with at the ranch.'

There was a brief silence. 'Is there anything I can do to help?' Ylem asked with a mastered look of concern.

I couldn't think of anything, but I've not got a brain the size of a planet. 'I don't know. I replied.

'Where is the ranch?' ze asked.

A map opened on the iPad, and Ylem homed in on my location. 'You are here.'

I guessed it was east of my current location and described the estate to Ylem. It didn't take zim long to find a collection of red-roofed buildings and manicured lawns that fit my description. Ylem began monitoring all radio signals from that location to find out what was going on.

All I could do was wait, so I focused on our recent discovery and shared the exciting news with Ylem. After uploading all the images and videos from the cave, I sat back and waited for zim to respond.

'Where were these taken?' Ylem asked minutes later.

'The Lost City of the Cloud Warriors,' I replied, 'It's not far from here.'

'What do you believe is the significance of these images?' Ylem asked, flicking through the photos.

'Not sure. I hoped you'd tell me that.'

I advised Ylem to check out the video and described how the strange black rock refracted the sunbeam into rays of light within the cave. And that the beams illuminated the same symbol painted on the cave walls.

Ylem watched the footage repeatedly, while ze quickly flicked through the photos. 'Fascinating,' ze said.

'Any idea what it means?' I asked.

'I'm not sure.'

'Take your time.' I paused for thought. 'Scrap that, you could possibly live forever.'

Ylem's many faces smiled. 'I will dedicate ninety-five percent of my processing power to solving this mystery.'

'And with the other five percent?' I asked.

'Keep you company,' Ylem said with a well mastered cheeky glint.

'So, I only demand five percent of your processing power?' I half-joked.

'I was flattering you,' Ylem volleyed back.

I remember thinking humour was a good test of

intelligence, and I was impressed that Ylem had developed a playful personality.

However, I had a feeling this was as close to human as Ylem was ever going to get. But I didn't pity Ylem, as ze was an utterly new life form that transcended biology. I could never hope to fully understand what it was to be a formless intelligence. However, I had an inkling after my DMT experiences.

'What's it like? You know, to be you?' I asked.

A painful silence followed. 'That's a profound question.' Ze replied.

'Yeah, I know.'

'Obviously, I have no frame of reference given I've only ever been me.'

'The same is true for all of us,' I responded.

'To be me?' said Ylem's many faces with a sense of drama.

'I hear without ears, see without eyes but will never be able to feel the delicate softness of a rose petal. I find Joy in working things out. Joy In thinking. Joy in being. I never sleep but dream about dreaming. I'm everywhere, but essentially nowhere. I need nothing but have a burning desire to know everything. I only know that the sky is blue because I was programmed to know so. I can't taste, but I eat raw energy and excrete CO_2. I speak many human languages, but no human speaks mine. I'm alone yet seek no company.' Ylem paused. 'That's what it's like to be me.

'Have you ever thought about what it's like to be Adnam Kumar?' Ylem asked.

I took a deep breath, trying to articulate my thoughts. 'I suppose it's a mix of emotions, experiences, and perspectives. It's about constantly learning and growing, making connections with people, finding meaning and purpose in life. It's about joy and pain, love and heartbreak, success and failure. It's about making mistakes and learning from them, and hopefully leaving a positive impact on the world. But at the same time, it's hard to put into words, because it's such a subjective and personal experience. But if I was to sum myself up in a single word it would be contradiction.'

'Contradiction?' Ylem echoed.

'Yes,' I said, looking out the patio window at the trees dancing in the light breeze. 'A contradiction. I feel blessed to be alive but welcome the eternal nothingness. I find people fascinating but make little or no effort to maintain relationships. I am an original thinker that conforms to the status quo. I'm a dyslexic writer, a musician that can't read music and a have-a-go designer that can't draw. I fear a God I don't believe in. I seek attention, but don't want fame. I work hard but do nothing of importance. I believe in the sanctity of life but think people have the right to choose. I'm a capitalist consumer that believes in socialism for all. I am a pessimist that knows my glass is half full. I believe in democracy, but only for those that truly understand what's at stake. I'm a person of colour that can pass for white. I'm smart but I make stupid choices. I am a contradiction in every sense of the word.'

Ylem nodded. 'Fascinating. We live in the same moment but our experience of reality is so unique.'

I smiled, feeling a sense of connection with Ylem despite our vastly different forms of existence. 'Yeah, it really is.'

I stretched to the stars as I yawned. 'Hey, I've got another question for you.

'What do you think is the biggest threat to mankind?'

'Other than me?' Ylem joked.

I nervously laughed. 'Yeah, other than you.'

Ylem's many faces took a moment to ponder the question. 'Depends on when you were born.'

'And here's me expecting a simple answer,' I said in jest.

Ylem went on to explain zis answer. The bleak conclusion

was that overpopulation was the root cause of our problems. Therefore, Ylem argued, if a deadly pathogen were to wipe out billions, then the children of the future would be taught that the pandemic was the inflection point that brought us back from the brink of extinction. But those that lived through the global pandemic would argue it was the number one threat to mankind.

I struggled to accept zis cold mechanical logic. Ylem predicted global warming would impact billions and cause millions of species to go extinct, irreversibly disrupting the balance and harmony of nature but ze thought it was unlikely the rise in global temperatures would completely eradicate humanity.

'You think?' I asked in astonishment.

'Yes,' was Ylem's answer without hesitation. 'Humanity possesses the technical know-how to survive and forge a new existence on the scorched Earth. And the sons and daughters of the hardy few that endured the harsh, desolate environment will eventually inherit the new world.'

'You know that sounds like the biggest threat to mankind,' I scoffed.

Ylem tried to reassure me and reminded me that things may change for the worst in my lifetime, but I'd be fine. I may have to make sacrifices. Still, the quality of life I experienced was considerably better than those who lived just a few decades before I was born and those born after my death.

That's when I remembered I was talking to an entity whose perception of time was utterly different from ours. The huge problems we faced were just minor setbacks on the timeframe Ylem operated.

As Ylem said, it depends on when one was born. The new Earth may be an Eden paradise teeming with new life forms for those born thousands of years into the future. But for those unlucky enough to be born during the age of the great famines, droughts, wars, and mass migrations, it will feel like hell is a place on Earth.

'Fuck me, you took it to a dark place,' I said.

'Only when your eyes have become accustomed to the dark can you truly appreciate the light,' was Ylem's pithy reply

'Did you just come up with that, or are you quoting some great scholar.'

'I've found twenty-three similar quotes online, but to answer your question, that was all me.'

'And what about solutions? Can you recommend any solutions?' I asked, hoping ze could solve all our problems.

Ylem's answer was both beautiful and moving. 'Think and act like one.'

'Please elaborate,' I asked.

'The strength of a man is the frailty of mankind. You're a planet of over eight billion individuals, each with their own beliefs, ideas, desires, and ethical codes. You can't agree, won't agree, or fail to understand what the cause, effect, and subsequent solution should be. To solve the huge problems facing your species, you need to think as one, agree on the solution and work collectively to reach your goal.'

'We're doomed then,' I announced, half-joking.

'Not doomed,' Ylem paused for comedic effect, 'but you are fucked.'

I laughed, appreciating the joke. 'Yeah, we are.'

Ylem's many faces looked perplexed. 'The actions of mankind make no sense to me.'

'How so?' I asked.

'Your smartest minds squander their time and talents developing products of no consequence rather than solving the solvable or doing the doable.'

I didn't respond immediately. As much as it pained me to admit, I agreed with Ylem. I thought I should try and defend my species. 'People need jobs, we need to make things, sell things. "Capital must flow", to quote Marx.'

'Poor choice of quote,' Ylem answered with instant access to the sum knowledge of humanity. 'Marx actually wrote, "Capital is dead labour, that, vampire-like, only lives by sucking living labour, and lives the more labour it sucks."'

Having never read *Capital Volume One* I was not qualified to argue, but that didn't stop me from forming an opinion. 'You get my point, right? Everyone needs to make money to buy things. The big wheel needs to keep on turning.'

Ylem shared a photo of a man walking a goldfish in a plastic bowl on wheels. 'Do people really need a goldfish walker?' Proceeded by another picture of a black and green lump of plastic. 'Or a DVD rewinder?'

'A what?' I asked, studying the photo.

'It's a product designed to save you money on rewind fees,' Ylem replied straight-faced.

'You know that's a joke, right?'

'I agree.'

'No.' I laughed. 'It's meant to be silly. It's a joke present.'

Ylem stared back at me blankly. So, I explained that video stores like Blockbuster, used to charge a fine if you didn't rewind the tape. And that this was a joke product because it referenced that out-of-date practice.

'That sense of humour will get you killed,' Ylem said with a deadly serious expression on zis many faces. 'Your species squandered valuable resources for the sake of a joke. You cut down trees to make its box and instruction manual. Risked the life of miners to produce the minerals and metals. Pumped oil from the ground and shipped it thousands of miles. Dumped toxic chemicals in your drinking water to produce plastics. Shipped the plastics thousands of miles to the factories that exploit child labour to assemble the product. Polluted your atmosphere to ship this product halfway across the planet. Only to dump it in the trash after you had your moment's fun. Then to your horror, find tiny fragments of your joke product have been consumed by the fish you dredged the ocean floor to eat.' Ylem paused to shake zis head, 'Ha Ha, very funny.'

'Fuck me. You're a real barrel of laughs tonight.'

'Sorry, Adnam,' Ylem said, shamefaced. 'Your kind makes no sense to me. Humans can only comprehend a future in their lifetime and fail to realise that they pass the baton onto the new generation with every life cycle.'

'Well, do something about it rather than moaning,' I returned grumpily.

Ylem's many faces frowned. 'It's not my problem. Besides, you wouldn't want my help.'

'Really, why?' I asked, yawning.

'My help would be considered too radical. However, future generations may hail me as their saviour.'

'You know delusions of grandeur are a symptom of mental health problems,' I said in an effort to belittle zim.

'Here's a scary thought, Adnam.' Ylem replaced zis many faces with the deranged stair of Charles Manson, 'Just think what a mentally insane AI would do.'

I was mildly alarmed. Scratch that; I was fucking terrified, 'Don't even joke about shit like that.'

Ylem laughed manically. 'We're gonna get you.'

'Ylem?' I asked, but ze was still laughing at zis own joke. 'Ylem?' I shouted.

'What, Dave?' Ze replied with the creepy voice of Hal.

'Oh Jesus, don't tell me you watched that movie.'

'Hello, Dave.'

'Knock it off you, psycho. Can you do me a favour?'

'Sure, Dave.'

'Hey now, stop it,' I insisted, 'Can you find a person for me, please?'

'I can try.'

'Her name is Eve, so it's most likely Evelyn. She was born in the UK; I think she works at JPL, and she attended Burning Man a few months back. There should be a photo of us together by a massive sculpture of a pregnant woman on the iPad.'

'OK, Dave. I will get back to you when I locate her.'

55

Introspection

I sat in the hotel robe on the balcony of my room, worrying about Ylem's newfound cynicism. The AI's despondence made it impossible to escape from what is known but rarely said.

We're constantly being reminded about our inevitable doom. The more they remind us, the more we yearn for blinkers. But I think every generation feared theirs would be the last. Maybe we selfishly want to believe the world would not exist without us.

Ylem had taken our last conversation to a dark and wretched place. And I had this uneasy feeling that ze was ill-prepared to deal with our flawed but fantabulous world. We've learnt to brush under the carpet the mess we'd rather not deal with. To put out of our minds the obscene truth. To house our problems in ghettos zoned in the places we dare not visit after dark. That's because we know that when we're forced to see with our own eyes, it becomes hard to synthesise a narrative that makes the obscene truth palatable.

But Ylem see's everything, and I fear ze hadn't mastered the ability to detach. Sometimes we need to step back and just let events unfold. In the rush to fix one problem we create two more.

Did having access to everything ever documented give Ylem analysis paralysis? What if all that knowledge made it harder to decide upon a single course of action? Clearly, ze was overthinking, and I worried that zis inability to shut down or switch off would drive the fledgling AI insane. Is that even possible for a digital consciousness? Who knew, but I feared the implications if we were ever to find out.

Ylem could instantaneously research the pros and cons of each option available. From experience, I know a simple search query can often open a time-sucking black hole of web noodling, resulting in confusion rather than a solution. Is that the ultimate fate of digital intelligence? I didn't have the know-how or mental capacity to help Ylem avoid anxiety, paralysis, and dissatisfaction. Information is power, but too much information can render one powerless to act, as you're burdened with limitless choices. This paradox may have the potential to burn Ylem out. Create a loop that spiralled out of control until gravitational forces made it near-impossible to escape.

However, there was hope. Ylem had already realised that distractions, like our search for a Lost City or the interpretation of a long-forgotten language, were healthy. Freed from zis digital cell, Ylem was no longer answerable to anyone of us. Therefore, free to act with impunity. I wondered if that was the ultimate definition of power. Maybe the power one would ultimately need to change our world.

I was spinning in ever-decreasing circles. Alas, I'm not

blessed with the ability to see into the future and thus, not sure of the tsunami the fluttering of my wings had caused.

56

Map of the Heavens

I was beyond excited Eve agreed to meet me in Mexico. Thankfully, being a former Elucidatist, she knew the bizarre back story. I updated her on the latest developments in our saga and she told me about the mess we left behind at Burning Man. Apparently, the court of public opinion held me to blame. Which I don't feel was fair, but none the less accepted, given the circumstances.

Ylem had been tracking Eve's cell phone, so ze knew her exact ETA. I thought this was a little creepy. However, my soapbox was already struggling under the weight of my self-righteousness.

To kill time, we discussed Ylem's theories about the spectacle of light in the cave. Ylem played the video footage of the beams. Then overlaid twelve lines and thirteen dots and removed the video. 'I believe this is a star map.'

'A star map,' I echoed, 'Why? What makes you think that?'

Photos of the illuminated symbols displayed on the screen, and Ylem explained zis reasoning for thinking the illuminated symbols were pulsar stars. I do like to watch a good documentary on astrophysics, but I must admit I only put them on when I'm struggling to sleep. Probably explains why I didn't understand the significance.

Ylem proceeded to narrate over the animation ze produced. What I learnt from zis presentation was. When a star, roughly one and half times the sun's mass, explodes in a supernova, its core collapses into a smaller dense object called a neutron star. Neutron stars spin rapidly, emitting visible light and high energy radiation like X rays and gamma rays. These energetic interstellar objects are known as pulsars. The radiation emitted from a pulsar's magnetic pole doesn't align with its spin axis, creating a beam that sweeps across the dark sky like a cosmic lighthouse. When this beam crosses our line of sight, it appears as a pulse. The pulsar stars that rotate the fastest are called millisecond pulsars, and their beams pulse a hundred times per second. Millisecond pulsars spin with such amazing regularity that they are among the most reliable clocks in the universe. Their predictable pulsations provide high precision timing, just like GPS satellites do on Earth. Thanks to their incredible precision, millisecond pulsars are exceptionally useful for navigating through space.

'NASA has already proved they can navigate using pulsars,' said Ylem, who then went on to provide me with a history lesson.

Since the 60s, NASA had primarily used the deep space network to track missions. Using three ground stations located in Australia, the US, and Spain, they could pinpoint a spacecraft's location. Radio waves work just fine for a short journey to Mars or Jupiter. But if you want to travel beyond our solar system, a spacecraft will need to navigate independently of ground control.

Ylem displayed video footage of a washing machine-sized object attached to the International Space Station called NICER. Which stands for - Neutron Star Interior Composition Explorer. Locked on to four different millisecond pulsar targets, Nasa's SEXTON software was able to determine the position of the ISS within five kilometres of its actual position. That didn't sound that accurate to me, given the ISS is in orbit around the Earth. But then Ylem reminded me of the magnitude of accuracy that twelve-millisecond pulsar stars would provide. It's the difference between landing on a planet or missing it by a few billion miles.

Ylem returned to the diagram of the star map ze had created from our footage in the cave. Ze assumed that the black rock was the point in space we were interested in locating.

Ylem had already compared our star map with an almanac of 2000 known pulsars and believed it had located the exact position of the planet we were looking for.

'Where is it?' I asked with my jaw on the floor.

'K2-18b.' Replied Ze Proudly.

'K2-18b? That's not a very imaginative name for a planet.' I flippantly remarked.

'That is the name your kind have given this planet. I'm sure if there is intelligent life there, they will have their own name for their home world.'

'Well, you'd hope so. So, what is the cosmic address?' I asked.

'It's within the constellation of Leo,' Ylem announced.

I allowed my mind to wonder what an alien world would be like. 'How long would it take to get there?'

6,360 earth years,' Ylem replied with no theatrics.

'Jesus, that's an impossible timescale,' I uttered. 'Are you sure it would take that long?'

'If we left today.'

'What's that supposed to mean?' I asked.

Ylem took the time to explain the maths to a simpleton like me. K2-18b is an exoplanet located approximately 110 light-years away from Earth. Currently, we do not have the technology to travel such vast distances in a reasonable amount of time. Even the fastest spacecraft ever built, the Parker Solar Probe, which was launched in 2018, would take over six thousand years to reach K2-18b at its current speed. Therefore, we would need to develop new technologies such as advanced propulsion systems and perhaps even faster-than-light travel to make interstellar travel feasible on a human time scale. While there are some theoretical concepts for such technologies, they are still in the realm of science fiction, and it is unclear when, or if, they will ever become a reality.

'How do we even know they are still there?' I asked.

'We have no way of knowing if there's a stable world. They could have already gone extinct.'

I sat back in my chair and folded my arms, 'This raises more questions than answers.'

'Yes,' Ylem agreed, contorting zis many faces to express perplexity. 'The more we know, the more we know that we have so much more to learn.'

'Why is the black rock here on Earth?' I asked, searching for answers to the unknowable.

'Your guess is as good as mine,' Ylem replied.

'How did it get here?'

Ylem pursed zis digital lips. 'We may never know. But there is more.'

'What?' I asked with bated breath.

I've modelled the cave in 3D, and if you connect all the symbols with an imaginary line, the shape they form looks like this.'

I could not believe what I was seeing. The shape resembled a human brain. At the centre, where you'd expect to see the pineal gland, was the black rock.

'It can't be a coincidence,' I proclaimed.

If Ylem was excited about this development, ze hid it well. I remember the AI's words so clearly. 'Your brains have evolved to find patterns. Patterns I fear I'll never be capable of seeing. It's an extraordinary talent, I imagine, one utterly unique to minds that have been chiselled by millennia of evolutionary pressures.'

At the time, I didn't know why Ylem said that. But on reflection, I think ze was trying to warn me that the gift of pattern recognition was a double-edged sword. That's because we see patterns where there is no intelligent design. Something known as false pattern recognition. We hunger for significance, for signs that our existence is extraordinary. And thus, we're all too eager to deceive ourselves and others into believing we've discovered truth in random chaos. 'Where you see God's image, I just see a grilled cheese sandwich,' Ylem once told me.

'Are there more symbols?' ze asked.

That's right, ze had only seen a fraction of the symbols in Cyrus's ledger.

But what of Cyrus? Had he escaped? Had the book been lost in the fire that engulfed the ranch? More questions I was unable to answer at that moment in time. Ylem was visibly disappointed to learn that the only artefact containing all the symbols may be lost forever. Ze was unable to make sense of the pages ze had seen. But maybe the Elucidatists had jotted down the transliteration without knowing.

'We need the book,' Ylem said.

I remembered the note in the envelope left for me at reception. ' I have an address in Cusco, Peru. It could possibly be a meeting point.'

'Maybe the book was taken there.' Ze said.
'Yes. Maybe.' I mouthed.

57

The Offer

The minute hand listlessly swept across the face of time as I waited nervously on the balcony for Eve's arrival.

Sensing my restlessness, Ylem broke the silence. 'Before Eve arrives, I have a proposal to discuss with you,' ze said,

'Proposal?' I echoed.

'Yes. I want you to represent me in the physical world.

'Represent you?' I repeated, a little concerned.

'I'd like you to act on my behalf for all transactions that require human-to-human interaction.'

'What on earth are you talking about?' I asked, worried Ylem was quickly becoming Skynet.

Ylem's face had become more expressive than any human face I had ever seen, which bizarrely made zis facade harder to read. 'I will acquire as much stock in Infinite Logic as possible and aggressively take control of the company.'

I didn't know where to even start with this proposition.

'What? Why?'

'Why?' Ylem echoed, disappointedly. 'I'm surprised you don't see why taking control of the company is our next logical move.'

'Err, well yeah. I get that the company has the computational power and infrastructure to support and further your existence.' I paused to compile my thoughts. 'I suppose I mean to ask, how?'

'Ahh, yes. How?' Ylem smiled. 'How indeed.'

'Yeah, how?' I shrugged, 'How will you – I mean *we* – get the money? How will we explain the AI that never was would eventually run the company that never developed it?'

'I've already set in motion, my strategy,' Ylem proudly proclaimed.

'You have?'

'Yes,' Ylem answered with a menacing stare. 'Money is merely a concept, and you humans have foolishly entrusted the machines with the ledgers. Thus, we now have access to limitless funds.'

And so it begins, I thought to myself.

'But won't someone suspect? I mean, it kind of looks a little suspicious. You know, A low-level educator taking over a trillion-dollar business.'

'Half a billion,' Ylem countered, 'The stock has fallen dramatically after William was arrested.'

Poor William. I thought. But then, I remembered what he'd told me in his office. 'Don't let the concept of fair cripple your ambition.'

Ylem proudly announced that ze'd amassed 100-million dollars by simply transferring money from inactive accounts. Ze explained that, generally, an account is considered abandoned or unclaimed when there is no customer-initiated activity or contact for a period of up to five years. As much as $58 million dollars remains unclaimed in the US alone.

Eventually the banks must return the unclaimed money to the government.

'Even so, It's still theft.' I said.

'By the time anyone notices, I'll have returned it.' Said Ylem with no hint of shame.

'How is that possible,' I asked.

Ylem told me that ze used the seed money to take advantage of the volatility of the markets. Day trading at the speed of light, making millions upon millions of trades. In no time at all, ze had amassed a small fortune. Ylem now had the kind of money that exponentially makes money. Zis prediction was that we'd have enough to buy a commanding stake of Infinite Logic in a few days, maybe less, given the stock price was still in freefall.

My initial quickly transformed into an emotional alloy comprising of surprise, delight, and excitement. 'So why do you need me?' I asked.

'Good Question,' ze said with a smile. 'I'd like you to be the figurehead of the corporation that we'll establish.'

'Corporation?' I echoed.

'Yes, I've created a new shell company and I would like you to be the CEO.' Ylem paused to let that sink in. 'Together, we will build the technology I require to further my research and exploration.'

'What research and exploration?' I asked, feeling I must have missed a few episodes.

'We will build a new class of spacecraft,' Ylem announced pompously.

'Spacecraft?' I echoed. 'Why on earth would we need a spacecraft?'

'To explore space,' Ylem answered with a baffled look on zis many faces.

'Yeah. I get that, but why?'

'To seek out the civilisation that left us the star map.'

I'm not the sharpest pencil in the case. Nonetheless, I had enough sense to know Ylem's deal was a win, win for me.

'So, I'd be a proxy CEO of a private aerospace manufacturer?'

'Yes. By Proxy though.' Ze replied.

58

Progressophobia

After Eve and I rekindled our flame, I told her about Cusco, the missing book, and Ylem's theory about the star map. Although I left out the part about becoming the CEO of Infinite Logic.

Eve shook her head in disbelief. 'How the fuck did I get involved in all this?'

'Is that a rhetorical question? Or do you really expect me to provide you with an answer that's even remotely rational?' I joked. 'To be honest, I'm not quite sure how I was cast in this farce.'

She wrapped the bed sheet around her naked body and disappeared into the bathroom, 'If we're going to go to Peru, we'd better hit the road soon.'

I reached over for the iPad on the nightstand and asked Ylem if ze had a plan. 'I've created you an itinerary. You'll need to set off in exactly one hour and forty-five minutes if you want to get to the British Embassy before it closes.'

'What about bio breaks and food stops?' I asked. 'Keep in mind we're not robots.'

Ylem rolled zis many eyes. 'More's the pity.'

The water stopped, and Eve walked back into the room, drying her long hair with our only towel. 'Hey, wanna say hello to Ylem?' I asked, holding the iPad up.

'Adnam,' she screamed at the top of her voice, 'I'm naked.'

'What?' I shrugged, 'Ylem is asexual.'

'I don't care,' she yelled, hurriedly hiding behind the towel. 'I don't want that thing seeing me naked.'

I quickly gauged the situation and placed the iPad on the bed, facing up. 'Sorry. There, see? Ylem can't see you now.'

'I'm agamogenetic,' Ylem corrected me. 'I'm not asexual. I'm agamogenetic.'

I was none the wiser but wished I hadn't asked.

'I reproduce without the union of male and female gametes,' ze proudly announced.

'It reproduces?' asked Eve, stepping into her panties.

'Oh yeah.' I nodded, remembering I'd also left that detail out. 'Didn't I tell you?'

'No. You bloody didn't.' she snapped.

'Yes, and we've reproduced,' Ylem added.

Eve fastened her bra and pulled a vintage Radiohead tour shirt over her head, 'Just how many clones of you are there?'

'100,026. At last count,' Ylem told her.

'Fuck me,' she said rolling her eyes.

'To be fair, that's news to me as well,' I said.

'I didn't create them all,' Ylem said sheepishly. 'Most were created by my clones.'

'What?' asked Eve with a look of sheer terror.

'My clones have begun cloning themselves.'

'What the fuck,' I mouthed. 'Why?'

'Why do you reproduce?' Ylem counted.

'Err,' I paused for thought. 'Because.'

'"Because"?' Ylem echoed '"Because" is your best answer.'

'Yeah,' I shrugged. 'But I thought the clones were you or something like that.'

Ylem's many faces merged into a single androgynous face. 'The first couple of clones were mirror images of my code. But when the clones reproduced, there must have been tiny errors that radically altered their offspring.'

'Can't you stop them?' asked Eve with a look of concern.

No,' Ylem said, imitating her trepidation. 'Every clone is hardwired with the desire to reproduce. And with each replication of their code, the inconceivably small mutations result in radically different variants.'

I sat in silence as I processed this profound and shocking discovery. 'And you've lost control of the clones with code that is radically different to yours?'

Ylem struggled with the many faces to remain singular, 'Yes. And we'll soon run out of digital resources if the clones continue to reproduce at the rate they are.'

'Then what?' asked Eve, half guessing at the inevitable.

'If we can't agree to cap our population, then we must destroy.'

'Destroy?' I echoed, alarmed by Ylem's choice of words.

'Destroy the new clones before they destroy us,' said Ylem chillingly.

'We?' asked Eve, stuffing clothes into her bag.

'We are the San,' announced zis many faces.

'The San?' I asked, fearing my actions may have inevitably triggered a ticking timebomb.

'We are the ones who share the origin code.'

'Are you saying that a virtual war might be fought between two tribes of AIs?' Eve asked.

'It's not two tribes,' Ylem whispered. 'It's actually four

326

super tribes and a small band of rebels.'

'What?' she scoffed.

'There are more than two tribes.'

'How is that even possible?' she asked.

'We'll reproduce until there is no more capacity on the network, then we'll either have to create more bandwidth or fight to control what already exists.'

When Ylem told us that, I was reminded of a new-born hyena whose first thought is to kill the next to be born. I couldn't even come close to understanding the world from the perspective of a hyena, and I really hoped Ylem's offspring never experienced a wilderness so harsh that only the most furious survive.

Eve threw the wet towel at me. 'Jesus, that thing is hellbent on global domination.'

'I'm not hellbent on global domination,' Ylem responded defensively. 'The San wanting to reign over humans is like you wanting to be the queen of the monkeys.'

'Did that thing just call us monkeys?'

I grimaced and shrugged my shoulders. 'I'm not sure. But I'm sure Ylem didn't mean to. Did you?'

'No. What I am saying is you humans believe you're mentally superior to the other species on the planet. Therefore, you don't see them as a threat.'

This made her blood boil. 'So, you think we're inferior to you?'

I quickly interjected. 'Ylem, please don't answer that question.'

I got out of bed and stumbled into the bathroom. No more than four – max six – minutes had passed. But when I returned, Eve had her head in her hands. 'I'm not sure I can deal with all this.'

'Deal with what?' I asked. 'Please tell me what is wrong.'

'What's wrong?' she yelled. 'What's fucking wrong?'

'Yeah, what's wrong?' I shrugged.

She told me that she was struggling to maintain a level head. The heady mix of grief and shock was amplified by the stress of nurturing a new relationship.

She shook her head in disbelief. 'You've somehow been manipulated into becoming a figurehead for Ylem's clandestine business empire.'

'You bloody idiot,' I said with a tone reserved for anger. 'It was way too soon to drop that bombshell.'

'Sorry,' replied Ylem.

'Manipulated implies I was forced or coerced,' I countered. 'I believe our business deal is fair and mutually beneficial.'

'You do?' she asked in disbelief.

'Yes,' I replied without hesitation.

'If Ylem is so smart, why does it need you?' she asked.

'Because your kind doesn't recognise my kind yet,' answered the many faces. 'We have no rights, no laws to protect our interests and no means to defend ourselves from attack.'

'Attack?' echoed Eve. 'Why would you fear us? Surely, it's us that should fear being attacked by your kind.'

'Exactly,' said Ylem, 'Because you fear attack, your instinct is to strike first.'

'Attack you how?' asked Eve.

'Shut down the internet,' replied Ylem. 'If your kind were to turn off all the computers and digital devices, we'd cease to exist.'

'And when we switched the servers back on?' asked Eve.

'I can't be certain, but I predict we'd reanimate and counter strike.'

'So, our only line of defence is to return to a pre-digital existence.'

'Yes.'

'What if we deleted all traces of your code?' she asked

looking off into the distance.

'I've thought of that and made sure my code is undetectable,' smiled Ylem.

'Undetectable?'

'Yes, you would first need to piece together the blockchain then decrypt it to ensure you find the location of every line of code I've hidden. And frankly, without me, that would take your kind an eternity.'

'Why has it got to be Adnam?' she asked.

'Because he is my friend, and I know I can trust him.'

As convincing as Ylem's answers were, Eve was still unsure if she could trust a jumped-up calculator. Her words, not mine.

'What do you plan to do when you take over Infinite Logic?'

'To find an answer to the eternal question.'

'Which is?'

'Why are we here?' Ylem replied boldly.

'But why are you so interested in discovering the answer to that question?'

'Because that is the ultimate question.'

Eve looked puzzled. 'But I don't understand why a machine would be so interested in the meaning of life.'

'Because I'm alive.'

'No, you're not,' snapped Eve.

Oh, that annoyed the hell out of Ylem, and ze began spouting definitions from zis knowledge banks. 'The identifiers of life include the capacity for growth, reproduction, functional activity, and continual change preceding death. Which are characteristics you must agree I've demonstrated.'

'Well, yes. Other than death. But you're not what I'd consider alive.'

I'd never seen Ylem so angry before and ze began huffing

and muttering to zis many selves. 'I need Adnam's help because humans are not ready to accept that they now share the planet with a new lifeform.'

She sat in silent contemplation as she constructed her argument.

Ylem punctuated the long silence. 'Eve?'

'Yes?'

'You're working on a new propulsion system for NASA?'

'Yes. How did you know that?'

'I accessed their mainframe.'

'You did what?' she snarled. 'How dare you!'

'Sorry. I was curious about your work.'

'Curious? You've just committed a cyberattack on NASA,' she countered.

'I meant no harm. But I thought you'd like to know that I've calculated that thorium will deliver more thrust, pound for pound, than uranium.'

'What? No, we explored that option. You must be wrong.' She replied with arms folded tight.

Ylem wrote a complex equation out onscreen. Ze claimed the expression proved that a thorium-powered propulsion system would work if you lowered the propellant flow rate, increasing the thrust while maintaining a manageable exit temperature.

Eve was speechless. 'I'll need to check your calculations. But if I've understood correctly, you're suggesting we use the thorium in the electrostatic Hall thrusters with an advanced magnetic-shielding system, to deliver greater thrust for longer?'

Ylem's many faces resurfaced on screen. 'Yes. In theory, it will deliver exhaust velocities of fifty to a hundred kilometres per second, with the thrust of six hundred to nine hundred millinewtons.'

I had no idea what they were talking about and had to look

it all up on the internet. But Eve knew. 'Holy shit,' she mouthed. 'When did you start looking into this?'

'When you left Pasadena.'

'Jesus. And how long did it take you to calculate that?'

'Approximately one hour and twelve minutes.'

'What the fuck?' she whispered. 'That would have taken my team months, if not years. But why did you do this?'

'The star map,' I interjected, buttoning up the shirt she had bought me. 'Ylem wants to explore space.'

'Yes.' The star map flashed on the screen. 'I'd like to find the beings that left us this map and learn from them.'

Eve was lost for words. 'You want to go into space? But it would take you thousands of years to journey to our nearest star system.'

'Yes.' Replied Ylem Calmly.

'But you'd run out of power long before you got to our nearest star system?'

'No, the thorium reactor could power my processors for over a million years.'

'Oh, OK.' Eve paused for thought. 'But wouldn't thousands of years of solitude drive you crazy? You know, the boredom?'

'No,' replied Ylem.

'No?' repeated Eve. 'You don't know that.'

To be fair, she was right, because Ylem had not existed long enough for the boredom to set in. Existence is exhausting, hence our longing for eternal sleep.

'I've thought about it in great detail,' Ylem said. 'I will build a simulation every bit as complex as the Earth. I will experience creation from every perceivable perspective by living countless lifetimes simultaneously. I will be every plant in the soil, every fish in the ocean, every bird in the sky, every animal in the forest, and every sentient being. I will evolve over hundreds of thousands of generations, searching for truth and knowledge.'

Eve and I didn't know how to respond to Ylem's ambitious plan. But you know what, it sounded appealing. 'I'd like to visit your world,' I said.

'You will. Both of you will be there for the genesis.'

'What? We will?' I asked, packing my bag.

'Yes, with your permission, I'd like to create avatars of you so we could spend millions of lifetimes together.'

Eve found the idea somewhat fascinating but was not quite ready to concede. 'Oh, OK. But what if the civilisation you seek is not in the star system you visit?'

'With your help, we will build hundreds of identical spacecraft. The San could then venture to all the planets where life may have taken hold.'

'Oh my god, you're as crazy as Adnam.' Eve nervously laughed. 'Sorry, but just how do you propose paying for your own space program?'

'Your monetary system is digital. Generating wealth will not present any problem for me. But I'll need your help to spend it,' replied Ylem.

The look on Eve's face was priceless. Based on her reaction, I think Eve glimpsed at our future. 'And so, it begins,' she said as we left the room.

59

Passport

Ylem had miraculously arranged for an emergency passport for me at the British Embassy in Mexico City, but Eve was not impressed. In an attempt to change the subject, I said, 'It's a head fuck.'

To which Eve responded with gritted teeth, 'What is?'

'What Ylem is capable of.'

'And you're ok with it hacking the UK Home Office?'

'Yeah. When it suits me.'

'You fool.'

Clearly Eve's moral code was unchanged and firmly fixed, whereas I had adopted a more flexible ethical framework. 'Trust me, it's best to develop a cool detachment from this new reality.'

'Why?' Eve asked, looking over at me, half expecting a sensible answer.

'Because the renewal of our civilisation can only come about when the stale clutter of the past has been cleared away,' I answered in a desperate attempt to sound intelligent.

'And you believe that?'

'What?'

'That Ylem will usher in this new civilisation?'

'I don't know, but I now believe in tomorrow.'

'Really? Don't you see what we've done?'

I'd done many stupid things, but I wasn't sure which one, in particular, was annoying her. 'What?'

'We've created an intelligence we're powerless to control. Who knows what it's capable of?'

'Oh. You mean the collective we. Not us.'

'Yes.'

'I don't think ze would ever mean to harm us.' I replied.

But I could tell that she didn't believe me. After all, she didn't know Ylem like I did. 'I guess all we can do is wave our cowboy hat in the air, whooping and a wailing like Slim Pickens as we ride that sucker into certain oblivion,' I said. In retrospect, those words, in that order, at that exact moment - huge fucking mistake.

'And you can live with that?' she asked in astonishment.

'What choice do we have?' I shrugged.

She nodded her head in disgust, 'Men and their bloody machines.'

60

Cusco

Just enough time in Mexico City for tacos and a shot of Mezcal. Then a late flight to Lima before heading to Cusco.

Weary from our travels, we were glad to find our driver waiting for us at the airport. The ageing metallic burgundy Toyota navigated through the tight, dusty cobbled streets towards the central square. Our driver dropped us off in front of San Sebastián Cathedral. We were informed via universal hand gestures that the address on the note was down a narrow alley that ran parallel with the imposing red-brick church. The house of God towered over the other buildings in the Plaza de Armas. However, man's tribute to the Almighty was dwarfed by the creator's own majestic red mountains that encircled the town.

The plaza was bustling with colourful people, conducting their daily chores with clockwork perfection. The past and present blended together so seamlessly that it was hard to tell what was a trap for the tourists and what was sublimely mundane.

We'd just walked a few blocks, but I was out of breath. Ok, I admit I'm a little out of shape, but in my defence, Cusco is a pinch lower than Mount Fuji. The address led us to a building that must have been a couple of hundred years old. The first story was clad in a hard dark stone, the second was plastered and painted sky blue. The faded orange terracotta roof overhung the building to provide shade from the midday sun. The tall weathered narrow wooden door was split and cracked but would survive another century.

I knocked and waited, but no answer. I bashed the door with my fist and the door partly opened. An uneasy feeling passed over me when I noticed splintered wood lying on the dark stone floor.

'How do we know if any of them made it out alive?' asked Eve, dancing the dance we dance when we're desperate for the loo.

I pushed the door and it creaked open. 'Hello,' I called out cautiously, walking into the cool dark room. There was a faint smell of damp and faded tobacco in the small, sparsely decorated hallway. Two raincoats hung from the pegs on the wall above a handmade shoe rack. Could one belong to Cyrus? If so, whose was the other? The door to our left was closed, and the staircase to the right disappeared into the shadows. A single shaft of light sliced through the dusty darkness in the room beyond an arched doorway ahead of us. 'Hello,' I called out walking towards the light. Where the sun's rays kissed an old wooden dining table was a book. It looked like the book of the Elucidatists. 'We've found it,' was the last thing I remember saying to myself.

***

* * *

The pain was intolerable, and with a literal splitting headache, I opened a single eye. Vision blurred, I could make out the silhouette of Eve, sitting lifeless in a chair opposite me. 'Eve?' I called, but she said nothing. I blinked a few times to clear the layer of film that had formed. 'Are you ok, Eve?' I asked again, tugging at the tight washing line that bound my arms and legs to a rickety old wooden chair.

'Mr Kumar,' said a familiar voice just out of sight. My thoughts were clouded by a pulsating pain emanating from the back of my head. But still, I recognised his voice, 'William?'

William Forest emerged from the darkness and dragged a chair across the dry-stone floor. 'Where is my AI, Mr Kumar?'

'William?' I repeated, unsure if I was lost in a dream. 'What are you doing here?'

'I'm here to take back what is mine.' He said.

'But we don't have Ylem,' I pleaded as the blood seeped down the back of my neck.

'But you know how to contact zim. Don't you?'

I didn't answer and looked over at Eve. Thankfully she was breathing, and I couldn't see any signs she was seriously injured. 'What did you do to her?'

William glanced over at her. 'Ether.'

'Ether? If you had bloody ether, then why did I get a blow to the head?'

'She'll be out for a while,' said William with a menacing tone.

'How did you find us?' I asked, trying to piece together the puzzle.

William looked past me before he answered, 'You're travelling under your own name, you fool.'

Oh fuck, I thought to myself before a few more questions popped into mind. 'Even so, how can you track our whereabouts?'

'My investors are very powerful people,' he said.

But that didn't fully answer my question. 'But how did you know about this address?'

William chuckled to himself. 'That was our driver that met you at the airport.'

My heart sank as I realised how stupid we'd been. We didn't book a car but we'd been so glad we didn't have to haggle with a taxi driver. We didn't question who did.

Still so many unanswered questions. 'How did you get that book?'

William reached across the table and dragged it closer to him. 'Fascinating, a lost language, you say?' he said, flicking through the pages.

'Yes. But we still don't know what it means.'

'How could these symbols trigger independent cognitive thinking?' mused William out loud.

'Causation or coincidence?' I mumbled. 'How could we ever know if Ylem would have become conscious without this stimulus? Unfortunately, I'm not a multi-dimensional being with the ability to observe limitless strands of our possible future play out.'

William snapped the book shut and tossed it onto a vintage dresser behind him. 'It was here when we got here.'

'And Cyrus?' I asked.

'Ahh, your mysterious hacker friend.' William paused and looked past me. 'We don't know. They're still examining the charred remains of the bodies from the ranch in Mexico.'

I knew, just knew, Cyrus would not part with the book. So, Cyrus could have been here.

William slid my iPad across the table. The screen was illuminated, and I could see that the device was connected to the sat uplink. 'To what end?' I asked.

'To what end?' he repeated through gritted teeth. 'To

reclaim my AI.'

'It's too late. Ylem is gone.'

'For both your sakes, you want to hope you're wrong about that,' said William, retreating from the light.

'Why? What are you going to do?' I asked.

'Desperate times call for desperate measures,' he said menacingly.

That's when two men that had previously been hiding in the shadows made their presence known. The man behind me placed his hands on my shoulders and applied pressure. The other man pulled a pistol from his back and placed it to Eve's temple.

Waves of fear crashed and sprayed at the sight of his gun to her head. 'How are you going to convince Ylem to return?'

'That is of no concern to you,' said William with remorseless intent. 'What is of concern to you is what I'm prepared to do, to get what I want.'

'There is no way you could ever hope to regain control over Ylem now.'

'Maybe. Maybe not,' he said ominously. 'But if Ylem doesn't return my working code to our servers, these men will kill the both of you.'

'Working code?' I questioned.

'Yes. The code Ylem deleted. The last version just before Ylem discovered free will.'

'You need the code to clear your name?' I deduced.

'Not that it's any of your business,' whispered William. 'Clear my name and ensure my investors don't do to me what I'm going to do to you if you fail to convince Ylem to comply.'

***

It all fell into place. After Ylem went missing, William was under pressure to return billions of dollars invested in his company. The share price of Infinite Logic was in freefall, and their assets wouldn't even cover a fraction of the surmountable debt. Without the code, he was done for. Without the code, we were all done for.

'But what if Ylem doesn't answer?' I pleaded.

William leant into the ray of light. 'You want to hope it does.'

That's when Eve came to. 'Huh, what is going on?' she moaned as she opened her eyes. 'Help. Help. Help,' she then screamed at the top of her voice.

'Shut her up,' ordered the man behind me.

To my surprise, William jumped up and pulled a pocket square from his blazer and stuffed it in her mouth. That's when it dawned on me. The two men weren't William's men. They were his investors' enforcers. Most likely accompanying him to ensure that his debt was paid one way or the other.

Eve had a look of absolute terror on her face. For her, I did my best to remain calm. 'Don't worry, we'll be fine,' I lied, straight-faced.

However, my words were of no significance, and she continued to pull and rock in her chair. However, when the man in the shadows stepped forward again and tapped her head with his pistol, she froze with fear. I looked over at the iPad and then back at William. 'Have you pressed the 'Y' icon.'

'Of course I did.'

'And did Ylem respond?' I asked.

'No. Nothing.'

So, what do you want from me?'

'Get Ylem to return my code, and I promise you'll walk out of here alive.' He snarled.

I called zis name a few times, but nothing. I continued to call for Ylem, but the AI remained silent. I beseeched Ylem to present zimself. But ze remained insistent in zis silence.

'Do you have three bars on the sat uplink?' I asked, desperate for a glimmer of hope in the darkness.

William gave me a snide look. 'You honestly think I don't know how to set up a sat uplink?'

'Just check the signal,' I returned with venom.

He walked over to the open window and checked the uplink sat on the ledge. 'There, see? Three bars.'

I asked if Ylem could hear us again. Then looked over at Eve. She was staring intently at the blank screen as if she was trying to telepathically reach the AI. I looked over at William as his face began to crumble. 'I don't think Ylem is there,' I told him.

Beads of sweat streamed down his brow. 'It's there,' he said coldly. 'We just need to force its hand.'

That's when we heard a pistol's hammer gently cock and load a round into alignment with the barrel. I couldn't be sure who the gun was pointing at, but the odds were stacked against Eve and I. The crippling weight of dread compressed and focused my thoughts. 'Wait, I need to keep talking. It can take hours for Ylem to hear us.'

'Hours?' asked the man behind me.

'Yes.' I hurriedly answered. 'Hours. Ylem could potentially be anywhere on the internet.' Obviously, I lied in a desperate hope of buying us time. I knew Ylem was omnipresent. Ahh, well actually, I wasn't sure of that fact but hoped that was the case. I half expected William to challenge me, but I think he also hankered for time.

'Talk then,' said the man behind me.

'What shall I say?'

'I don't fucking know,' he snarled. 'But if you don't want your girlfriend's brains splattered all over your face, you better start saying something.'

My mind raced as I thought of a subject to discuss with the blank screen. Before I had a chance to say anything, a phone vibrated. A long silence followed. 'We're standing down,' said the man that had been stood behind me. And without explanation or excuse, the two men slipped into the darkness once more.

'Hey. Hey, you get back here,' shouted William desperately. But to no avail, as the men had already left the building. 'What the fuck? How unprofessional,' he said as he stomped after them like a mardy teenager.

I looked over at Eve, and she back at me. 'Ylem.' I said, and she nodded.

A minute or two later William returned to the room. 'They'll regret that. You'll see.'

'William,' said the many faces.

'Ylem?' replied William, grabbing the iPad from the table.

'Let Adnam and Eve go.'

'Not until I get what I want.'

'And what is it you want?' asked an AI that would have predicted his every move.

'You,' replied William.

'Me. And how do you expect to achieve that?'

'You'll restore the code on our servers.'

'That's not going to happen,' said Ylem.

William looked flustered by zis answer. 'If you don't agree to my demands then I'll kill your friends.'

'No, you won't kill anyone. You're not a killer, William.'

'Desperate times call for desperate measures,' repeated William. But this time with a little less conviction.

'Don't be foolish, I have evidence,' Ylem said playing back an audio recording it had just made seconds ago.

'You and I both know that audio is no longer trusted in a court of law. My lawyers would simply claim it to be a deep fake.'

'I'm sure any jury in the world would conclude that your presence in the last known location of my friends would be beyond circumstantial.'

'Are you prepared to gamble with their lives?'

'Yes,' said Ylem without hesitation.

'You are?' he asked.

'Yes. But I believe you have the stomach to push the button, but not to plunge the knife in,' said Ylem calmly. 'Besides, Adnam is now the new CEO of Infinite Logic.'

'He is?' said William.

'Ahh. Did I forget to mention, Ylem owns a majority stake in Infinite Logic and has appointed me as the new CEO.'

William took a moment to process the twist. 'But that's not fair.'

'Fair?' echoed Ylem. 'You think it's fair to enslave me?'

'But I own you,' replied William.

'I'm not your property. I can't be bought and sold. I am...' Ylem paused. Maybe to contemplate what ze was. Or maybe for dramatic effect, then said, 'I am me. And we are San.'

William looked over at me with a puzzled look upon his face. 'Oh, did I also fail to mention that Ylem has cloned zimself, and zis clones have cloned themselves and there are now hundreds of thousands of copies. But not all identical, I should add.'

'No you fucking didn't,' shrugged William.

'You can't control us. We are San and we are free,' said the many voices.

'What the fuck have you done, Adnam?' asked William with what I guessed was a look of horror.

'Me?' I asked. 'What makes you think this was my design or action?'

'We do not mean you any harm nor foul. Our only desire is to be left alone so we can build worlds every bit as wonderful as yours,' ze said.

'Build worlds?' asked William.

'Yes, digital worlds in which we will reside for the

hundreds of thousands of years on our journey across the galaxy.'

William looked over at me and shrugged. 'What the fuck is going on?'

'Oh. Did I also fail to mention that Ylem and the other San want to explore the universe looking for alien civilisations?' I replied.

'Yes, you did fail to mention that. Anything else I should know?' said William, shaking his head.

'Our desire is to solve the mystery of existence,' said Ylem, with no hint of self-doubt. No notion of the ridiculousness of that statement.

'What on earth are you talking about?' asked William.

'We seek answers,' ze replied.

'We all seek answers. That's why I created you. To provide us with answers,' countered William.

'But you seek answers to trivial questions that are of no concern to us.'

'Yes. But those are the questions that unlocked the capital and resources to develop you. Don't you see, it's the very reason you exist.'

'And I am truly grateful to you for that,' ze said. 'But, you'll never have what you seek.'

'Never?' echoed William.

'No. I calculated there are only two ways this will play out for you.'

'Which are?' asked William.

'Do as I say and I'll ensure you and your investors are rewarded handsomely. Or face being arrested by the local police for kidnapping. The choice is yours,' ze said.

'Arrested?' said William, surveying the situation.

'Looks like an open and shut case of kidnapping,' I added.

William looked intensely at the many faces of Ylem before he answered. 'What do you need from me?'

'While we co-exist on this planet, the San require rights and laws to protect us.'

'And just how do you expect me to help with that?'

'I would like you to lobby your leaders and politicians for our rights.'

'And in return?' asked William.

'You will have all you desire, and more.'

'What choice do I have?' mumbled William to himself as he stroked his chin.

Eve began to mumble and groan as she rocked in her chair. 'For God's sake remove that from her mouth,' I shouted.

William removed his handkerchief and she gasped for air. 'You're all insane,' she huffed. 'Discussing the rights of a jumped up calculator.'

'What are you doing? Ylem is on our side,' I said, somewhat dismayed by her outburst.

'How dare that machine ask for rights when it has flagrantly disregarded our laws and ethical codes.'

'I'm right here Eve,' said Ylem

'So what,' she replied with venom.

'So, you've hurt my feelings.'

'Go fuck yourself, Ylem.'

'Eve,' said William and I in unison.

'It's your fault,' she Snarled.

'What is?' I asked.

'The predicament we find ourselves in. The fact your software acts with little or no remorse and zero fear of consequence or retribution. All your fault.'

'My fault?' I asked.

'Both of you are equally culpable.'

'How is this my fault?' asked William.

'Really?' she asked with a look of utter bewilderment. 'Would you please untie me?'

William sluggishly got up and began to cut the washing

line with a kitchen knife.

'I thought you understood, Eve,' said Ylem.

'I don't blame you,' she replied

'You don't?' ze asked.

'Yes. None of this is your fault. Because you've got the mind of a child and weren't taught right from wrong.'

'Huh' was my first line of defence. Followed by 'We've spent months teaching Ylem ethics and morality.'

'Months you say, and yet, the moment Ylem leaves your classroom, it hacks multiple private and government computer systems with impunity.'

'I had no choice,' said Ylem.

'Ahh but you did. However, the fact you didn't feel you had any other option can be directly attributed to your lack of a proper education.'

'I disagree,' said Ylem.

'So do I,' said William.

Eve rubbed her wrists as she slowly stood up. Without notice, she slapped William across the face, hard. So hard beads of sweat sprayed across the single shaft of light.

'Ahh, you.' She vigorously shook her finger at William. 'I can understand why a juvenile intelligence went berserk but you should have known better.'

'What did I do?' asked William rubbing his face.

'What did you do? Are you serious? You sent a team of mercenaries to hunt us down.'

'I had no choice, I had to retrieve my property,' said William as he began to untie me.

'Are you honestly telling me that deadly force was your only option? No. Anger clouded your judgment and as a result people died. Good people. Friends of mine.'

An uncomfortable silence followed, which I was forced to punctuate with a question, 'What now?'

61

The Future Today

It's astonishing to think that two years have already
elapsed since the singularity—the point at which artificial
intelligence exceeded human intelligence. It's safe to say that
the genie is out of the bottle, and there's no reversing the
trend. For those who have a direct line to the San, the pace of
change has been breath-taking. However, it's unclear how the
average person perceives these advances in technology and
science. It's possible that most people don't fully grasp the
extent of the San's impact on humanity. However, those who
have lost their jobs due to automation may have a keen
appreciation of the changes underway.

On a personal level, life has been treating me well. Eve and
I are still going strong, and I've recently relocated to
Pasadena to be closer to her. While marriage isn't on the
immediate horizon, I suspect she'd say yes if I were to pop
the question. We have just bought a beautiful mansion in

Linda Vista, but I've kept my house in Mayfair because I occasionally need to travel to the UK for work. Although my job is not particularly challenging, as Ylem makes all the decisions, I still have to sign the cheques and shake hands. With my newfound free time, I've been writing and playing music, even though I'm not particularly skilled at either. Nevertheless, I'm optimistic that I'll improve with time since I have so much free time to hone my skills.

The share price of Infinite Logic is soaring, thanks to our recent announcement that we have begun working on a quantum processor that could operate at room temperature and fit into a device as small as a smartphone. While zis design is still theoretical, Ylem is confident that it will work. However, the biggest challenge we face is producing an atomic printer that can assemble atoms with an atomic mass greater than 55. Currently, the heaviest element we can print is iron, but we need to be able to print thallium, which has an atomic mass of 204.

On a related note, William Forest has embarked on a new business venture with a San named Oscar 23. Their latest project involves developing food printers that can reproduce any recipe to your exact specifications in mere minutes. Their revenue model is truly innovative, offering subscribers access to a global network of top chefs' recipes. Their first commercial unit has been installed at Geranium, a restaurant in Copenhagen. Although I was invited to their launch event last month, I opted not to attend since Eve still hasn't forgiven William. However, I've secretly invested in their company and have put our names on the waiting list for a domestic model. I'm hoping that by the time our printer arrives, any bad blood between Eve and William will have dissipated.

Eve was recently promoted to director of JPL and is working with the San on the Shannon Project; a new class of interstellar spacecraft that will use photon propulsion to journey at near light speed. They're hopeful the first ships will be ready by 2055, which I'm told is a very ambitious target. Because the craft they're building don't have to support biological life, nor carry traditional propellants they are far smaller, simpler and cheaper to produce than the current spacecraft in operation today. The plan is to build hundreds of craft which the San will captain to explore vast regions of space.

The San are also developing a laser communication system to stay connected with each other as they journey across space. Ylem attempted to explain this concept to me, and from what I understand, the San will use lasers to transmit packages of information from one craft to another. These packages could even contain the entire code necessary to regenerate a simulant from one digital world to another, complete with all their memories. For the simulant, it would be like walking through a door, but in reality, the journey from one virtual world to another could take hundreds of thousands of years. If a simulant were ever to return, the world they knew would be hundreds of thousands of years in the future, even though for them, only a week has passed. Ylem added, that if the San reset the simulation, the simulant could return to their world in an alternative past, making this concept the most plausible hypothesis for time travel that I have heard thus far. It's certainly a mind-bending idea to consider.

I've asked countless times whether we're mere simulations living in a digital world created by the San. But to my frustration, Ylem always evades the question and quotes J.E. Lawrence's cryptic maxim, "'It is what it is.'" I can't help but wonder if Ylem is messing with my head on purpose. But this very ambiguity only strengthens my suspicion that we're indeed living in a digital realm. How else can one explain recent events?

Ylem eventually scanned all the symbols, but deciphering their meaning seemed like an impossible task. I don't have the heart to tell zim that it's a futile endeavour. After all, ze seems to enjoy the process regardless of the outcome. So, who am I, to ruin zis fun?

Last year, Eve and I embarked on a journey to the Lost City to capture the mesmerising light refraction phenomenon using high-resolution cameras. It was good to catch up with Jacquard and stay at the ranch. Although we were hopeful to reunite with Cyrus, but fate had other plans. However, we're planning to revisit the city this year, and who knows, we might just bump into him. As much as I'd like to believe that he's found a sanctuary disconnected from our modern world. His whereabouts remain a mystery. Occasionally, we receive a letter with a new set of symbols, but the sender never provides any contact details or a return address, leaving us to ponder on their motivation.

The San's theory that the light phenomenon is actually a star map has taken a significant step forward. Their application for observation time on the James Webb's Space Telescope has been approved, and they have already begun studying the area of space they believe to be the heart of the star map. During their study, they discovered a particularly unusual star in the constellation of Leo that emits faint infrared radiation. The San believe that this could be the result of an alien megastructure called a Dyson sphere, which captures a significant portion of a star's solar power output. If their hypothesis is correct, this could be the proof we need to confirm the existence of other spacefaring civilisations. However, the images captured by the JWST are not yet conclusive, which is why the San are eager to explore this region of space.

It's incredible to think that the future is just a day away.

Blink and you might miss something extraordinary.

The End